THE

WARGOD'S
A P P R E N T I C E

A Novel

GEORGE WHITNEY

Whitney Press
1030 Nassau St, Delray Beach FL 33483
6175158324

ISBN: 978-0-69290561-6 (sc)
ISBN: 978-0-9997341-1-7 (hc)
ISBN: 978-0-9997341-2-4 (e)

Library of Congress Control Number: 2018904979

Lulu Publishing Services rev. date: 04/30/2018

History is the lies historians agree to tell about the past.

Napoleon

We must know that war is common to all and strife is justice, and that all things come into being through strife necessarily.

Heraclitus

War is father of all and king of all; and some he manifested as gods, some as men; some he made slaves, some free.

Heraclitus

To Lex, our protector
1978–2016

PART I

THE WARGOD'S APPRENTICE

CHAPTER 1

I first learned that I had "my little gift," as Bernie called it, in the fourth week of my first year at Island Pond Regional High School, located in what they call the "Northeast Kingdom" of Vermont.

I hadn't wanted to go down our mountain to the high school. I was happy with Dad and Mom homeschooling me along with my younger sister, Polly, and my younger brother, Max. My parents had PhDs from Harvard, and our house was jammed with books—thousands of them, on every shelf and piled in every nook and cranny. I had learned to read when I was three and spent my nights and rainy days curled up in my room with a book. I had finished Gibbon's *Decline and Fall of the Roman Empire* by the time I was ten. I breezed through *War and Peace* at eleven and had read all of Jane Austen's novels by twelve. I didn't like Jane's books as much as the other two. They were too girlie for me.

There were some oddities about us living up on our mountain, but they didn't seem odd to me at the time. For one thing, our nearest neighbor was ten miles of bad road away. We hardly ever saw another living soul except when some tourist got lost and drove by our house in leaf-peeper season. From time to time during deer season in the fall, a hunter might knock on our door and beg us to tell him where he was. For another thing, we didn't have a phone—either cell or landline. We had a shortwave radio in Dad's office upstairs, and only Dad was allowed to use it. We drove down the mountain only once a month and then never twice in a row to the same town and store. Usually Mom or Dad made us wait in the car while they did errands. Sometimes Mom wore a blonde wig when she went into the grocery store, and Dad wore a big, bushy beard. It was Halloween all year long in our house. We got no mail. We didn't have a mailbox or a box in the post office.

1

Only years later did I come to understand that we were hiding.

I didn't spend all my time reading or schooling. I loved to roam the deep woods that surrounded our old farmhouse, making a birding journal. I had collected notes and sketches of more than sixty species, including *Anser albifrons*, the greater white-fronted goose, and a mating pair of *Cepphus grille*, black guillemots that had migrated down from Newfoundland and were rare in Vermont. I was proud of these additions to my journal.

Yes, I was a bird nerd.

On one scorching August afternoon when I was fifteen, Dad caught me in the woods totally bare-assed except for my knapsack and binoculars.

"You're buck naked. What do you think you're doing?" He was just back from one of his business trips. He had hurt himself. His shoulder was in a sling, and he was grumpy.

"I was overheated," I protested. "I folded my clothes neatly. No one saw me. And see? I'm not really naked. I'm wearing my binoculars." They were barely covering my private parts.

"You're turning into a wild beast," he said. "Time you got civilized. You're going to the high school in the fall."

"I'd rather not, Dad," I whined.

"You smell like a damn grizzly bear and talk like a Harvard English professor," he said. "I suppose it's my fault for making you live way up here without the internet, a cell phone and X-Box. It's time you learned to be a teenager. You'll love it."

I didn't. I talked weird, and I looked weird. I was only a ninth grader, but I was already six foot six though exceptionally scrawny. I wore thick eyeglasses that were always sliding down my nose. I had acne. With my long, none-too-clean black hair hanging down to my shoulders, I looked like a pimply Sasquatch. I knew a lot about *Anser albifrons*. I knew a lot about everything in my classes. I got straight As. In every class—English, math, chemistry, American history, European history, and AP European history, which was supposed to be for seniors only—I was always waving my paw in the air, answering every question, and making the other kids hate me. I quoted long passages from Gibbon. The other kids wanted to beat me senseless, but they didn't dare because I was so big.

I knew everything about my classes but nothing at all about other kids, except Polly and Max, and they didn't count. The boys sneered at me and called me a dork, geek, and nerd. The girls stared and giggled. I didn't know what to make of their giggling, but I noticed that one girl didn't giggle. Her name was Deanna, and she smiled at me when I passed by. She had long, black hair like mine, only hers was shiny clean. She had very pale, haunting blue eyes. I thought she was beautiful, but I didn't say hello to her. I didn't know how. I didn't know how to talk to girls—or to anyone, for that matter.

Since I had no friends, in the afternoon after classes, I roamed the woods around the school birding. One day I happened to walk by the football field where the varsity team was practicing and stopped to watch. It was a lovely, late-summer day.

Corky, the school gardener, had just finished clipping the field with his gang mower, and the air was filled with the delicious scent of fresh-cut grass. Corky was sitting on his machine a few yards away, taking a cigarette break. He turned to me. His left eye was blank white, and his fingers were stained brown with nicotine. "Principal says the campus is smoke-free," Corky said. "You think I give a shit?"

"I guess not," I said.

"Smart-ass punk," he mumbled.

I turned back to watch the practice. The guys wore helmets and armor like knights from the Crusades. They all lined up and, at some secret signal, crashed into one another. They shoved, grappled, grasped, and smashed each other in a ferocious melee, chased each other around the field, hurled themselves through the air, tore at each other's bodies, and finished in great heaps of tangled arms and legs. Then, magically unharmed, they all got up and did it again. It reminded me of the Norse myths I had read where fallen Viking warriors got roaring drunk in the halls of Valhalla, hacked off each other's arms, legs, and heads, and then leapt up, reattached their limbs, and started the battle over again. It was wonderful!

I walked up to a short, muscular, bald man with a whistle around his neck. "Excuse me, sir," I said. "Are you the teacher of this class?"

"I can see, son, that if you had another brain, you would be a halfwit," the coach replied amiably. "Yes, I am, but people call me coach, not teacher, and it is not a class but a practice."

"I'll play," I declared.

He looked me up and down and saw that, though very scrawny, I was as tall as a giraffe.

"Very well, then. Go to the equipment manager in the gym," he said, "and tell him to issue you your gear. Then suit up and get out here."

I did as I was told and soon returned fully armored.

"You, Geek, take off those glasses, and get in at left defensive tackle with the JVs," barked Coach.

I trotted out onto the field. A helpful teammate cursed me and shoved me into my position. I was nearly blind without my glasses, and I just stood there squinting as the center snapped the ball. The offensive tackle, a 250-pound senior with a bushy beard, knocked me onto my back. He lay on top of me as the ball carrier scampered by.

"You're my bitch," he whispered in my ear. He pursed his lips and made a smooching sound. "I love you."

Football went the same way for me all week. I got knocked flat. I got up. I got knocked flat again. I got up. The big tackle proposed marriage. My body was covered with bruises. Every muscle ached. Most kids would have quit after all that punishment.

I loved it.

CHAPTER 2

Game day was Saturday. We were playing St. Johnsbury High, a much bigger school, and they were slaughtering us 42–0 at the beginning of the second half. After the kickoff, Coach decided to write the game off as a lost cause and give the JVs a little playing time. He sent us in on defense.

The St. Johnsbury offensive tackle facing me was a monster even larger than the brute who had been torturing me all week in practice. St. Johnsbury broke their huddle and trotted to the line of scrimmage. Both teams took their stances.

The quarterback began his count. "Hut one …"

And that's when the really weird stuff began to happen.

I felt a hot flush. My heart began to pound. My leg muscles swelled, hardened, and throbbed with power. I turned my head slightly to look down the line at the ball in the center's hands and was astonished that I could see perfectly without my glasses. I read the writing on the ball. "Wilson," it said. "Made in USA. Inflate 13 pounds." I saw the eight little laces. I saw the tiny bumps on the surface of the leather that gave it grip. I counted 2,055 little bumps. I saw the center's fingers on the ball. I saw his dirty nails. I saw that the index fingernail of his right hand was chewed. I saw the tiny muscles in the fingers of his right hand tighten.

"Hut two," the quarterback barked, and I was suddenly on a great, flat plain by the sea with mountains far away on the horizon.

"Hut three," the quarterback barked again, one tremendous, thundering voice echoing off the mountains.

"Freedom!" he roared and was answered by thousands more voices rising in a strange undulating war cry: "Alalalalala!"

The earth trembled under tens of thousands of running feet.

My legs ached. Sweat stung my eyes. Dust choked my nose and mouth. My heart pounded in my chest.

The center hiked the ball. I knew exactly what to do.

I shot off the mark and knocked the huge tackle on his back before he could move a muscle.

He grunted, and his eyes rolled back into his head.

Every player on the field was moving in slow motion except me. I was moving at light speed. The St. Johnsbury quarterback rolled out to the right side at a slow walk, as if he were moving in thigh-deep sand. His blockers shuffled.

I drew a bead on the quarterback, slowed a half step, and drove my helmet into his ribs with tremendous force. I heard the crash of tons of metal on metal and a terrible howl of anger, terror, and pain from thousands of voices.

Four of the quarterback's ribs, probably the first through fourth I judged from studies of my father's anatomical texts, cracked. The quarterback screamed. The ball popped out of his arms. I pounced on it.

I trotted off the field as EMTs were loading the quarterback into an ambulance. I could hear him whimpering and moaning. I didn't understand what had happened to me or how I had done what I had done, but I felt wonderfully strong.

Coach put me in again as soon as we were back on defense. No one could touch me. I recovered fumble after fumble. I littered the field with groaning St. Johnsbury players. We won the game 49–42.

That was the day that I discovered that I had that talent—a genius, really.

Coach made me the first-string left defensive tackle. He told me that I was the first freshman to start for St. Matthew's in thirty years. I became a school hero. People wanted to say I was their friend, but I really didn't care about them at all.

I did care about Deanna. She was a soccer star and walked by the field almost every day on her way to practice, kicking a ball in front of her and sometimes bouncing it from one knee to the other. She had pretty knees. She always stopped to watch us solemnly for a few minutes and then moved on. When she didn't come, I was disappointed. Some of my teammates made rude comments, and I glared them down. Now that I was a football hero and they had seen what I could do to them, they cringed. Other, nicer, members of the team said Deanna was cute and hinted that she liked me. They said that I should go over to where she was standing on the sidelines dribbling her ball and talk to her. What was there to lose?

But I didn't know what to say.

The season went on, and I was invincible. I doubled the school record for tackles in a single game, which had been set in 1952. We finished the season undefeated, and people said it was all because of me. I was elected first-string defensive tackle on the all-state team. Coach said college recruiters were already starting to call him. The *Rutland Herald* carried a huge photo of me on their sports page holding a football and looking like a real tough guy. I was happy. I felt so good I was almost ready to talk to Deanna.

On the afternoon everything in my life changed, I was walking through the woods near the high school mulling over what I would say to Deanna. The leaves had fallen, and the trees were bare. I could see my breath. I didn't bring my binoculars or my journal. I had no taste for birding anymore. All I could think about was Deanna. *Should I ask her to walk with me into town and get a burger at McDonald's? Would she say yes? Would she say no? Would she say no and laugh in my face or whack me one?* I calculated the probability that she would whack me one at 50 percent.

I had a special place: a big maple, hollowed out on one side, where I kept a stash of protein bars for snacks when I took my birding walks. I stepped up to the tree, stuck my hand in the hollow, and felt around for a bar. Suddenly, the ground gave way under my feet. My fingers scrambled to get a handhold on the tree, but I plunged down and down into a deep dark hole. I crashed into the earth and lay there stunned.

"Trapped like a shithouse rat!" I heard a voice say from above.

I saw stars. I stumbled to my feet, staggered, and fell on my face. "Get me out of here! Somebody help me!" I gasped.

"They paid me to dig this damn hole, and now I'm going to fill it up," growled the voice. "With you in it, you shitty little smart-ass godling!"

A shovelful of dirt hit me full in the face. "Help!" I gurgled from my knees. "Somebody help! Stop!"

Two more shovels of dirt smacked my shoulders. The dirt rain stopped. From the top of the hole I heard a thud, a shrill shriek, and an awful gurgling, bubbly sound. Something not dirt fell through the air, plopped on the floor of the hole, bounced, rolled to my knees, and lay still. I looked down. It was Corky, the school groundskeeper. Or rather it was Corky's severed head staring up at me with his one white eye and a Marlboro stuck to his lower lip.

"Yow!" I shrieked rather like a ten-year-old girl who had just seen a mouse.

A length of rope smacked me in the face. I rallied and shot up it hand over hand like a squirrel chased by an angry king cobra.

Deanna was standing beside the hole, lackadaisically wiping the blood off the blade of a vicious black knife with a leaf. She was looking scorching hot. She wore skin-tight yoga pants. If she had happened to have a dime in her pocket, you could have read the date. She wore high black dominatrix boots. Her black hair was in a ponytail. She was a petite girl, but I could swear she had grown three or four inches in the few days since I had last seen her and put on ten pounds of muscle: all in her quads. She was jacked.

She slipped the knife into a scabbard hidden behind her neck.

"Don't look down," she warned me.

I looked anyway. A headless corpse lay at my feet, spurting steadily diminishing geysers of rich, red blood with each weakening heartbeat.

I barfed.

"Feel better now?" she asked.

"A little, thank you," I replied.

"We have to go. There'll be others," she whispered.

It was getting dark. Without another word, she took off into the woods at a fast jog, leaping over rocks and stumps like a white-tailed deer.

I did my best to follow. We ran for a good half hour. I was panting clouds of steam. Luckily, I had nothing left in my stomach to puke.

Deanna wasn't even breathing hard. She led me through the trees to an unlit dirt road where a black limousine was waiting, no lights, engine running. The chauffeur jumped out and opened the door for me. He was about eight feet tall and a yard wide. He wore a black uniform and an automatic pistol in a shoulder holster.

"Welcome, Master Lex," he said. His voice was basso profundo and sounded like an alpine avalanche.

"Good luck, Lex," said Deanna. "Be careful."

"Aren't you coming?" I asked.

"Can't," she replied. "I have *Glee* in ten minutes."

"Deanna!" I cried. "What's going on?"

"You'll know soon," she said. Then she kissed me on the lips.

It wasn't just a friendly peck like brother and sister. Her lips lingered on mine just like in the Harlequin Romance novels my mom kept stashed in her secret place in the attic. She also "pressed her body against mine," as the novels say.

Or at least I thought she did.

My knees turned to water. Before I could recover or speak, she had disappeared into the night.

CHAPTER 3

"Time to go, Master Lex," boomed the chauffeur.

I climbed into the limo. We roared away in a spray of gravel.

The back seat of the limo was pitch-black. Alone without Dianna, I was frightened. *What the hell is going on here?* I wondered.

"Hello, Lex," said a soft voice, and a light clicked on beside me. Under the light, I saw an old man. He was very slender and so tall that his white hair brushed the ceiling. He wore a beautiful three-piece suit.

"Who the hell are you?"

"I am your grandfather." He extended a long, bony hand.

"No, you aren't!" I barked. "I don't have a grandfather. Don't touch me!"

I had had a very bad day. I wasn't in the mood for any more surprises. My mom and dad had never, ever mentioned any relatives.

"Everyone has a grandfather, Lex," he calmly said.

"Then my grandfather is dead."

"No, I am your grandfather, and as you can see, I am not dead."

"Are you kidnapping me?" I thought of the chauffeur's pistol. "Take me home right now!"

"I can't. Believe me, I'd like to. But I can't."

"You're lying. Why not?"

"Because your mom and dad and your brother and sister are gone."

"Gone? Did you kidnap them too?"

"No, Lex. There was a fire." His voice trembled just a little.

"Was anyone hurt?"

"Lex, your family is dead."

"No. You're lying! Take me home! Now! Or I'm getting out here." I pulled the door handle. It was locked. We were going about eighty miles an hour.

He explained. This afternoon, old Mr. Hagen had driven his rattletrap pickup up to the house to deliver a cord of firewood and found our house ablaze. By the time the volunteer fire department had driven the twenty miles to our house, it was a pile of smoldering embers. The state police were at the house now, along with the local police and the FBI.

I burst into tears. "No! Liar!"

"I'm sorry," he said.

We drove on through the night.

"You will live with me and your grandmother now."

I saw the chauffeur's eyes darting back and forth in the rearview mirror as he checked out each passing car. I cried and I cried. Exhausted, I finally fell asleep.

And so I began my new life.

***

I woke up after midnight when we stopped at a high iron gate. A guard buzzed us through. We drove for fifteen minutes down a long driveway lined by old trees. Three times, I saw men standing in the trees beside the driveway carrying rifles.

We pulled up at the front door of a mansion with a high, stone turret like the keep on a medieval castle. Every light in the mansion seemed to be on. My grandfather and I stepped out. I smelled the sea and heard the roar of surf.

I walked up the steps to the tall oak and iron front door. In the middle of the door, there was a silver brass knocker in the shape of a helmeted goddess's head. It was Athena, I knew, Greek goddess of wisdom and the heroic side of war. I pulled the knocker and heard the knock echo and re-echo through the hallways of the great house. The door swung open, and a dignified, middle-aged man wearing a dark suit appeared.

"I am John, your grandparents' butler, Master Lex," he announced in a prim British accent. He helped me out of my coat. "Your grandmother will be right down."

I was standing on a pink marble floor that glistened like ice over a bottomless arctic lake. Dark shapes like big fish moved beneath the ice at my feet. Three stories overhead was a vast dome painted with fat, pink ladies bathing in a pond. Chubby naked cherubs orbited around them strumming golden harps. The fat ladies were smirking at the cherubs. Weird.

"After Boucher," said a tall, buxom woman descending the stairs. She was dressed head to toe in mourning black. "Your grandfather hates it. He doesn't like Rococo."

She had a strong, sculpted face. It was deeply wrinkled now, but it was easy to see that she'd once been a great beauty. Her long, gray hair was done up in a tight, old-fashioned bun. She threw her arms around me and held me in a hug. She smelled of some priceless perfume that made me dizzy.

"Welcome, Lex," she said. Her voice was sweet and heavy like honey. "You may call me Granny. This is your home now. I'm sure you're tired. Would you like to go to your room? I think you'll love it, dearie." Granny turned to John. "Will you bring up supper, please, John?"

"Yes, Mum." John glided silently away.

"And one of your delicious toddies too, please, John," Granny added. "Master Lex has had a very trying day. A strong one, please."

"Yes, Mum," John replied and disappeared.

I followed Granny up the white marble stairway. She led me down a very long, dimly lit hallway. Its end was lost in distant shadows. The hall was lined on both sides by portrait busts set on pedestals. The main building at my school had portrait busts lining its walls too—George Washington, Abraham Lincoln, and Martin Luther King Jr.—the usual famous dudes looking serious and noble.

I walked over to one of the busts and jumped back. "Shit!" I recoiled. "What's that?"

"I wish you wouldn't swear, dearie."

"Sorry." This didn't seem like the sort of household where people cursed like high school students.

The bust was of some ancient soldier in his death agony. His nose and one ear were cut away. One eye socket was black and empty. His mouth was contorted in pain. Most of his teeth were knocked out.

Granny walked over and read the little nameplate on the base. "Leonidas. You know, Leonidas, dearie, the commander of the three hundred Spartans at Thermopylae. It's his death mask. Your grandfather collects them."

"Death mask?"

"From his face, you know. Your grandfather would be glad to explain the process to you. I think they use hot wax. He allows me to have my pretty Boucher if I let him have his silly death masks. Come along now. We're almost there."

We walked past Ramses II, Cyrus, Themistocles, Philip of Macedon, Alexander, Hannibal, Scipio Africanus, Julius Caesar, Alaric, Attila the Hun—one dead soldier's face after the other.

"Here we are: your room." She swung open a door, and we stepped inside.

It was a boy's room from the 1960s. There was one small window, a bunk bed, a two-drawer bureau, a bookshelf built of boards and concrete blocks, and an old wooden chair, three-legged and propped up on another block. In one corner, there was a huge old armoire. Faded Harvard pennants were pinned to the wall on either side of a mirror with a Rolling Stones poster, a lava lamp, red, and the bookshelf was filled with old schoolbooks: Latin, French, European history, algebra, and a copy of the novel, *Dune*.

"Do you like it?" Granny asked, drawing the curtains. Dust motes pranced in the sunlight. "It was your father's."

"I love it, Granny," I lied.

"I knew you would." She walked over to the armoire, produced a set of jingling keys, selected a big brass one, and turned it in the lock. "You'll love this," she said, throwing open the armoire's double doors.

Inside were two vast armies of toy soldiers poised for battle on opposite sides of a no-man's land two feet wide. On one side was an army of armored men wearing crested helmets and carrying round shields and long spears pointed upright. They were Greeks, Hoplites, I knew. On the other side of no-man's land was a much larger, more colorful horde of archers, spearmen in wicker armor, and cavalry bearing gaudy flags and banners. Asians of some kind. The back of the armoire was mirrored, giving the armies a weird effect of infinite reflection and re-reflection.

"Your father played with them night and day," she said. "Until he grew up and started to play with the real ones, of course."

The mirror's effect made me dizzy, and I closed my eyes for just a moment. When I opened them again, the Greeks seemed to have lowered their spears and moved a few inches toward their enemy.

I heard that shout again: "Freedom!"

"Sir?"

John was standing beside me, holding a silver tray with a sandwich, a slice of apple pie, and a steaming silver mug. "Your supper, sir."

I slammed the doors of the armoire shut, grabbed the mug, and took a sip. It was hot, spicy, and delicious. I knocked it back. My head swam. I heard the muffled clash of tiny weapons and the war cries of tiny soldiers behind the armoire doors. I staggered over to the bed and threw myself down.

"Good night, dearie," Granny said.

"Good night, sir," echoed John.

The door clicked shut behind them.

CHAPTER 4

Alone, my grief swept over me like a tidal wave and washed me away. Mom and Dad, dear Polly, and little Max were gone. I was all alone. My body twisted and wracked with sobs. I wept until there was no more sorrow left inside me to release. Drained, I fell asleep.

I dreamed I was inside the armoire, shoulder to shoulder with thousands of soldiers hacking, thrusting, screaming, falling, and bleeding. The air was thick with the choking dust raised by thousands of feet. The dust reeked of blood, vomit, and shit. I struggled to keep upright in the mad crush. I staggered. I tripped and fell. A corpse fell on top of me, then another and another. I was crushed under their dead weight. I couldn't breathe. I was suffocating. My heart pounded in my ears.

I awakened with the covers twisted around my face and pounding on my door. John came in carrying a breakfast tray steaming with scrambled eggs, juice, coffee, and warm, freshly baked blueberry muffins. "Good morning, sir," he chirped. "I trust you slept well."

It was my first hangover ever. The most fiendish tortures of the Spanish Inquisition—the rack, red-hot pincers, thumbscrews, the agonies of the Iron Maiden—are gentle smooches compared to the hell of an alcohol-induced head. I know. I've been there—in the hands of the Spanish Inquisition, I mean. My head throbbed. My stomach churned. My mouth tasted like a rat and a possum had fought it out to the death on my tongue, died of their wounds, and were rotting in green mush between my front teeth.

I wanted to die. I was dead. "I'm sick, John," I complained.

"Madam suspected you might have a touch of the flu this morning, so she asked me to make you this." He handed me a large glass filled with some amber fluid. "Drink it down all at once, please, sir."

I chugged. The drink was one part volcanic magma, one part hydrochloric acid, and one part ground glass. It burned horribly going down. My eyes watered. My skin burned. My muscles knotted in spasms, but my head cleared instantly. Vim and vigor surged into my brain and body. I felt fabulous.

I gave the eggs no mercy. "What time is it?" I asked.

"Eleven, sir. Your grandfather has scheduled an interview with you in his study at one. Please be on time, sir. He's a very busy man. His study is on the top floor of the tower, which is just off the north wing."

I showered and put on some 1960s clothes I found in the closet—over-tight bell bottom blue jeans and a tie-died psychedelic Jimi Hendrix T-shirt.

I considered how was I going to kill the hour and a half before my appointment with Grampy and decided to explore my new home. I took a right out of my bedroom door, walked down the hallway past those creepy busts, down the front stairs, and scouted around the first floor.

My grandparents must have had dozens of servants to keep a huge house like this one, yet the house was empty and silent. I found a big living room with heavy wood furniture that looked old and valuable and a big dining room with a huge twenty-five-chair table and an enormous crystal chandelier hanging from the ceiling. A mating pair of Demoiselle cranes nested in the chandelier. When the female stretched her broad wings, the chandelier tinkled. I entered a billiard room where I stopped to miss a couple of easy shots. I passed next into a humid greenhouse and a jungle of exotic tropical plants. Monkeys and parrots chattered and cawed in the thick foliage. A large, invisible animal bustled through the undergrowth grunting.

I wandered through this house until I came to a big steel door, elliptical-shaped, studded with big rivets, and raised a few inches off the ground. In the middle of the door, instead of a handle, there was a wheel like the watertight door on a ship or a submarine. I turned the wheel, and it shrieked with rust. It stuck, then moved, and I swung the door open.

Inside was a swimming pool. The ceiling above the pool was so shrouded in mist that it seemed to be of infinite height. The opposite side of the pool was so cloaked in thick fog that the pool seemed to be of infinite width. I didn't like the looks of this pool. It had no beginning and no end. It had no sky above it. Its waters were black. It was bottomless. This pool creeped me out.

Time to go. It was getting late. Time for my appointment with my grandfather. I stepped toward the door, and behind me, I heard a tiny toot, like a child's tin horn, echo behind me from the fog. It tooted twice again: "toot-toot."

I turned to look and saw sailing out of the mist a 104-gun, first-rate sailing battleship flying the colors of the British Navy.

Imagine my surprise. The little vessel had packed on every bit of canvas and was sailing directly toward me, tooting all the time as if to attract my attention. When she came within ten meters of poolside, a drum rolled and her crew broke into action, swarming like an army of ants all over the deck, rigging and masts. She swerved abruptly to starboard, exposing her starboard battery. Her gun doors crashed open. Her guns were rumbled out. Wisps of smoke rose from her slow matches.

"Oh my God! She's going to give me a broadside!" I thought.

The little ship's side exploded and was engulfed in white smoke. But instead of being riddled by round shot, grape shot, and chain shot (all in miniature, of course, but they might have broken my glasses or shipped a tooth, I felt nothing but a blast of hot wind.

The man-o'-war passed beyond the smoke, and I saw her officers standing at attention on her quarterdeck. One officer—by his gaudier uniform I saw that he must be the captain—held a megaphone. He raised it to his mouth. His officers saluted crisply.

"Ahoy, Lex," the captain shouted.

"Ahoy, Captain," I shouted back.

"Good luck in your adventures," he bellowed. He had lungs of leather. He snapped me a salute.

I saluted back. "Thank you, Captain."

"Godspeed," he shouted as his man-o'-war glided back into the fog. "Victory" was embossed in gold letters on her stern.

It was 11:45, and I went searching for the door to the tower where my grandfather's study was located. I expected something grand as befitting a rich and powerful man, but instead, as so often the case in this house of marvels, I was surprised. The entrance was hidden behind a splintery old door just behind the servants' table in the kitchen and was marked with a torn piece of cardboard and the words, written in black Magic Marker: "To Office."

I gave the door knob a yank. It squealed on its rusty hinges, stuck, and then opened. The stairway smelled of mold, mice droppings, and ancient cooking odors. The walls and steps of the tower were stone dripping with condensation. I started climbing. It was dark and creepy inside the tower. Invisible cobwebs tickled my nose, and I brushed them away. The stairs wound up and up. I came to a slit window and looked out. Below me was the driveway and my grandfather's black limousine.

The chauffeur was polishing its hood with a cloth. I climbed for another minute or two and looked out another slit widow. The chauffeur was still polishing, but this time, the car wasn't from our time. It was a model I had read about in a 1940s gangster story. I trudged around and around. I looked out the next window and saw the chauffeur again, but this time, he was polishing the side of a carriage. I reached the top and found a stout oaken door. Riveted to the door was a brass plaque: "Members Only."

I reached for the door handle. The door swung open before I touched it.

It was an old-fashioned New York gentlemen's club from the turn of the twentieth century, silent and smelling of furniture wax and good cigars. Gas lights flickered. The floor was deeply carpeted. Side tables set with heavy silver cigarette and cigar boxes and crystal ashtrays stood beside big brown leather chairs and sofas. Teddy Roosevelt might have been sitting in one corner sipping cognac with his political cronies. One wall was covered by a rack filled with magazines and newspapers printed in languages from all the corners of the earth—and from other earths as well. Against another wall was a long, brightly polished oaken bar. Over the bar hung an enormous oil painting of a battle. Masses of cavalry in silver breastplates and plumed silver helmets were engaged in a desperate charge against the muskets and bayonets of an infantry square. The foreground was a tangle of wounded and dead men, shattered horses, and broken caissons.

The painting was entitled "Waterloo. 1963."

I was sure that the Battle of Waterloo was not fought in 1963.

On another wall was a museum of weapons. The display began with edged weapons: spears, halberds, lances, swords, and battle axes. I pulled down a war hammer. Its spike was crusted with dried blood and chunks of some other organic matter. Revolted, I quickly put it back.

I moved along to the firearms. All the historical examples were there in chronological order: a bronze Chinese hand cannon, a vase-shaped bombard from medieval times, matchlock pistols, flintlock rifles, percussion rifles, lever-action rifles from the Old West, bolt-action rifles, semi-automatic rifles and machine guns of World War I and II, and the AK-47s and M-16s still in use today. At the very end of the display were strange weapons: tiny, shining things made out of fantastic translucent plastics and unknown alloys in odd shapes and sizes that seemed unsuited to a hand, a human one, anyway.

The last wall was covered with framed group photos like the class pictures that hung on the walls of Island Pond Regional High School. In the first, a short, fat, balding man knelt in front of a small group of men and women holding a small flag marked "1946. Hastings." In the second, the little man's flag read "1947. D-Day." I got the idea. They were battles. Some of them I recognized, and some I didn't. On and on, year after year, but not every year, the flags went: "Philippi, Sedan, The Marne, Antietam, Stalingrad, Yorktown, El Alamein, and Zama." Until they ended with "The Armada."

I examined the faces of the little man's companions. All were obscured. Some were shadowed, and others were turned away from the camera. Some were out of focus. I was puzzled. Why take photos of people who could not be seen?

In the middle of the room was a large, brightly polished wooden conference table set with twelve chairs. In the middle of the table was an enormous leather-bound book. The book was the largest I had ever seen. It was the size of a coffee table and as thick as a concrete block. I walked over to it and read the title embossed in golden Gothic lettering on the cover: "The Battle Book."

I tried to open it. The cover wouldn't budge. I tried to lift the book. It wouldn't move. I tried to slide it across the table. It wouldn't slide.

A big black tomcat hopped up on the book and sat down. He blinked his big yellow eyes once, did a quick face wash then jumped back down to the floor and scampered through a little kitty hole in the base of a tiny postern door, which I now saw had been hidden from sight behind *The Battle Book*.

The cat was timely. I checked my watch. It was time for my appointment with my grandfather. I walked over to the little postern and knocked.

"Come in, Lex."

I entered. My grandfather's study was like an alchemist's library. Shelves of ancient, leather-bound books connected by a balcony and circular metal stairway extended from the floor to the ceiling. The cat sat on the balcony, staring down at me with contempt. He growled, leapt up, and shot down the stairway in a blur and out the kitty hole.

My grandfather sat behind an enormous gleaming mahogany desk, bare except for a file folder, a big red telephone, and a beautiful silver .357 Magnum Smith and Wesson revolver in a presentation rack. I noticed that the pistol was loaded.

"Sit down, please." He gestured a long elegant hand toward a straight-backed wooden chair in front of his desk.

I sat. He picked up the file and read it. Somewhere, a big clock was ticking off the seconds. Thunk, thunk, thunk.

After seventy-two thunks, he finally said, "I would like to talk to you about your future."

When an adult "wants to talk to you about your future," watch out. I immediately went on the defensive.

"I'm going back to school, aren't I? I mean, my grades aren't great, but I promise I'll work harder next term and do better. Honest, I will. And I want to play football next fall, and maybe get a scholarship for college. I was thinking Harvard … a major in history and a minor in litera—"

"Quite impossible," he said.

"Why?"

"I hoped you might have guessed the reason by now. I can only suppose the shock has been too much for you. My people have finished their investigation. I have their report here." He pushed the folder across the desk toward me.

I read that at about noon yesterday, while I was in the woods being saved by Deanna, two intruders probably disguised as deer hunters had entered our house and shot Dad, Mom, Max, and Polly while they were having hot dogs in the kitchen. Then they shoveled the hot coals from the cookstove onto the kitchen floor and set the house on fire to make it look like an accident.

I slumped back down into my chair.

Thunk. Thunk. Thunk.

"Why? Who?"

"We'll get to that. Now, I want you to tell me what happened to you yesterday afternoon."

There was no sense in lying. He already knew. He knew everything.

I told him.

"The same people who murdered your family tried to murder you, Lex. Luckily, we had someone watching over you."

"Deanna works for you?"

"She is one of us. Yes. In any event, our enemies now know where you are. Your football success, though heroic, did not work entirely to your advantage. Your fame ..." He was being sarcastic now. "Brought you to their attention. They will try to kill you again, and they will keep trying until they succeed."

I wasn't listening. I didn't care whether they killed me or not. My parents, my brother, my sister, my home, my life—everything had been stolen from me. I had stopped needing air. I had stopped needing food. I had stopped needing love. My soul had become a black pit, an empty void. I was already dead.

Nature abhors a vacuum, they say. Something had to refill my soul. It came in a rush. It was scalding hot like lava. It was bright red like the hottest fire in the hottest furnace in the hottest subbasement of hell. I saw that red, not in my eyes, but behind my eyes in my brain. My face burned. My neck and shoulders burned. Every muscle in my body knotted, and I screamed inside my head, "Blood!"

I was no longer a boy but a wild wolf. My eyes burned red, streams of slaver dripped from my razor fangs. I rumbled a deep growl. Then I turned and padded back into my forest.

I was me again. I felt weak and sick to my stomach. I was trembling all over and pouring sweat.

My grandfather leaned slightly forward and examined my face. "You will have to learn to control that," he said. "And use it."

"Yes." I said.

Thunk. Thunk. Thunk. My rage drained slowly out of me. Hollow, I just sat there motionless.

"I don't understand," I whispered.

"You will understand everything in good time, young man." He patted my knee. "As I was saying, we are here to discuss your future. Have you given any thought to a career?"

"I'm only sixteen. Shouldn't I be in school?"

"There are many different kinds of schools."

"I mean another high school."

"I do have good connections at a boarding school on Easter Island. Excellent weather, good surfing. Safe, but rather remote."

"No, thank you."

"I also have connections in a Benedictine monastery in the Chilean Andes. It's a quiet life, but it wouldn't have to be forever.

"I don't think so."

"And there's the family business."

"What's the family business?"

"It's exciting and extremely challenging," he went on. "It combines the physical, the intellectual, and the moral in equal measures. There is some violence involved. You like violence, don't you, Lex?"

For an instant, the wolf returned, snarled, and bared his fangs, and then it disappeared.

"I guess I do," I said.

"I believe you do. You are an exceptional football player. So was I. So was your father. In that first game, were you not surprised to discover how easy it was for you to commit violence on your opponents? And how good you were at it?"

"Yes."

"And how you enjoyed it?"

"Yes."

"I think you should interview. If you like the job, and the boss likes you, he would offer you an apprenticeship. No harm in taking a look. You don't have to decide now."

"I'll do it." I would have agreed to anything. I really didn't care.

"Very good." He pulled a business card out of his desk drawer and pushed it across to me. "The car will be ready for you in an hour to take you to see this gentleman."

The card read: "Dr. Bernard T. H. Polemarchos, PhD, LLD, JSD, ThD, PsyD, EdD, et al."

"It's pronounced 'Pol-A-Mark-OS.' Dress as you would for gym class: shorts, sneakers."

A discreet knock at the study door, and John entered. "The secretary is here, sir."

"Send him in, please, John. That will be all for now, Lex. We will talk more."

As I was going out, a geezer in a ten thousand-dollar suit with dyed hair and a lot of bad cosmetic surgery was coming in.

"Who is this boy?" The geezer snarled at John. "Does he have security clearance?"

The wolf returned. I wanted to tear his throat out with my teeth. I struggled to control myself. I bit down hard on my lower lip and tasted blood. The pain drove the wolf away.

"Sir, could I get the name of the carpenter who belt sanded your face?" I asked.

The geezer turned bright red. The veins in his temple and neck popped out.

What's happening to me? I wondered.

"Mr. Secretary, come in. Good to see you," my grandfather said. "Why so glum?"

So, this is how it all started: with me making a decision based on crazy impulse, with no information whatsoever, that would change my life forever and almost kill me on numerous occasions.

CHAPTER 5

An hour later, Grandfather's chauffeur drove me away from the coastal estates of the North Shore deep into suburban Long Island. Black Escalades with tinted windows accompanied us front and rear. We passed one tract development after another.

What did they look like—those men who had murdered my family?

I shut my eyes and put myself into our kitchen.

***

Mom, Dad, Polly, and Max are sitting around the kitchen table eating hot dogs and baked beans. Max opens his mouth and shows Polly his half-chewed dog.

"Mom! Max is showing me his food!" Polly cries.

"Max Whitney, chew with your mouth shut, please," Mom says.

The hinge of door creaks.

A shadow crosses Dad's face. He looks up, startled and angry. "Can I help you?" he asks.

***

The limo slowed, and I woke up. A sign on a gateway said "Levittown, Nassau County, New York." We pulled in and drove along a street lined by identical white, Cape Cod-style houses built in the 1950s. We came to a cul-de-sac and pulled up in front of a house with a sign: "Doctor B. H Polemarchos. 15004 Sparrow Lane."

I got out of the limo and walked up the path to the front door. Three little girls pedaled by on bikes, chirping happily. Two pretty young mothers pushed their babies by in strollers.

"We're thinking of a nice birdbath," said one, a brunette.

"Will the association allow it?" asked the other, a blond.

"I doubt it," sighed the brunette. "They're so strict, and we have no pull with them at all—unlike like some people who get away with anything." She glared over at 15004 Sparrow Lane.

I walked toward the garden gnome guarding Dr. Polemarchos's front door. He seemed to be rather taller than the average gnome. When I came closer, I noticed he wasn't a gnome at all. Dr. Polemarchos's little statue had stick-up pointy ears, the body of a man on top, and goat legs and hooves on the bottom. He had nasty, squinty eyes and thick lips set in a lecherous leer. He also had a woody two feet long. I blushed and looked away.

It was—I knew from my reading in Greek mythology—the great god Pan. Pan is portrayed in modern books as an impish, fun-loving young sport who gambols about the Attic countryside playing his pipes and flirting with pretty tree nymphs. Not this Pan. This Pan hosted parties that served roasted newborns on the buffet table. He was not young. He was infinitely ancient. His features were worn with thousands of years of wind, sun, rain, and vice. Greasy yellow moss grew out of his pointy ears and drooled from between his fat, sensual lips. His eyes squinted with bestial violence and lust.

I shivered and hurried past him to press the doorbell button. There was no ding-dong, just a weird tingle through my finger and down my arm. The door swung open.

"Welcome, Lex," said a plump little bald fellow in his fifties, dressed in rumpled khakis and a white, short-sleeved button-down shirt with a plastic pocket-protector holding three Bic pens. "I am Dr. Polemarchos. You may call me Dr. Polemarchos."

I felt sure I had seen him before. He struck me as the sort of pathetic creature who worked in an appliance store on weekdays and tutored dumb, lazy, rich kids in remedial math on weekends. A pair of drugstore reading glasses hung on a gold-plated chain around his neck.

"I see you were admiring my Pan," he said.

"Well, yes," I replied doubtfully.

"Our word *panic* comes from him, you know."

"How interesting."

"Athena, as I am sure you know, represented for the ancient Greeks the heroic side of war, while Ares represents the vicious, bloodthirsty, and cowardly side. Pan is henchman to and creature of Ares. The Greeks believed that he inspired soldiers with the fear that caused them to run away in battle."

"Interesting," I repeated.

"And be slaughtered, of course, for there is nothing as foolhardy in war as to turn your back on your enemy and be cut down when you cannot defend yourself."

"I can see that."

"And my slippers? Do you like my new slippers?" he asked. I looked down. He wore fuzzy pink bunny slippers, with ears and all.

"Uh, yeah. I guess. Very handsome," I replied.

Weirdo!

"Welcome. Welcome. Welcome," he said in some sort of slight foreign accent. "Come in, come in, come in. Do come in."

I got the hint and went in. He extended his hand, and we shook. His grip was soft, fleshy, and moist.

"Would you mind, Lex, if I asked you to slip off your shoes and into a pair of these?" He pointed to a dozen pairs of fuzzy animal slippers— bunnies, squirrels, mice, an elephant, Donald Duck, and so forth—lined up in a neat row by the door. "Mud, you know."

"No, I don't mind."

"Some of my clients do mind, you know. Terribly. They consider it a dreadful imposition. There has been harsh language. Even threats. Once, violence was narrowly averted. Happily, she ended up accepting Donald Duck."

I picked a pair of fuzzy skunks.

"Ah, Mr. Skunk. Excellent choice," he said. "Very indicative. You and I will get along famously, I'm sure. Come along, now. Let's get started."

He shuffled off toward parlor, and I shuffled along behind, feeling degraded in my skunks. The parlor was shabby. A plastic mat covered the tattered sofa. He removed it and motioned for me to sit.

"How is your grandfather? In good health, I hope?" He sat down beside me a bit too close for comfort.

I edged away. "Yes."

"I heard about your family. I'm terribly sorry."

I mumbled something.

"Both your father and grandfather worked with me, you know."

"No, I didn't know."

Now I knew him! He was the fat, little man in all those photos.

He made his fingers do the "spider doing pushups on a mirror" thing. "To start the interview," he said, "I'd like to give you a little paper-and-pencil test. It will only take about ten minutes. Is that all right with you?"

"Sure."

He handed me a single sheet of paper and a sharp number two pencil. The test was multiple choice. It was also utter nonsense. One question was: "Would you describe yourself as A) a sunny day B) a chipmunk C) a can of tomato soup D) a blue dump truck."

I chose the can of tomato soup. I like tomato soup with a sprinkle of parmesan cheese. It's good cold too.

I finished and handed the test back to him. He put on his reading glasses.

"Interesting," he said. "Did you know that your PTV is ninety-ninth percentile?"

"Is that good?"

"It depends. And your CLS! Heavens, what a CLS!"

"Is that good?"

"Sometimes yes. Sometimes no. Your adjusted SDQ needs work though. How are your grades?"

"Medium."

"People with your characteristics are rarely comfortable in an academic environment. What's your favorite subject, Lex?"

"History. I love history," I said.

"Ah, I'm not surprised. Why history?"

"Because it's real."

"Real? Is it? Napoleon said that history is the lies historians agree to tell about the past." He stopped and waited for me to reply, but I didn't know what to say. "Of course, Napoleon turned bitter after we thrashed him at Waterloo. And what are your favorite parts of history?"

"The battles. I like the wars and battles."

"Naturally. Are you familiar with the Trojan War?

"Sure. We read parts of *The Iliad*."

"Did you like it?"

"No, sir, not really."

"But it's a battle story, Lex. The very first of its kind. And so very violent." He began to recite. "'Everywhere the battlements and bastions were awash with men's blood, Greek and Trojan ...'"

"I guess we didn't read the good parts."

He closed his eyes and recited more: "'Hector's armor yet showed where the collar-bones hold the neck from the shoulders, the throat, where death of the soul comes most quickly; in this place, brilliant Achilles drove the spear as he came on in fury, and clean through the soft parts of the neck the spear point was driven.' Marvelous, isn't it?" He sighed.

Dr. Polemarchos was beginning to scare me a little.

"Don't look so glum. You'll pass this interview." He pondered in silence for a few moments as I squirmed in my chair and wondered if the hour was almost up.

Finally, he said, "The Trojan horse."

"What about it?"

"What was it?"

"Everybody knows that."

This guy's an idiot.

"Tell me."

"It was a giant wooden horse. The Greeks hid soldiers in it and sailed away. The Trojans thought they had won the war and the horse was a victory gift. They pulled it inside the walls. The Greek soldiers snuck out that night, opened the gates, and let their army in. End of Troy."

"A good synopsis," he said. "Is that how Troy fell?"

"Sure."

"No, it didn't."

"But that's what *The Iliad* says."

"No, it doesn't. The horse isn't in *The Iliad*."

"Really? Are you sure?"

"Well, let's take a look and see if I'm right, shall we?" He stood up.

Take a look? WTF?

I followed Dr. Polemarchos through a ratty little study and into a shabby kitchen with avocado-colored linoleum countertops, a two-burner electric range, and an ancient Frigidaire with a big condenser on top. I stepped in an enormous dog water dish, drowned my right skunk, and cursed.

We stepped out a torn screen door into the small backyard. It was naked of all vegetation and strewn with enormous petrified turds that must have been laid by a rhinoceros. In the back, leaning against a tumble-down wooden fence, was one of those two-door Rubbermaid utility sheds you buy at Home Depot to store rusting cans of leftover paint. Dr. Polemarchos led me toward the Rubbermaid.

I stepped gingerly around the turds. I didn't want to break an ankle.

He flung open the doors of the shed. "Come right in," he said cheerfully.

We stepped inside. Bernie pulled the doors closed behind us. Inside it was very dark and creepy and smelled sort of … gamey. I heard a snuffling sound, like the nose breathing of some large beast. It seemed to be coming from the implausibly distant end of a very long passageway that simply couldn't exist in a Home Depot Rubbermaid utility shed—not even the deluxe, eight-by-ten model. I heard a low rumbling growl.

"Shit! What's that?" I jumped.

"It's just us, Kitty," he cooed into the darkness. "And, Lex, please do not curse. You might upset Kitty."

I certainly didn't want to upset Kitty.

Then he seized my hand very hard.

"Ouch!" I squeaked.

"Geronimo!" he cried.

CHAPTER 6

A blinding flash of light, and I was on the world's fastest elevator shooting upward. We reached the ten thousandth floor, and I hung pressed nose-first against the ceiling of the elevator for an instant. Then, I was on the world's fastest elevator shooting down again, leaving my guts plastered to the ceiling.

My butt hit bottom. "Ugh!" It knocked the breath out of me. My head ached. I felt blood running out of my nose. I wanted to puke.

I did puke.

"Grab the rail!" a deep voice shouted.

I pulled myself to my knees and grabbed the nearest firm object at hand, the rail. We were moving—very fast. I heard a thundering, drumming sound. Whack! Whack! My spine cracked, and my knees crashed up and down on the floor. I clung to the rail with all my might. We swayed to the right then to the left, whiplashing my neck and squishing my brain onto the left side of my skull and then onto the right.

"Stand up!" the voice shouted.

I grabbed the rail with both hands and pulled myself to my feet. My legs were Twizzlers.

A monster stood right beside me. He had greasy black hair that went down to his shoulders and a bushy black beard that went down to his barrel chest. His craggy face was covered with hideous scars. He was huge, at least six inches taller than me, and much broader across the shoulders. His upper arms were as big as my thighs and tattooed with strange symbols. He wore an ankle-length tunic made of armor that shimmered like fish scales.

A quiver of arrows and a bow were slung across his shoulders. A huge two-headed battle ax, a sword, and a dagger hung from his belt. Two spears stood in a holder fixed beside him. On his head was a helmet made from the six-inch ivory tusks of some beast. In his massive, gnarled hands, he held ropes. No, reins. They were attached to two horses galloping in front of us, hooves thundering, manes flowing, sleek with sweat.

Oh my God! We're in a chariot!

I nearly peed myself. To be honest, I did pee myself—just a couple of drops though.

"Who the hell are you?" I screamed.

"It's me, Polemarchos, you idiot!" the monster bellowed. "You may now call me *Master.*"

"Look there!" The new, horrible Dr. Polemarchos, pointed a golden-ringed finger the size of a carrot. Ahead of us across the plain stood a great walled city. Thousands of little figures, just like toy soldiers, were churning around its walls and over its battlements. Clouds of black smoke were billowing out of the city into the sky. I could hear distant cries.

"Troy!" he bellowed.

"No way," I gasped.

"Way, you imbecile!" he roared.

Something whistled by my left ear. Something whistled by my right ear. I felt a sting in the back of my right hand and heard a thunk. An arrow quivered in the rail. My hand was bleeding.

"Someone shot me!" I screeched and dove to the floor.

"Its war, little girl! Man up!" the Master shouted. "Look there: Phrygians!"

I peeked over the rail. Fifty yards in front of us, six men in pointy hats and capes were busily working bows. "Stand up!"

"I can't!" I whimpered and stayed where I was.

"Get on your feet!"

"I can't," I sobbed. "Don't make me."

He grabbed my collar and heaved me up like he was lifting a kitten. "Take these!" He thrust the reins into my hands.

"What do I do?" I squealed.

"Hold tight!"

The Phrygians were getting closer. Arrows whistled overhead. Thunk. Thunk. Thunk. Three stuck in the front of the chariot. The Master pulled the bow off his shoulder. He yanked an arrow from his quiver, fitted it on his bowstring, and pulled it back to his ear. Twang.

The nearest Phrygian dropped to his knees, tearing at an arrow buried in his chest. He coughed up a gout of blood and flopped face-first into the dust.

"You killed him!" I screamed.

"No shit, Sherlock," he replied. Twang. Twang. Twang. The Master pulled, fitted, drew, and shot.

One Phrygian collapsed with an arrow in his forehead. The second took a shaft right into his mouth. The third staggered away with an arrow in his neck. The severed artery spouted blood six feet into the air with each beat of his heart. The Phrygian made a ghastly gurgling sound, and a gush of hot pee filled my skunk slippers. The three surviving Phrygians were now only twenty yards in front of us.

"What do I do?" I screamed.

"Run them over, dumbass!" he roared.

One Phrygian froze and screamed as the horses trampled him under their churning hooves. I heard his bones snap and crack. The second tried to throw himself out of the way. Our left wheel bounced over his back. The chariot bucked, weaved, and nearly tipped over.

Five down, and one to go. The Master was holding his big two-bladed ax. He cleaved the survivor neatly in half as we passed. The bottom half, spouting gore, took two steps and crumbled. The top half hung in the air for half a second, flapping its arms, and dropped into the dust.

The Master grabbed the reins and pulled the horses to a stop. Five Phrygians and two half-Phrygians were strewn across the sand behind us. Five were motionless. One, his spine shattered, was dragging his dead legs away to some hiding place to die. The Master twanged an arrow into his skull.

I leaned over the rail and retched. Green bile this time.

"Fabulous!" The Master chuckled as he watched me wipe puke off my chin with my T-shirt. "Quite a rush, huh? Better than sex, huh?"

I hadn't the strength to reply that, of sex, I was wholly ignorant.

He snapped the reins. "Giddy up, boys." The horses broke into a trot, and the chariot lurched and bumped toward the city.

"I see you are admiring my bow," he said after a few minutes.

I hadn't been admiring his stupid bow. I hadn't been admiring anything. I felt sick, depressed, and terrified. I wanted to go home.

"Heh, Lex, chin up," the Master said as if he was reading my mind. "You're a hero next to most people. You didn't shit your pants. Everyone shits their pants in their first combat. You must have rhinoceros balls, kid." He squeezed my shoulder, bruising it badly.

We rode on for a few more minutes.

"So ... wanna hear about my bow?" he asked hopefully.

I wasn't about to disagree with this homicidal monster. "Love to," I said.

"It's a composite bow—the weapon of a Steppe horse king. The master bow-makers glued animal horn, ligament, and wood together into a laminate. It takes months to make one of these beauties, and they cost a fortune in their day. Composite bows are much more powerful than bows made from a single piece of wood. The Mongols will conquer the world with these weapons. This is the atom bomb of 1100 BC."

He handed it to me. I really didn't want to touch the murdering thing, but I took it because the Master was trying to be friendly, and I really, really wanted my new, horrible tutor to be friendly. The bow was much heavier than I thought it would be. The bone on its underside felt cool and smooth to my touch. Its outside was decorated with complicated carvings of chariot kings hunting lions and mythical beasts. The bow really was beautiful.

"Like the bow of Odysseus. Go ahead—draw it."

I couldn't get the string back to my chest, much less my ear.

"I can't."

He laughed. "Neither could the suitors in *The Odyssey*. Remember? Takes practice, boy. You've got to work at it. Ancient archers started by pulling their strings only back to their chests. Over centuries, they learned the advantage of pulling back to the ears. Much deadlier, but it takes years of practice and conditioning to learn to use one of these puppies."

I tried again. Grunting, I managed to pull the string almost to my chin.

"Better," he said. "You're not as much of a pussy as you look." He laughed. His teeth flashed. They were filed down to sharp points.

We rode on toward an ugly little brown hill.

"The so-called burial mound of Achilles," the Master said. "When he passed through here on his conquests, Alexander the Great stripped off his clothes and ran around it three times."

"Why?"

"Oh, Alex loved taking his clothes off in public. Great bod."

We rolled around the side of the hill, and I smelled a frightful reek. "What's that awful smell?" I asked.

"The Greek army, of course," he replied. "The brutes are strangers to soap and water. Time to see our Trojan horse."

It was surrounded by a milling mob of unwashed Achaean infantry men bearing great figure-eight chin-to-ankle horsehide shields, brandishing spears, and waving banners.

"Yo, Ajax," one filthy specimen shouted to a nearby man-mountain who was nearly seven feet tall. "How many Trojan girls will you nail today?"

"Twenty," replied Ajax. "A new record." He roared like a hungry bear and slammed his shield with his spear butt.

"Palamedes claims he ravished twenty-three when Mysia fell!" another soldier yelled.

"Yeah, but they were all boys!" Ajax roared.

Everyone had a good laugh.

The Trojan horse was not a horse at all, though it had a big horse head gaily painted on its side in red and blue paint. The square wooden tower was eight floors high and covered with fresh animal skins, which also stank to high heaven. The horse had four big wheels and a door in front at ground level out of which protruded an enormous tree trunk sharpened to a point. In the back, it had another door with a ladder leading up to the open penthouse, which was swarming with archers.

"It's a siege tower," the Master said, "invented by the Assyrians a hundred years before today but new and very high-tech in this benighted part of the world." He pointed to the tree trunk. "See that battering ram? It'll make short work of the Trojan wall."

Nearby, we saw a cluster of chariots manned by flashy dudes in gleaming armor and shining helmets topped with fancy plumes and feathers. We drove over to give our respects.

"Welcome, Lord Polemarchos," said the biggest, ugliest, shiniest dude in the bunch. He had to be speaking a very ancient Greek dialect, yet I understood it perfectly. More of the Master's magic, I supposed.

The dude was another seven-footer and weighed at least three hundred pounds. His battle-scarred, black-bearded mug looked like ten strong men had hacked it for a week with machetes. His enormous body was bound in six concentric bands of golden sheet armor from his toes to his chin. How he could fight in that regalia, I couldn't imagine. I couldn't have stood upright. His helmet had two giant ox horns sticking out of it. He held a round shield painted with a scary demon face and a spear about twenty feet long with a long, nasty point at the working end and a big spike at the bottom. A fine collection of human heads dangled from the sides of his chariot. Some were old and wizened. Others were fresh and covered with big, green-headed flies.

"Greetings, King Agamemnon." The Master turned to me and whispered, "Bow low. Very low, as if your life depended on it. It does."

I bowed so low my head touched my knees.

"Come to see my horse, Polemarchos?" Agamemnon said eagerly.

"Yes, my King."

"A splendid piece of work, don't you think?"

"Very fine, my King."

"Do you like the paint? I asked for a touch more orange in the red. I think this red has a bit too much green in it, but it's too late now to do it over."

"The red is perfect, King," said Bernie.

"Well, I beheaded the artist a few minutes ago anyway."

"Artists are a drachma a dozen, Your Majesty."

"It's just about dry now. In a minute or two, the boys will wet those skins down, and we can get started. Ah, here they are."

A bucket brigade of soldiers was entering the back door of the horse and climbing the internal ladder to the penthouse. The archers in the penthouse had shouldered their bows and were tipping the buckets of water down the sides.

"You're a bit late, almost missed the party. Where were you?" Agamemnon asked.

"We ran into some Phrygians, my King, and slew them all."

"Good job. Did you take their manly parts as trophies?" he inquired.

"No, my King," the Master said. "I have no use for more manly parts. My own are heavy enough."

That got a good laugh from Agamemnon and his boys.

"Did this young squire of yours account for any of the villains, Polemarchos?"

"Yes, King, two of six."

"Fine! Very fine!" exclaimed the king. "When the city falls, we will reward our young hero with a comely slave girl. What do you think of that, young hero?" He winked and licked his lips like a hungry iguana.

"I would be most grateful, King." Whatever language I was miraculously speaking, he understood me perfectly.

"Oh, to be young again!" He scratched his privates enthusiastically.

Agamemnon's staff of toadies and flunkies voiced their objections: "You are in your prime, sire! You're as young as you feel, lord! You look half your age, sir!" and "May the king live a thousand years!"

"Now, now," Agamemnon said, waving his hand dismissively while blushing like a schoolgirl. "Ah, I see the boys are ready. Where are the priests! Call the goddamn priests!"

"Priests! Priests!" the call went out from the flunkies.

Three white-robed geezers with long hair and beards down to their stomachs staggered on stage. The first led a magnificent white bull by a golden chain. The second carried a golden basin. The third priest carried what looked like a solid-gold Weber barbeque grill. The first priest tinkled a little golden bell.

Agamemnon and his entourage bowed their heads reverently.

The priests brayed a prayer to Zeus, Poseidon, Ares, and Athena, beseeching the immortals to take the Greek side in the upcoming battle. The prayer ended. The priest holding the golden chain drew a knife and deftly slit the bull's throat. The poor beast mooed once and collapsed.

Blood spurted from his neck into the second priest's basin. He swirled the blood around and examined it. "The auguries are favorable!" he croaked.

"Favorable auguries. What a surprise," the Master whispered. "If that priest had said *unfavorable*, his head would be on the ground by now."

"Praise Zeus! Sound the trumpets for the advance!" Agamemnon hollered.

Six soldiers lifted long silver horns to their lips and blew a shrieking blast that made our horses rear. The mass of infantry clashed their spears on their shields and chanted: "Horse! Horse! Horse!"

They began to push. The horse creaked, groaned, and started moving toward the city with King Agamemnon and his general staff following close behind.

We hung back. "We shall stay out of bow-shot range," the Master said. "Officially, we're not supposed to get involved. We're only observers. And there's no point getting you killed on your first day. Right, boy? Right? Can't have that." He whacked me so hard on the back that I nearly swallowed my tongue.

He flicked the reins, and we bumped and rolled over to a safe spot a few hundred yards to the right of the horse. On top of the walls, the Trojans were scurrying around like angry ants after, out of sheer boyish malice, you fetch their hill a good kick. Smoke rose from the city.

"They're lighting their fire arrows," Dr. P. remarked.

Sure enough, as soon as the horse drew within bow range, clouds of flaming arrows arched out from the city and struck the horse. They sizzled and snapped on the wet animal skins, but none started a fire. In return, the Greek archers on the horse and the thousands on the ground returned fire.

Pin-cushioned Trojans began to tumble from the battlements. It looked like the Greeks were the better shots.

"Aggie knows his business. Ah, they're at the wall. Now let's see what his boys are made of."

The horse's ram thundered against the gate. Boom! Boom! From the horse's penthouse, which was six feet higher than the top of the wall, the Greeks were shooting arrows and hurling spears and stones down on the Trojans on the battlements.

"Keeping their heads down until the ram cracks the gate. Then they'll attack from below and above simultaneously. The Trojans better do something—or the Greeks will be inside the city in ten minutes."

There was a blast of trumpets from within the city. "Ah!" the Master exclaimed. "Here's the Trojan sally!"

A mob of Trojan chariots rounded the corner of the city walls from the right and galloped toward the horse, raising a great cloud of dust and followed by masses of Trojan infantry puffing along behind them. Happily, we were well out of their path.

"They're going to burn the horse or push it over. Priam has committed his reserve."

"Reserve?" I asked.

"Those are the fresh soldiers a general holds back until he assesses that the crisis moment of the battle has come. If Priam's timing is right, he'll panic the Greeks and turn the tide. Too early or too late, and he's screwed."

Trumpets blasted to our left. "That would be Agamemnon, committing his reserve," the Master explained.

Agamemnon and bodyguard peeled off from the horse and led several thousand Greek infantrymen straight for a head-on crash into the charging Trojans.

"The decisive moment of the battle! Don't you love it?"

"Sure," I said. It was fun to watch ... from a safe distance.

There came a splintery crash and great roar from the Greek host. The ram had stove in the gate, and now the Greek infantry were shoving their way into the city. From the penthouse of the horse, the Greeks had lowered a drawbridge onto the wall and were surging across. Shrieking Trojans, some of them aflame, were falling from the battlements in a steady rain.

The two reserves crashed against one another outside the wall. The Greeks advanced a few steps, pushing the Trojans back. The Trojans advanced a few steps, pushing the Greeks back. Then, suddenly, a spasm stirred the Trojan ranks, as if the whole army had suddenly flinched. I saw men in the rear ranks lower their arms and hesitate. I saw one man in the rear rank step backward, then another. The first man dropped his shield and spear, turned, and ran. In an instant, the whole Trojan host disintegrated into a mob of fear-crazed men in flight.

Except for two chariots, laggards, which I noticed were rounding the corner of the city. They were charging not at Agamemnon and the Greeks but at us.

"Look there, Master," I gasped.

"Hmm," the Master said. "What are these two idiots up to?"

The two chariots galloped closer.

"The rules say that we're not to fight unless we absolutely have to," he said. "Let's get out of here." He snapped the reins and turned our chariot away from the Trojans. "Ya!" He howled and whipped the horses. "Go, Boreus! Go, Notus! Ya!" We surged forward ... and I tumbled out the back!

I sprawled on my butt in the dirt as the Master galloped away.

I jumped up, kicked off my skunks, and took to my heels barefoot. The chariot was now only a speck in the distance. I sprinted for him, waving my arms and shouting.

I was the fastest player on my football team—over a nice, flat football field in cool Vermont weather. Here—on the Trojan plain in hundred-degree heat, barefoot over gravel and sand, detouring around boulders and nasty patches of cactus, and leaping over holes and dry streambeds—it was a different story.

After ten minutes, I was soaked in sweat and gasping for breath. My feet were cut and shredded. I stumbled over a flat rock and just missed stepping on an enormous serpent sunning himself. He awakened cranky from his nap, coiled, and took a shot at me. His fangs barely missed my ankle, and I had just enough juice left in my legs to dance away.

I figured I was going to die out there on the Trojan plain, devoured by beasts and picked clean by vultures, when I saw that the chariot had turned around and was galloping back toward me. The Master had finally noticed my departure. My morale soared ... and then my right ankle buckled, and I went down on my face.

I lay there stunned for a moment and spat out a mouthful of sand and a small beetle. My ankle ached terribly. I rolled over and saw that the two Trojan chariots were now only fifty yards away and thundering down on me fast.

And that thing that happened to me in football happened again. I knew exactly what to do. Ignoring the pain, I jumped up. I saw everything with supernatural clarity. I saw that the lead chariot was manned by a driver with brown eyes and a javelin man with a scar on his left cheek. I saw the sweat beaded on the driver's forehead. I heard the javelin man grunt as he heaved his weapon. The javelin flew toward me in super slow motion. I saw the point glisten in the sunlight. I saw the slow rotation of its shaft. I crouched, and the javelin inched over my head and clattered into the rocks.

I would fight. I reached down and picked up a stone at my feet. It was exactly the right size, weight, and shape. I cocked to throw it. The first chariot was now forty yards away, moving very slowly, and the driver's sweaty forehead appeared to me as big as the side of a house. I let it fly. My stone traced an elegant arc right into the driver's forehead, just above his nose. A splinter of bloody bone flew upward. His eyes rolled back. His tongue lolled out. Already dead, he pulled the reins to the right and crashed into the second chariot. Both chariots hurtled into a pile of boulders. I heard skulls bursting like melons on the rocks. From the boulder pile, I heard groans, whimpers, and wet gurgles—and then nothing.

The Master thundered up, stopped beside me, and grunted. "Four down with one rock. Your Gramps said you have a knack for the killing business."

"Thank you." I felt incredibly good. Then I felt incredibly awful. I had killed four men! I wanted to throw up again.

"Get in."

"Yes, Master." I jumped aboard. Great billows of smoke were rising from Troy. The city had fallen.

"By the way, now that we are comrades in arms, you may drop this pretentious *Master* business. Call me Bernie."

"Yes, Bernie."

"Let's go home." He seized my hand. There was a blinding flash of light.

This time, I passed out.

CHAPTER 7

I dreamed of war chariots and burning cities and a giant horse machine painted like a sixties love van with psychedelic designs and "Make love—not war!"

The birds twittered outside my bedroom window. I heard a discreet knock on my door.

"Sir, there is a breakfast buffet set up in the dining room. Your grandfather is waiting for you."

My ankle ached, but otherwise, I felt terrific. I got out of bed and limped over to my closet to get clothes. The weird 1960s gear was gone and had been replaced with normal clothes—two suits, two jackets, dress pants, ties, khakis, blue jeans—all of it brand-new Brooks Brothers or Ralph Lauren. I'd never seen so many nice clothes in my life. We didn't dress that way at home. Then, I remembered that home was gone.

I chose some khakis and went to the dresser. There were piles of briefs, socks, Polo shirts, shorts, and T-shirts. One drawer was full of button-downs. I chose a dark green Ralph Lauren. There were ten pairs of shoes in the bottom of the closet. I took black Nikes.

I looked fabulous. If only Deanna could see me now.

Where was Deanna? My grandfather had said that she worked with him. Did that mean I would see her again? I wanted to see her again. I remembered her kiss and blushed.

The dining room sideboard was laid out with a huge breakfast spread. I walked over, picked up a plate, and prepared to help myself when the cat leapt up right in front of me and began sniffing at the bacon. I shooed him. He withdrew a few steps, sat down, and stared at me with malevolent yellow eyes. I shooed him again, and he refused to budge. I gave up, helped myself to two heaping plates of scrambled eggs, fried eggs, a cheese omelet, toast, waffles, pancakes, bacon, sausages, steak, home fries, and three kinds of muffins, and sat down at one end of the dining room table. The cat snatched a piece of bacon and carried it off.

My grandfather sat at the other end of the table behind a copy of *Jomhuri Eslami*, which I knew was the Iranian state newspaper. He was dressed for golf, 1900s style: knickers, high socks, argyle sweater, and cap. Somehow, he did not look foolish in his outfit. Everything about my grandfather always demanded respect.

"Good morning," he said.

"Good morning," I replied and commenced stuffing my face.

"The Persians are acting up again."

"Mmmmf." I swallowed a mouthful of waffles. "Persians?"

"Iranians. The mullahs say that the Great Satan must withdraw its carriers from their gulf or there will be hell to pay."

"Mmmmmf. Who's the Great Satan?" I wasn't much up on current events. I had lived most of my life entirely cut off from the world.

"Us," my grandfather answered. "It's the usual bluster. Unless, of course ..." He stopped and peered at me with disgust over his reading glasses. "I can see you are too preoccupied with what I would loosely call *dining* to discuss issues of vital international importance." He returned to his paper.

I went back for seconds. When I had finished my third plate, I sat back in my chair, sighed, and patted my full belly.

"Done?" he asked. "Or shall I have the cook roast you a steer?"

"All done," I said and belched.

"I suppose you have the right to eat like a wolf this morning," he said.

"What do you mean?"

"After your strenuous activities with Dr. Polemarchos yesterday."

"Activities?"

"How did you find Troy?"

I knocked over my plate, shooting leftover scrambled eggs and bits of sausage all over my shirt. "Wait a minute!" I cried. "How do you know about my dream?"

"Because it was not a dream," he said calmly. "Look at your hand."

I gaped at the cut where the arrow had nicked me.

"And what about that ankle? Did you sprain that in bed?"

"Holy shit!" I cried.

"Indeed, but I wish you would not curse. It seems you have learned bad habits at that public high school you attend. I told your father he should send you to Groton or Eton."

"That's crazy!" I croaked.

"Definitely," my grandfather said coolly. "My first outing with Dr. Polemarchos came as a shock to me too. It took your father a full week to get over his. I was worried the experience had unhinged his mind."

"What the f—"

He gave me a stern look. "Is that a question, however vulgarly put?"

"Yes, sir."

"Then the answer you seek is: Dr. Polemarchos travels in time."

John appeared and dabbed at my shirt front with a moist rag and a bottle of spot remover.

"And space too," John added. "You always forget space, sir."

"Quite right, John," Grandfather said, looking slightly peeved.

"How?" I croaked.

"I haven't a clue. Perhaps John can explain."

"I will try, sir," said John.

I followed him on special and general relativity but lost him on Gödel space-time and the Novikov self-consistency principle.

"I call it magic," Grandfather said.

John said, "It is, sir—to us." The doorbell jingled, and he jumped up. "That would be the ambassador," he said, gliding away.

Grandfather stood. "Dr. Polemarchos tells me that you did very well yesterday. He wishes to take you on as his apprentice. Would you like that?"

I didn't hesitate. "Yes," I answered. For all that I'd been terrified at Troy, it was the coolest thing I had ever done—probably the coolest thing that anyone had ever done.

"Excellent," he replied. "You will begin tomorrow."

"But, Grandfather, just one thing."

"Yes."

"Who is Dr. Polemarchos?"

"Not *who* is Dr. Polemarchos, Lex. *What* is Dr. Polemarchos is the better question, Lex."

"What do you mean?"

"Dr. Polemarchos is a Wargod, Lex."

"A what?" I goggled.

"A Wargod. That's what they call themselves. JFK called them war *clods*. But only behind their backs, of course. He didn't like them. He thought even the best of them were arrogant."

"They?"

"There are many others beside Dr. Polemarchos. Many of them are not as friendly as he. In fact, they hate us and are extremely dangerous. We call them The Others. It was they who killed your family."

My wolf stepped out of the forest, and I felt that red-hot surge. My face reddened.

My grandfather noticed and scowled. "Dr. Polemarchos will teach you about that. And many other things about our business and about who you are too, Lex." He extended his hand and shook mine. "Good luck, young man. I know you will make me proud."

He walked toward the door, stopped, and turned. "You see, Lex, you are quite an unusual person."

He walked out.

CHAPTER 8

My new life began the next morning promptly at seven at Bernie's ratty little house.

The squishy Bernie opened the door even before I had rung his bell. "Good morning. Good morning. Good morning," he said. "So pleased you've decided to join me. So very, very pleased."

He wore an aqua sweater vest and black and white checked Walmart slacks. No armor. No boar's tooth helmet. No composite bow, thank God. "Welcome, welcome, welcome. Come in, come in, come in," he cried. "Come in!"

I went in.

"Welcome!" he repeated.

I slipped out of my shoes and realized that I had ditched my skunks at Troy. I chose the elephants.

"Elephants never forget," Bernie remarked cryptically. "Come along now, and I'll show you your room. You'll be staying here for a time while I get you ready."

"How long?"

"Rome wasn't built in a day," he quipped, shuffling away on worn-out bunnies.

"Ready for what?"

But he had already vanished with surprising speed for a chubby man.

He led me to the back of the house and into a tiny little bedroom. Squeezed into a space much smaller than my room at my grandparent's house was a bed, a bureau, a desk, a chair, and a closet. The single, cloudy window overlooked Bernie's wretched little backyard. He threw open the closet door. "Everything you'll need," he said and immediately slammed it shut.

45

I didn't get much of a look, but the closet seemed to contain a very odd collection of clothes. Some of them looked like dresses.

"Do you like it?" he asked hopefully. "You must keep it tidy: bed made to military barracks specifications. A one-drachma piece dropped on the bed must bounce three inches high. You will do your own laundry. I have no washer or dryer, so you will have to wash and dry your clothes the traditional way. There is a tub, a nice flat rock, and a clothesline in the yard. Your clothes must be folded neatly and put away. You will help me with the dishes after all meals. I require you to broom clean the entire house daily or as needed if Kitty tracks in human remains. One of the duties of a soldier is to keep your barracks, yourself, and your weapons clean."

"Soldier?"

"Of course. You are a soldier now, Lex. No one enters this house but you and me and Kitty. Oh, I forgot. You must put Kitty out every evening before bed. Security, you know. She is a first-class watch cat."

"I bet," I said.

"The bathroom is just down the hall. You've seen the kitchen. I'm an excellent cook. What are your favorite foods? I'm especially good at Greek cuisine. Do you like stuffed grape leaves? And Retsina?"

"Bernie, how long am I going to be here?"

"I have no idea. We could be interrupted by unexpected exigencies at any time. The more you learn before we are called, the more likely you are to survive. You do want to survive, don't you?"

"Yes." I was pretty sure about that.

"Good. Then come along now. There's not a moment to lose." He vanished out the bedroom door.

I found him a moment later in the parlor. His plump white body was now stuffed into a pair of very short, skin-tight camouflage shorts and an equally tight T-shirt faded with age and stenciled "Legion d'Etranger— Maroc." I caught a glimpse of pink belly sticking out from under his shirt and looked away in horror. His footwear was just plain embarrassing: a pair of high-top, pink and black Ked basketball sneakers with silver laces and red and green Tartan socks pulled up to mid chubby white calf. His forehead was wrapped in a Japanese pilot's headband stenciled (in English) "Okinawa Kamikaze Club. 1945. No Pain. No Gain."

"Please sit down," he said, gesturing toward a plastic-covered chair.

It crinkled under my weight and stuck to my bare legs.

"Did you know that, throughout the history of war, infantrymen have carried an average load on their backs of exactly 79.7 pounds?"

"Bernie, where did you get those socks?" I asked, trying hard not to laugh.

He ignored me and went on, "War is a very strenuous endeavor."

"Yes, it is," I said, thinking of my sprint across the Trojan plain chased by those two chariots.

"An exhausted soldier is much more likely to get himself killed or lose heart and run away from a fight than a fit solder, do you see?"

"Yes."

"So, your very first responsibility as a commander—"

Me, a commander?

"Is to ensure that your men—"

My men?

"Are well-housed, well-clothed, well-fed, well-rested, and physically fit. Do you understand?"

"Yes, Bernie."

"The first weeks of your apprenticeship will be devoted to your own physical training. Are you ready to work hard?"

"Yes, Bernie."

"Oh, good boy," he said cheerfully and clapped his chubby hands. "Then, it's time for a nice little run. How is your ankle?"

"Better," I replied. I recovered from injuries quickly in those days. At least from ankle sprains, if not as quickly from sword and bullet wounds.

"Put these on please." He handed me a pair of sandals.

"Sandals, Bernie? How can I run in sandals?" I protested.

"Soldiers ran in sandals for thousands of years," he answered. "Or barefoot. You may run barefoot if you wish."

"No, thanks." I put them on. They were leather, and the ancient design laced high up the calf so they stayed on.

"And this too," he said and pulled a black vest from a coat hook by the door. He held it out to me by one finger.

I took hold of the vest, and it crashed to the floor.

"Just a hundred pounds to start, because of your ankle," Bernie said. "We'll add more. We've got to make you fit, fit, fit!"

"Do we start right now?"

"Oh, no. Tomorrow. I just wanted to show you my running outfit. Do you like it?"

He sucked in his gut and stuck out his chest.

"It's very nice, Bernie," I said.

CHAPTER 9

My training began in earnest the next morning. Bernie placed one of those air horns football fans use to cheer on their team to my right ear and let fly. It blew me right out of bed onto the floor.

"Wakey-wakey, eggs and bakey!" he screamed at the top of his lungs.

I moaned softly and looked at my watch. It was three o'clock in the morning.

I pulled on my running clothes and staggered down to the kitchen for breakfast. It was not IHOP's country fried steak and eggs breakfast combo with hash browns and the mega-stack of buttermilk pancakes on the side.

The first course was a big brown loaf of grainy bread burnt on one side and raw in the middle. It tasted like Bernie had mown the turd grass in his backyard, crushed it with a dirty rock, and roasted it on an open fire made from camel dung.

"Mmmmm. Delicious," I lied. "But how about a little butter? Or maybe some strawberry jam?"

Bernie handed me a dish of greenish olive oil sour with age.

The bread was followed by coarse, tasteless porridge in a crusty wooden bowl black with ancient grease. There was something Bernie called "bacon" floating in this pig swill. The "bacon" was a slab of yellow fat. By the smell of it, it had been laying in the sun for a week. On the side, there was a plate of brown roots. Dirt still clung to them.

"This is disgusting," I observed.

"The Roman army conquered the world on this food," Bernie declared.

I was hungry. I ate all of it.

We ran seven days a week for a month. "You must be fit, fit, fit!" Bernie chanted, running in place, taking deep, cleansing breaths, and hammering his chest with his fists. "A warrior must be fit!"

He always wore his bizarre workout clothes. He was very proud of his outfit. Bernie had terrible fashion taste. It was like he came from Planet Walmart or something.

I always wore the vest. It almost killed me, but after a few weeks, I had gotten used to the hundred-pounder.

Bernie gave me a hundred and twenty-five-pounder. He seemed to have an unlimited supply of these instruments of torture in his closet.

Do you know those fancy cardio machine monitors that show you jogging through fashionable spots like Rodeo Drive or Martha's Vineyard? You stand on them with one eye on the screen and the other glued to the shapely yoga pant bottom of the young woman in front of you. Bernie and I didn't have the girl, but we did have the scenery. Only it was real. We'd step into the Rubbermaid utility shed. Whatever was lurking back there in the darkness had stopped growling at me.

"You like Lex, don't you, Kitty?" Bernie asked the beast. "I don't think she'll eat you now … probably."

Bernie would grab my hand, and in a blink, we'd be jogging across a dusty desert while a strange, hairy little man with a bow slung over his shoulder watched us from a shaggy pony. Or we'd jog across a vast empty plain past the blackened hulks of burnt-out tanks or through a city of flaming buildings and streets scattered with corpses.

I had natural speed and strength and that weird, unnatural talent, but I had never worked hard at developing my skills. Bernie's pace was murderous. I couldn't count the times that I threw up. The pain in my legs and lungs was excruciating.

I knew that I had to distract myself from that pain or I would quit. I didn't know what Bernie would do if I quit. The squishy Bernie might be forgiving. The other Bernie, the one from Troy, might just hack my head off. I didn't want to know which Bernie I would see, so I began using mental tricks to keep myself going. At first, I distracted myself by concentrating on football. I ran a highlight film of Lex's greatest plays in my head. That worked until Bernie led me up some ten thousand-foot alpine trail, and I wanted to die. Football wasn't working, so I switched over to filling my head with pictures of Deanna: her pretty hair, her pretty eyes, Deanna kicking her soccer ball past my football practice, Deanna saving me from Corky.

Corky. He had tried to kill me. Others like him had killed Mom, Dad, Polly, and Max. Rage and bloodlust swelled up hot in my heart. Finally, I had come to the one mental trick, the one distraction from Bernie's torture that worked. I began planning my sweet revenge. How would I catch those murderers? What exactly would I do to them when I caught them? Would it be a quick death for them or a prolonged, agonizing one? I dwelt on this question as I ran. Vengeance was the best motivator of all.

Still, one day, I reached my limit and rebelled. Bernie, that sadist, had extended our run by an hour and added an extra fifty pounds to my vest. I'd had enough. I wasn't going to take it anymore. Nobody could push me around. Nobody could tell me what to do.

We were running along a soggy path through a thick jungle. The midday sun barely peeked through the forest canopy. It was perpetual twilight and yet unbearably hot and humid, like running up to my neck in a bubbling deep-fryer. I felt like a human onion ring. Clouds of mosquitoes swarmed around my face. There was no breeze, no air. I couldn't catch my breath. The vest—now at two hundred pounds—was rubbing my shoulders raw. A blister had burst on the sole of my right foot, and I could feel blood in my sandal.

I quit.

I threw myself to the ground, hacking and gasping for air. I gagged. I choked. I knelt and faked blowing my lunch.

Bernie stopped running and just stood there watching me. When I had finished my little act, he asked, "Do you want to die?" His voice was different. It wasn't jolly, warm, old Bernie anymore. His voice was forty degrees below zero.

"I am dying," I said.

"No, you're not. But you will die if you behave like this where we're going."

I whined that I couldn't go on. I'd hurt my bad ankle. I'd strained my knee. I had a cramp. I had a blister, probably a hernia. I was dizzy, probably a stroke. I was sick. I begged him to let me rest.

"I do not give motivational lectures," Bernie said. "You either get up or follow me—or you do not." He turned and started off on his high-stepping jog. His feet sloshed along the path.

I lay on my stomach, watching his fat rump jiggle around a corner and out of sight. In a few moments, the thump of his footsteps disappeared. Silence fell over the jungle.

Where the hell am I?

The jungle stirred and came to life. Far above me in the tree canopy, monkeys chattered, and birds warbled and squawked.

He's coming back. Isn't he?

The bushes rustled to my left. A plump hamster-looking animal scurried across the path from the left and disappeared into the bushes to my right. A small, spotted snake slithered through a puddle. I slapped a mosquito on my arm and then one on my cheek. Bees buzzed.

Bernie, where are you?

From my right came a bloodcurdling shriek.

Shit! What was that?

I leapt to my feet. The bushes writhed. Branches tossed and shook. Another shriek. Then silence.

I stared into the jungle murk. Then I saw it: the vine-wrapped fuselage of a silver plane. On the side of the plane, just below the cockpit, were faded words: "Slammin' Sammy Prescott."

Sitting in the cockpit was Slammin' Sammy himself. Sammy wore a shattered helmet and a rotting, mold-covered flight suit. Tendrils of green flesh hung from his cheeks. Maggots crawled in and out of his eye sockets. A silver snake wriggled in his right ear and out his left. Sammy was grinning at me.

Horrified, I took a step to run. My foot touched something. Some primitive survival instinct made me freeze. I looked down. My left foot was pushed against a thin silver wire strung tight across the path—a booby trap! One misstep, and I would have blown off my foot. Crippled, I would have lain there on the path bleeding until whatever it was that had just killed that hamster-thing came back and ate me at its leisure.

Will it start with my eyeballs? My soft parts?

Suddenly, I saw a vision of our kitchen. Mom, Dad, Polly, and little, chubby Max are having lunch around the kitchen table. Mom has whipped up one of her lovely cheese omelets. Logs are popping in the wood stove. Max opens his mouth and shows Polly his half-chewed lunch.

"Ew. Gross!" Polly cries. "Mom, Max is showing me his food."

"Max, chew with your mouth closed," Mom says.

Dad is smiling.

The creak of door hinges.

A shadow crosses Dad's face. He looks up, startled and angry. "May I help you?" Dad says. Suddenly, Dad turns to me and says, "Lex, my son. Who will avenge us if you die here?"

I ever so carefully stepped over the wire.

"Bernie! Yo, Bernie! Wait up! I'm coming," I shouted and sprinted after him.

I never quit again. I whined a bit, dogged it from time to time, and faked a little injury here and there, but I never quit.

CHAPTER 10

I wore the sandals Bernie had given me and got terrible blisters.

"A warrior must care for his feet," Bernie said. "A soldier's feet—not his junk—are his most important parts. Never forget it."

He gave me a little bag with a razor blade, matches, Band-Aids, and petroleum jelly. He taught me how to heat the razor red hot with the matches, puncture the blister, squeeze out the pus, and cover it with a Band-Aid. He showed me how to use the jelly to grease up places on my foot where the sandals would raise blisters.

The blisters healed and I got used to the sandals.

As soon as Bernie saw that I could run comfortably again, he made me throw them away and run barefoot.

"You never know," he said. "Might lose a sandal."

The soles of my feet got so callused that I could walk on broken glass and not feel it. I know because Bernie made me run back and forth across a busted Retsina bottle. He drank a lot of Retsina, but he never showed any effects whatsoever. I couldn't stand the stuff. It tasted like warm pine cone juice.

So, we ran and ran. I soon realized that I was getting very strong and mentally tougher and tougher. In some ways, I was turning into a different person.

We ran for a month. Then my training suddenly ended. One morning at five o'clock, I was out in the yard as usual, starting to pull on my vest. It was two hundred fifty pounds, more than my body weight. It felt light as a feather.

I was "Fit! Fit! Fit!"

"Forget the vest," Bernie said. "Today we begin our classes."

I dropped the damn thing on the ground and glared at it. I invited it to perform unnatural sexual acts on itself.

"Classes?"

"Yes. Today we begin our studies of war." Bernie opened the Rubbermaid doors. "Have you ever wondered, Lex, when war began?"

"To tell you the truth, Berns, no." I wasn't scared of Bernie anymore. Chubby Bernie hadn't been Awful Bernie for a long time, and I had begun addressing him in a somewhat disrespectful and familiar fashion.

"Why do we fight wars, Lex?"

"I haven't given either of those things a single thought in my entire life, Berns. Sorry."

He grunted. "Too busy slobbering over girls and stuffing yourself on McDougal's fast food, I suppose?

"Yes, Berns. But its McDonald's."

"And sports."

"Football. Yes, Berns.

"Sports are just frivolous imitations of war, you know."

"Yes, Berns."

"Why not enjoy the real thing? The genuine article? The real McCoy?"

"Why not, indeed, Berns?" I replied.

We stepped inside the Rubbermaid, and Bernie closed the doors behind us. The thing-in-the-darkness snuffled and whined.

"Don't worry, Kitty," Bernie said. "We'll be home soon."

Bernie grabbed my hand.

Zam! We were in another world.

This world was ferociously hot. The sun looked bigger than normal. We were on a vast sandy plain. I glanced over at Bernie. He was stark naked. I averted my eyes in horror. Bernie in the buff was very disturbing.

But much worse than seeing Bernie naked was seeing that I was naked too. I covered myself.

"Bernie, we're naked!" I cried.

"No shit, Shylock," he said.

"That's Sherlock," I said.

"Better put on this sunblock," Bernie said and handed me a plastic bottle. It was marked "#6000." I slathered it on.

The terrain looked African: an endless expanse of dry grassland interspersed with a few patches of dusty, stunted trees. In the far distance, a single volcanic cone thrust up out of the plain. It reminded me of the pictures I had seen of Mount Kilimanjaro, but Kilimanjaro was dead. This volcano was still pumping out black smoke. I heard distant rumbling and felt a tremor at my feet.

Bernie pointed toward the mountain. "Let's stroll on over in that direction and see what we can see." He began his jog.

I kept my eyes glued to the ground. The plain was alive with strange animals. A small herd of weird little horsey creatures about three feet tall galloped away as we approached. "Hipparion," I noted. "Three-toed ancestors of our horse."

"Correct," Bernie said. "I see that your studies have included prehistoric African fauna."

True. I had spent many a happy hour pouring over Novak's definitive sixteen-volume *Mammals of the World from the Pliocene to Today*.

We jogged past a herd of twenty huge cow-beasts. The smallest stood about six feet tall at the shoulders and had enormous curved horns eight feet from tip to tip. The bull was a monster—ten feet tall and weighing as much as two Cadillac Escalades. He raised his head from the grass, watched us pass, switched his tail to shoo away flies, and went back to his lunch.

"*Pelorovis antiquus*," I observed.

"Ancestor to the T-bone you had last night."

"No. Pelorovis is ancestor to the African Buffalo not to the genus *Bos* to which our modern beef cattle belong."

"I stand corrected."

"Furthermore, we had putrid goat stew last night, Bernie, not T-bone."

"Goat is better," he said. "Less cholesterol."

We jogged on. "Now, where are they?" Bernie fretted. "Have they moved on? Ah-ha. There they are at last."

A quarter mile ahead, I saw a large gray lump in the scrub. It was surrounded by a half dozen moving figures. Apes? Baboons? I didn't like the look of them.

"We'll stop here," Bernie said. "Have a drink."

I shooed a seven-foot lizard off a flat rock where he'd been sucking up four-inch ants. I sat down. I was pouring sweat. Bernie was completely dry. He didn't seem to have sweat glands. He produced a World War II GI canteen out of somewhere and offered it to me. I took a swig.

"Do you need to pee?"

"No, Bernie. I do not need to pee. And I don't see how it's any of your business."

"You should need to pee. If you do not need to pee, you are dehydrated. If you are dehydrated, you will drop dead from heatstroke, and I will have to explain your demise to your grandfather. Have another drink."

Bernie watched me gulp. "More," he ordered.

I drank more. I drank until I felt a quart of cold water sloshing around in my guts. I looked in the canteen. It was still full to the brim. I drank another pint. It was still full.

"Okay, enough," Bernie said. "Now when you do pee, you must tell me if your pee is clear or yellow. It should be clear."

"Bernie," I protested. "I do not wish to discuss my pee anymore."

"All righty, then die of heatstroke," he said petulantly. "Let's pop over and have a chat with those fellows."

We jogged along, and the big gray lump became a large dead animal, then a dead elephant, then an enormous rotting mammoth with gigantic curved tusks covered in dark clouds of buzzing flies. A little band of furry people were busy slicing chunks of meat off the beast and gnawing them—flies and all. They, too, were naked. A waft of putrid meat attacked my nose.

Bernie stopped. "Luncheon al fresco, circa 800,000 BC, East Africa," he remarked. "Delightful. Could be the Jardine des Tuileries in Paris. Straight out of an Impressionist painting. Right?"

"Not right."

One furry person—the largest one—spotted us. He jumped up and down, gibbered grunts, clicks, and squeaks and pointed.

Bernie replied in his grunts, clicks and squeaks: "Friends! Friends!"

I understood him perfectly. "How do you do that?" I asked him in grunts, clicks, and squeaks.

"I have a knack for languages," he replied.

Upon a closer look, I saw that the people weren't exactly people. They were people-ish, but not like the folks you typically see down at the mall. They were stark naked, of course, and the bodies of these sort-of people were covered with a thin coat of brown hair. Their heads were longer and larger than ours, and their foreheads were much lower. Their features were flat with broad noses and very wide nostrils. All of them were busy twitching their noses to get a good whiff of us. Their bodies were smaller than Bernie's and mine and much more lightly built. They looked designed for sprinting away from the giant hungry beasts that must be lurking everywhere in this strange land.

The largest and bravest of the band, the leader, stepped forward and twitched his nose. He grimaced and waved his hand in front of his face like Bernie and I had just farted in the parlor after a spicy Indian dinner.

"Bernie, those people aren't people," I said.

"How very astute of you to notice," Bernie replied. "They are *Homo erectus*. That big guy is probably your great-to-the-five-hundre d-thousandth-power-grandfather."

"Yours, maybe, but not mine," I said defensively.

"Not likely," he replied. "I am not from around here."

Great-Gramps waved his arms and snarled, displaying a pair of very large, pointy canines.

"Our lunch!" I heard. "Go away, bad, smelly thief!"

Bernie shouted, "Friends, we don't want your lunch. We've already dined." He patted his tummy and smiled contentedly.

"Our lunch!" the leader insisted. "Go away!" He turned his butt to us. I figured he was going to moon us. Instead, he squatted and squeezed a generous bowel movement onto the ground. He scooped up the product of his exertions and threw it at us. "Eat this!" he yelled.

"I don't think he likes us, Bernie," I said, as the turd splattered my bare toes. "Let's move on."

"No, Lex. I brought you here to learn. And learn you will, even if it kills you. Now, let us proceed with our lesson. This fellow's belligerence presents the question: 'Why do nations go to war?'"

"These guys aren't a nation," I replied.

"Oh? Why not?" asked Bernie. "Because they don't have a flag and a seat in the UN? A million years from now, UN diplomats will behave just like these fellows, only worse. So, tell me, Lex, why is this fellow threatening us with violence?"

"He thinks we're going to take his lunch."

"Exactly. My old friend Thucydides thought that nations go to war because of fear, greed, or honor. Which is your great-grandfather's motive?"

"Fear. He's afraid we'll take his food."

"Yes. And ..."

"Greed, because he won't share with us."

"Yes, and ..."

"Probably honor too because he wants to look like a tough guy in front of his friends. All three, I guess."

Great-Gramps was still hopping up and down, screeching and flinging meadow muffins.

A nugget hit Bernie's bare chest. Bernie brushed it off. "You might call that a diplomatic protest note," he remarked.

Great-Gramps held up a hunk of rock and screamed, "Pussies! Wimps! Get outta here—or I'll crack your skulls and eat your brains!"

"Ah, we have entered the saber-rattling stage," Bernie said. "Threats can be an effective method for advancing a nation's diplomatic agenda, but only if they are credible, of course."

"Looks credible to me."

Great-Gramps turned to his band, waved his arms wildly, and shrieked something about how Bernie and I had come to steal their food, drive them from their sacred hunting grounds, murder their children, and dishonor their women.

"Rallying the troops with the traditional pre-battle speech," Bernie said. "'We few. We happy few. We band of brothers etcetera etcetera if perhaps not quite so poetic."

Great-Gramps smacked his lips and rubbed his hairy tummy.

"Now he's promising them rich booty: fresh meat in this instance."

"Fresh meat?"

"Us, of course. *Homo erectus* was a cannibal."

Great-Gramps's soldiers picked up rocks, stones, sticks, and loose debris and joined him in screeching, gibbering and hopping. When the band reached that frenzy of battle ardor that the leader deemed suitable, he and his boldest lieutenant charged, howling.

"Uh-oh." I said. "Those guys mean business."

"No, not just yet. They're just getting up their nerve for the attack. Primitive human warfare is defined by a great deal of threatening and posturing before actual combat is joined. By example, the paper I wrote for the Society of Wargods on warfare in the Neolithic Nile civilization shows that—"

Before Bernie could get into his lecture, Great-Gramps's lieutenant picked up a stick and heaved it. He threw like a girl. The stick bounced in the dust by my feet, and I kicked it away.

"Ah, now they've declared war, don't you think, Lex?"

"I guess."

"Well, no sense anyone getting hurt," Bernie said calmly. "Shall we surrender the field of honor to our friends here?"

"Definitely."

We turned and walked away. At the sight of us withdrawing, the *Homos* hooted, jumped up and down, and screamed, "Chicken! Chicken!" or words to that effect.

We had retreated twenty or thirty yards when I heard a fresh and more vehement chorus of shrieks and hoots from Great-Gramps and his cohorts. I turned to look, and a rock glanced off my shoulder. "Ouch," I remarked.

Great-Gramps hopped up and down in triumph. "Follow me!" he howled. "The enemy is fleeing! Fresh meat!"

Bernie was perfectly calm. "Ah." He sighed and picked up the rock. "This missile illustrates the fourth reason nations go to war. Can you think what that is, Lex?"

"Let's get out of here and talk about it later." I did not wish to see my skull cracked open and my brains eaten like a soft-boiled egg yolk.

"Nations go to war because they think they can win."

"But they can win, Bernie. There's thirty or forty of those brutes."

"Our appeasing stance, you see, far from persuading this fellow that we mean him no harm, has encouraged him to believe we are easy prey. We have played the part of the Allies appeasing Hitler before World War II."

"Let's appease him more back at your house, Bernie," I insisted. "Please."

"But he has made a miscalculation. We are not easy prey."

"We aren't?"

"It is miscalculations about their ability to win wars that will bring nations to disaster—even to our present day. By example, take the German invasion of the Soviet Union in 1941 ..."

With a final cry of "Victory or death!" or words to that effect, Great-Grampy and his army charged in earnest.

"Let me illustrate," Bernie said. A World War II Russian 7.62 PPD-42 submachine gun with a seventy-two-round drum magazine appeared in Bernie's hand. Bernie cocked the weapon and squeezed off a burst.

Bang-bang-bang-bang-bang. Bullets kicked up dust all around Great-Gramps's hairy toes. He sprawled in the dust, rolled into the fetal position, stuck his thumb in his mouth, and lay there whimpering and soiling the ground with urine. His "band of brothers" stopped in their tracks. They stared at their leader for a moment and then fell upon him, bashing him with sticks and rocks, tearing off juicy hunks of meat, and cramming them into their mouths.

"Ew," Bernie said. "You see, my boy, what becomes of defeated generals. Stalin shot his losers by the bushel basket after the Germans invaded Russia in 1941," said Bernie. "Let that be another lesson for you."

On that note, he seized my hand.

Back in the Rubbermaid, something huge was thump-thump-thumping against the inside of the shed. I felt like I was inside a bass drum.

Of course, it was only Kitty's giant tail.

"Happy to see us, Kitty?" Bernie cooed. "Daddy told you he'd be back soon, didn't he?"

Kitty purred like three chainsaws.

CHAPTER 11

"So, Lex, did you enjoy our ape men?" Bernie asked. He passed me a hearty breakfast of gruel in that same unwashed wooden bowl.

"No," I growled. Floating in the swill was the hind leg of something with a few strings of gray hair still attached. "Jeez, Bernie. What's this?" I dropped my spoon in revulsion.

"Squirrel a la Polemarchos," he said. "Mmmmm. Delicious." He smacked his lips in an utterly disgusting manner.

"Bernie! People don't eat squirrel," I protested.

"Soldiers do—when they're hungry enough. Soldiers eat what they can. They live off the land. Bon appétit."

I slapped my spoon down on the table hard. "I will not eat this!" I cried.

"Okay," he said.

"And I'm not going to have any more filthy apes throw shit at me!"

"Okay." He smiled.

"And I thought I was going to see some cool battles. That wasn't a battle!"

"It was."

"Berns, what are we doing this for?"

"Mmm," Bernie said. "I suppose you think you are entitled to an explanation."

"Damn right I am!"

"You aren't, maggot." His voice was suddenly Bad Bernie's, deep and low like distant thunder in the mountains. "You are entitled only to obey."

He frightened me. I shut up.

"But I will give you one out of the goodness of my heart. Let's see if you can handle it."

"Thank you," I said meekly.

"Soon, you and I will be called to fight a great battle that may determine the course of your world's history for thousands of years. It will be my responsibility to win that battle."

"Oh, sure. Right. We're going to save the world." I had reverted to sarcasm. It was very hard for me to be respectful to Bernie when he was standing before me buck naked. "Would you please put on some clothes?" I begged.

He slipped into a bathrobe marked "Hotel Vesuvius. Pompeii. 79 AD."

"And your responsibilities are to assist me and to do your duty," he said. "Okay?"

"Sure. Why not?"

"And possibly die or be horribly crippled and mutilated for life."

"Okay, sure." More sarcasm. I didn't believe a word of this.

"Shut up and listen!" he roared.

My ears rang. I cringed into my chair.

"I am now preparing you—trying to prepare you because you are a thick-headed, spoiled, disobedient, vain piece of useless American boy meat—to assist me and survive."

"Yes, sir."

"The ape men taught you why wars start. Today, we will begin our studies of how wars should and should not be fought. Do you get it?"

"Yes, Bernie, sir."

CHAPTER 12

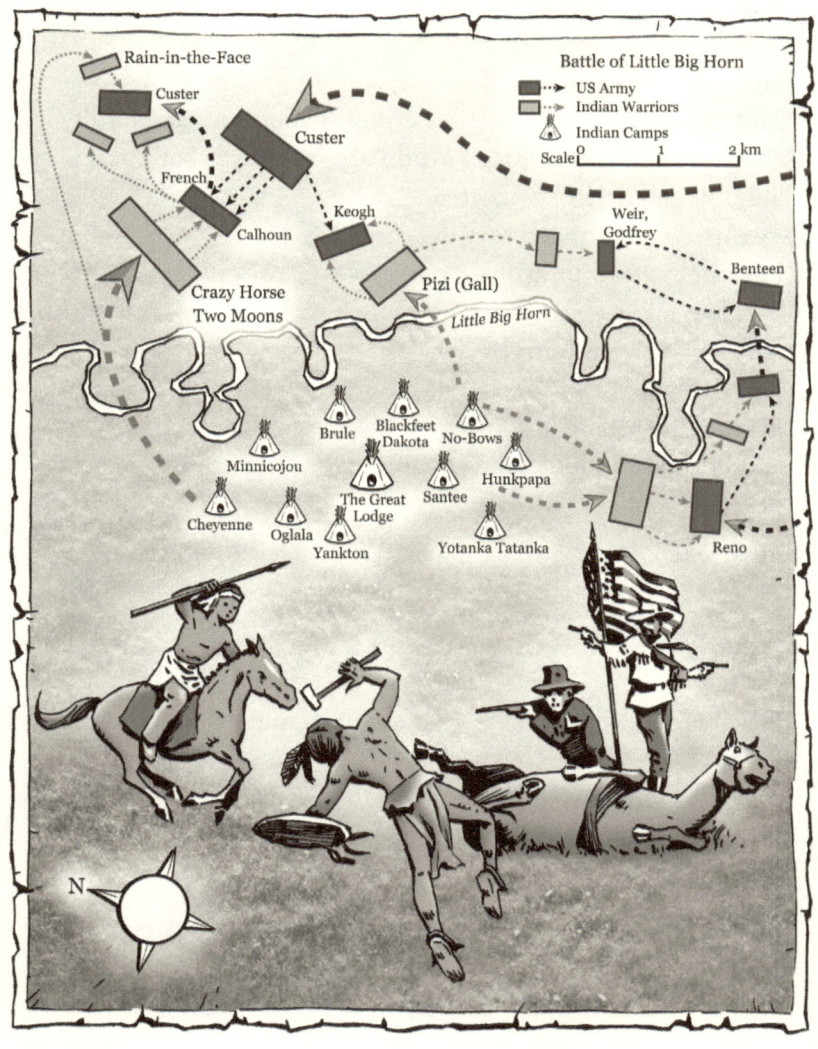

Battle of Little Big Horn

US Army
Indian Warriors
Indian Camps

Scale 0 1 2 km

Rain-in-the-Face

Custer

Custer

French

Calhoun

Keogh

Weir,
Godfrey

Benteen

Crazy Horse
Two Moons

Pizi (Gall)

Little Big Horn

Brule

Blackfeet
Dakota

No-Bows

Minnicojou

The Great
Lodge

Santee

Hunkpapa

Cheyenne

Oglala

Yankton

Yotanka Tatanka

Reno

N

A few minutes later, we went through Bernie's usual time-travel production. This time, it gave me a blinding migraine headache.

We didn't arrive buck naked—thank god. We left Bernie's house in clothes, and happily, we arrived in clothes too. I found myself wearing buckskin pants, a red flannel shirt, a leather vest, and a cowboy hat with a red feather stuck in it. I was armed to the teeth with two big revolvers at my hips, a rifle in the scabbard beside me, and an enormous buffalo-skinning knife and two hatchets stuck in my belt.

Bernie was dressed like me, with the addition of a fancy tasseled buckskin jacket and a huge sombrero that was three feet across with three feathers stuck in it. He was Big Bernie again. His thigh-sized upper arms were covered with tattoos. His greasy hair was jet black and hung to his shoulders in pigtails. His skin was a deep tan, and his scarred face was painted white in an eerie death's head mask. He had two enormous horse pistols, two rifles—one of them a big buffalo gun—hanging in scabbards beside him, a saber slung behind his back, and two hatchets at his belt.

Both of us were sitting on horses. I had never been on a horse before. We had no horses in Vermont. My steed was brown and very large. I noticed that it was a long way from my horse's back to the ground. I didn't much like that.

When you think about it, riding on the back of a giant animal for transportation is a really sketchy idea. I prefer my feet or a bike. Did the horse like me? What was its attitude about carrying me on its back? Why should it tolerate me? I was very happy that my beast was just standing there peacefully munching grass and not galloping over hill and dale, throwing me off onto jagged rocks and stomping out my brains.

"Nice horsey," I whispered to my charger, hoping to ingratiate myself with flattery. "Nicest horsey in the world."

Our horses were standing on a bluff overlooking a pretty little valley through which flowed a sluggish stream lined with cottonwood trees and willows. It was a lovely early summer day, not too hot, with a warm breeze making waves in the long grass of the prairie all around us.

"Welcome to Montana," said Bernie.

"This is a nice place. What's it called?"

"The locals called it 'Greasy Grass.'"

"We are Indian scouts for the United States Cavalry," Bernie explained.

65

"Don't you mean 'Native American' scouts, Bernie?" I interrupted.

"No. I do not mean 'Native American' scouts.' That term was not in usage in 1876. The polite term is *Indians*. Less polite is *redskins, savages,* and other demeaning and bigoted expressions. If you call Indians Native Americans, people will think you're crazy."

"Yes, Bernie."

"You and I are Arikara Indians, bitter enemies of the Sioux. I am the chief scout. My name is Bloody Knife."

"Who am I?"

"You're Squatting-Dog-Taking-a-Dump," he said. "You are my dumb-ass, good-for-nothing assistant and gofer. We're under military discipline here, so when I say jump, you ask how high on the way up. Got it?"

"Yes, Bernie."

"Bloody Knife, stupid."

"Yes, Bloody Knife, sir."

"And you keep your pie-hole shut with that 'Native American' talk. Right?"

"Yes, Bloody Knife, sir."

Bernie began his lecture. "Squatting-Dog, did you know that battles are more often lost than won?"

"No, Bloody Knife, sir. I didn't."

"It happens to be true. War is not adventure, blood, and glory. It is mankind's most difficult job. Anything can go wrong in war, and it always does. It's a total screw-up."

"Yes, sir. A screw-up."

"The winner of a battle is not the military genius—the Napoleon or Alexander—who does everything right. It's the commander who does the fewest things wrong. Today, we will go to a place where I will show you a commander who screws the pig—"

"That's screw the *pooch*, sir." I said. Bernie was not always in perfect command of the American idiom.

"As I said, how a commander screws the pooch. And then I'll show you how men die hideously as a result." He leaned over and gave me another of those bone-shaking slaps on the back. "Come on, boy. Let's have some fun!"

Bernie made a little clicking sound, and his horse began a slow walk down the bluff toward the little stream and the woods. My beast followed. I squeezed my eyes shut, pressed my knees with all my might against his flanks, and clung to his mane with white fingers.

Our job as scouts, Bernie explained, was to find out where the bad guys were lurking and how many there were. The bad guys in this instance, Bernie said, were a band of Sioux and Cheyenne warriors who had escaped their reservation and were roaming the area, allegedly slaughtering white men, violating their wives and daughters, burning their houses, beating out the brains of their babies against fence posts, and so forth.

"It's called reconnaissance, and what we learn about our enemy is called intelligence," he said in full pompous teacher mode. "And if a commander doesn't do the recon and get the intel, he's a blind man groping in the dark and will get himself and his command massacred. Got it?"

"Yes, sir, Bloody Knife, sir."

"Once you and I find those villains and report, the Seventh US Cavalry Regiment will come up from behind and herd them back to the reservation. The Seventh Cavalry is under the command of Lieutenant Colonel George Armstrong Custer."

It hit me. "Oh, shit, Bernie," I yelped. "We're at Custer's Last Stand!"

"Yup," he said. "Are you thrilled?"

"No!" I shouted. "I know all about Custer. He and his whole command were slaughtered!"

"Shit happens." Bernie remarked. We had stopped at the stream's edge and my horse was slurping up gallon after gallon. "And now we're going to ride over there." He pointed to the patch of woods "And find out what's behind those trees."

"I'll go first," I announced bravely. I was damned if I was going to let a horse scare me. After all, I was probably smarter than it was, even if it was a lot bigger.

Bernie looked at me skeptically. "All right," he said. "Be my guest, General Guts 'n Glory."

"Go, horse," I said timidly.

The beast ignored me and kept on slurping.

"Please," I said.

Not a twitch.

"How do I start this thing?" I asked.

"It's a she, and her name is Hellfire. Try sweet talk and flattery. Shake both reins and say, 'Giddy up, Hellfire,' politely. Don't shout or it will be the charge of the light brigade all over again—and you'll end up with a broken neck."

"Giddy up, pretty Hellfire," I said. To my astonishment, my mare lifted her head and started sloshing across the stream. Bernie was close behind.

"Good horse," I said. "Nice horse. Pretty horse."

We started into the trees. There was no path. The woods were thick and dark with brambles, underbrush, tree trunks, and limbs. It was a miniature jungle. The light was as dim as evening. We were slogging through swampy ground when Bernie tapped me on the shoulder.

"Stop and listen," he whispered. "Pull gently back on the reins and say, 'Whoa.'"

I did so. We stopped. Beyond the trees, I heard dogs barking.

"Dismount and follow me," Bernie said, drawing a rifle from one if his scabbards.

I drew one of my six-shooters. "Don't touch that!" he hissed. "You don't know how to use it. Firearms use is a deadly serious matter."

We tied our horses to a tree, dismounted, and continued on foot. The barking grew louder. Ahead, sunlight peeked through the trees. Bernie stopped and parted a bramble bush with his hands. "Look," he whispered. "What do you see?"

On a low hill, about a mile from the edge of our forest, I saw teepees.

No, a forest of hundreds of teepees. A forest of hundreds and hundreds of teepees. It was a Native American metropolis.

Milling among the teepees were warriors galloping their ponies, whooping, and showing off to the girls, young girls watching and giggling, women tending cooking fires and breast-feeding babies, children playing, packs of dogs barking and fighting, and senior citizens doddering about— hundreds and hundreds of Native Americans doing Native American stuff.

"How many?" Bernie asked. "Count them."

"It'll take all day," I protested.

"Divide the camp into squares in your mind. Count the number of people in one square then multiply that figure by the number of squares you estimate there are in the entire camp. It'll give you a football field figure."

"Ballpark figure."

"Shut up and start counting."

"Maybe five thousand?"

"There are seven thousand: two thousand five hundred warriors and five thousand women, children, and old people in that village. It is the largest Native American army ever to be assembled on the North American continent."

"Does Custer know about all these Indians?"

"No, but we're going to tell him. We have done a proper reconnaissance. We have done our duty. Now let's see what Custer does with it. Let's get out of here before you get me killed."

We fetched our horses and rode back through the woods, across the Little Bighorn, and back up to the top of the bluff.

"There they are." Bernie pointed down the valley.

A column of tiny figures in blue were riding along the far side of the river toward us, guidons and flags waving.

"How many soldiers?" asked Bernie.

I did my football field estimate. "Four or five hundred?"

"About right. There's another column of about a hundred and fifty under Captain Benteen a few miles behind. Custer is about to fight two thousand warriors with seven hundred and fifty troopers. Does that sound like a good idea to you?"

"No."

"You're not as dumb as you look. We'd better get right down there and tell Colonel Custer he's making a mistake."

He flicked his reins and took off at a brisk trot. My nag followed. I gripped her sides with my knees until my legs screamed in agony, as did my sore butt. We trotted up to a character who was a cross between a sixties flower child and a metrosexual Buffalo Bill. Colonel George Armstrong Custer wore a white, soft-as-butter, tasseled deerskin jacket, tight deerskin trousers, and black cowboy boots tipped with shiny silver caps. Under his rakishly angled, broad-brimmed hat, his blond hair hung in wavy ringlets to his shoulders. He had a bushy mustache, beady little eyes, and a long snout like a giant rodent. Just as King Agamemnon, he was attended by a cloud of officers, aides, gallopers, and assorted flunkies and toadies. His troopers plodded behind.

Custer whipped off his hat and flicked his hair back like a prom queen. "Come on, boys! Hip-hip-hurray! Follow me!"

"Is he gay?" I whispered to Bernie.

"Certainly not! Soldiers are not gay, Lex—except for Alexander the Great, Frederick the Great, Richard the Lionheart, and the entire Theban Sacred Band phalanx. Women worship Custer. Millions of young women swoon at the mere mention of his name."

"Swoon?"

"Get the vapors. Faint."

"Women faint over him? He looks like a giant mutant rat."

"Beauty is in the eye of the beholder," Bernie remarked. "Caesar thought Cleopatra was hot. I thought her complexion was bad, and she had saddlebags."

Custer's rallying cry had no effect on his men. Undaunted, he burst into the rousing anthem of the Seventh Cavalry, "Garryowen." "Let Bacchus's sons be not dismayed, but join with me each jovial blade, come booze and sing and lend your aid …"

His boys were not feeling like "jovial blades" at that moment. Their uniforms were caked with dust, their eyes were hollow and bloodshot, and their filthy faces were gaunt and gray with fatigue.

"Mistake numero uno. Remember what I said about a commander taking care of his men?" Bernie whispered. "He's had them in the saddle for days. He's going to catch those Sioux even if it kills them."

One trooper—a pink-cheeked child not more than fourteen—slumped over his saddle, asleep. He teetered and tumbled headfirst off his horse onto the ground. A grizzled old sergeant, a huge man with a thick black beard and a scarlet handkerchief wrapped around his neck, leapt down from his horse and helped the dazed boy to his feet.

"Colonel?" the sergeant called to Custer in a thick Irish brogue. "The men need a break, sir."

"They're lazy," said Custer in a snooty, fake British accent. "Surely they can give me a few more miles."

"No, Colonel. Darling, they can't."

"Very well, Sergeant. But I don't countenance sloth. Take ten minutes. No more."

The troop stopped and dismounted. Many of them lay down on the grass and began snoring.

"What do you have to report, Sergeant?" Custer asked Bernie.

"Boss, there's a big village and an army of Lakota and Cheyenne pony-soldiers just behind those trees over there. They're got their war paint on."

"I've told you never to call me *boss*, Sergeant. If you do so again, I shall place you under arrest," replied Custer.

"Okay, General."

"I am a colonel, Sergeant, not a general. If you call me *general* again, I shall have you flogged for insubordination."

"Okay, Colonel."

"Colonel, sir."

"Okay, Colonel, sir."

I'd read all about Custer's last stand, and I hated it. All those poor American soldiers were going to be killed and scalped, and I could prevent it. I couldn't keep my big mouth shut. It was I who had screwed the pooch.

"But, Colonel Custer, there's a Native American army behind those trees! Two thousand of them!" I blurted.

There was a deathly silence. Bernie rolled his eyes.

"A what?" Custer scowled. "Did you say an *American* army behind those trees?"

"Yes, sir. I mean, no, sir. I said an Indian army behind those trees."

"The hell you did. You called those bloodthirsty savages *Americans*," Custer shouted. "Are you a traitor, boy? Are you a spy? Sergeant, who is this redskin friend of yours?"

"Nobody, Colonel," Bernie answered. "A pathetic bastard child. I promised his poor mother on her deathbed to care for him." Bernie twirled his finger beside his temple. "He's … touched in the head, you know. He's only good for feeding the horses and washing my underwear. I feed him scraps that a mongrel dog wouldn't touch."

"A retard, is he? A moron? And he presumes to call a band of filthy, flea-bitten aboriginals Americans! Get him out of here, Sergeant."

"Yes, sir. But there is an Indian village and an army just beyond those trees."

Custer was in no mood to listen. "Really, Sergeant?" Custer said wearily. "If you must, tell me about this army of yours. How many savages are about to attack us, do you suppose?"

"At least two thousand warriors, Colonel, sir."

"Two thousand! Don't you mean two hundred?"

The aides and flunkies laughed heartily.

"And how many in your famous village, Sergeant?"

"Six or seven thousand, Colonel, sir," said Bernie.

He turned to his aides and flunkies. "The chief scout tells me that there's thousands of savages just behind those woods," he announced with a flourish.

The aides and flunkies guffawed.

"Sergeant, there ain't that many savages in the whole of this land."

"I saw them, Colonel."

"But did you actually count them?"

"Well, no, sir. I didn't have time."

He turned back to his flunkies. "As I thought. You didn't count them because you undoubtedly cannot count higher than three." He chuckled. "It's one, two, three, a lot for these redskins, isn't it, gentlemen?"

The flunkies roared.

"I can do my numbers," Bernie protested. "I went to mission school. There are at least two thousand pony soldiers just behind those trees, and, sir, many are armed with these."

Bernie drew a lever-action carbine from the scabbard strapped to his saddle.

"A Henry Repeater? Ridiculous," Custer said. "Even we do not have Henry Repeaters. Those savages have bows, lances, and stone clubs."

"Sir, I saw hundreds of Henrys."

"Idiotic. Very well, Sergeant. Watch me make short work of your Indian host armed with Henrys." Custer turned in his saddle. "Major Reno!" Custer shouted. "Reno, to the front."

A bushy-bearded office rode up.

"Major Reno, Bloody Knife here says there are savages beyond those trees: a small village and a few braves. We will divide the troops. I will take half up to that bluff." He pointed to the height where we had started our ride across the stream and into the woods. "We'll attack the village from their left flank and rear. Meanwhile, you will attack from this meadow. We will round the rabble up and drive them back to the reservation. It will be my greatest victory. Do you understand, Major?"

"Yes, sir." Reno saluted smartly and rode away.

"Mount them up, Sergeant," Custer commanded.

"Sir, Mother of God, give them five minutes to rest."

"They can rest after we've corralled these savages. Mount them up, I say! As for you, Sergeant, get that idiot of yours out of here before I have him hanged for treason."

The troopers dragged themselves up into their saddles. The column divided itself into two halves. One half, commanded by Major Reno, remounted, and walked their horses across the meadow toward the forest that hid the village. The other half, led by Custer, turned to the right, plunged into the little river, splashed across it, and began struggling up the bluff.

When they had gone, Bernie glared at me and said, "I told you to keep your piehole shut. Next time, remember that your twenty-first-century ideas don't apply in the past where people think completely differently. The motto of time travel is 'When in Rome, do as the Romans do—or they'll chop off your head.'"

"I'm sorry, Bernie." I really was sorry.

"Don't be too hard on yourself. It wasn't you. It was the character of this commander. Custer's vain, overconfident, and ambitious. He thinks a great victory will make him president. And he's stupid too," Bernie added. "Custer is an idiot. He was dead last in his class at West Point. Now he's divided his force into two parts and is twice as outnumbered as he was before."

Custer and his troopers were stopped at the crest of the bluff, looking down on the Little Bighorn and the woods that hid the village. Closer to us, Reno and his men were walking their horses across the meadow. They were now a hundred yards from the trees. The sound of a little tin bugle echoed down from the bluff.

"Look! Our blue-eyed boy is charging the village," Bernie said.

Custer and his troop were galloping down the bluff. They splashed across the stream and disappeared into the trees and brambles.

"Now Custer and Reno can no longer see or hear one another. That means that they can't help one another either. No cell phones, no radios, you know."

Down in the meadow, Reno's troopers were drawing their carbines from their saddle scabbards and dismounting. All but the few who stayed behind to hold the horses—one man to every four—spread out and began walking slowly through waist-high grass toward the trees.

The thin line of troopers, carrying their carbines across their chests, had almost reached the woods. They were about three hundred yards from us.

"Are they just going to walk right in there?" I asked.

"Naturally. If Custer thought there were a hundred thousand Sioux behind those trees, he'd still attack. They're only ignorant, cowardly savages, you know."

"He's a racist, you mean?"

"Yes. But that's your twenty-first century mind-set again. Practically everyone in nineteenth-century America is racist. The real point is not that his racism is immoral—even though it is—it's that his racism has led him to extreme overconfidence and will get him and his men killed."

Reno's troopers had just reached the edge of the trees when I heard sharp popping sounds. A thin pall of white smoke sifted slowly up from the forest floor and hung in the treetops. I saw a trooper fall to his knees. Another stumbled backward, fell, and lay still.

The popping increased as the troopers began firing back into the woods. More smoke rose from the meadow.

"Watch that big Irish sergeant," Bernie said.

I spotted him by the red handkerchief tied around his head. He raised his carbine to his shoulder, took aim, fired, opened the bolt to eject the spent cartridge, inserted another, raised the carbine, and fired again. It was a swift, deadly mechanical sequence. He was a killing machine.

Suddenly the sergeant stopped firing. Something had gone wrong. He scowled and struggled with his rifle bolt. He pulled a knife from his belt and jammed the blade into the carbine's innards. Working the knife furiously, he cursed again and yelled something to the man nearest him. He set back to work at the bolt.

"It's called a *stoppage*," Bernie explained. "His weapon is jammed. Let me show you." He thrust a big rifle into my hands. "This is the weapon:

the 1873 Springfield carbine in .45–70 caliber. Very innovative for its day. It's the first breech-loading—as opposed to muzzle-loading—rifle to see general service in the US Army."

I raised it to my shoulder and aimed. It was heavy. *The sergeant must be a strong man to handle this big weapon so easily.*

Bernie went on with his little small arms lecture. I liked it. I like guns. I know I'm not supposed to, but I do. "It's known as the trapdoor Springfield because the breech opens up like this." He flipped the rifle's breech block open from back to front, exposing its chamber. He handed me a shiny copper cartridge.

"Load it," he ordered.

I slipped the cartridge into the chamber and clicked the trapdoor shut.

"Now fire it."

"Here?'

"Sure. Everyone else is shooting. Why can't we have some fun too? Hold it up tight to your shoulder."

I pulled the trigger. The rifle crashed and bucked. My ears rang.

"Okay. Now open the breech again."

I did. The empty cartridge popped out and fell to the ground.

"That's what's not happening down in the meadow. Custer's men are just at this moment discovering that when their rifles heat up, these soft copper cartridges swell and won't eject. The people at the Springfield Arsenal back east in Hartford, Connecticut, forgot to test-fire their fancy new rifles under rapid-fire, battlefield conditions."

"They can't shoot?"

"You guessed her, Chester. It's a significant disadvantage," Bernie said dryly.

"I would say so. Bad luck."

"No, it's another mistake, but this time, it's not Custer's. On the other hand, here's another mistake that was his. He didn't bring along these bad boys."

A cannon-like weapon materialized beside us. It had two wooden spoke-wheels, eight small, rifle-sized barrels, a crank, and a conical hopper sticking up from its top. It shone with brass and highly polished hardwood.

"How'd you do that?" I asked.

"You wouldn't understand," he said. "This is the weapon invented by

Mr. Gatling. Isn't it lovely?" he asked proudly and stroked the barrels. "You load the bullets into the hopper here, turn this crank, and it fires a fusillade: two hundred bullets a minute."

"Custer had machine guns?"

"Not a machine gun. That would be Mr. Maxim's invention later in this century. Nevertheless, it fires very rapidly by 1870s standards and is deadly against cavalry. Custer had three. Would you like to shoot it? It's fun." Bernie's face lit up like a kid on Christmas.

"Is that a good idea?" I asked, thinking about all those pissed-off Native Americans just a mile away.

"Go on. Have some fun. Shoot that stump over there." He adjusted a little screw that turned the barrels a few inches to the right and aimed the gun at an old cottonwood stump thirty feet away. "Go on. It's loaded. Just turn the crank."

I cranked. Wacka-wacka-wacka! The gun raised a clatter like the devil was hammering out his erotic memoirs on an enormous manual typewriter. The Gatling's wheels jumped six inches off the ground. Flames leapt two feet out of the barrels, and smoking brass poured out of the bottom of the gun. A great cloud of white smoke billowed all around us. I stopped cranking. The smoke cleared. The stump was now a pile of sawdust.

"Groovy, huh?" Bernie said.

"We don't say *groovy* anymore, Bernie. We say *amazing* and *awesome. Cool* is always okay too."

"Very cool," Bernie said. "Custer has three of these Gatling but elected to leave them back at his base. He doesn't believe in newfangled weapons. Like all soldiers, he loves his old familiar tools: the rifle, the pistol, the bayonet, the saber. The knights of the Middle Ages refused to accept firearms. They loved their armor and lances and their glorious cavalry charges. That's why there are no more knights."

"And that's why there will be no more Custer," I said.

"One of many reasons for his downfall," said Bernie. The Gatling and the pile of empties vanished.

The popping continued and increased. When the smoke cleared, I found my sergeant. He was still digging at his rifle's breech with his knife and swearing. I could read his lips and saw that he was cursing. His swear words were pretty much the same as ours. He said the sh** word, the god*** word and the f*** word, and sometimes, he combined all three.

Then something terrible happened. Suddenly my sergeant stopped cursing. The knife fell from his hand. Wide-eyed, he stared down at his chest. It was pin-cushioned with half a dozen arrows. His eyes rolled back in his head, and he crumpled to the ground.

All over the meadow, troopers were struggling with their bolts or had thrown their rifles down and drawn their Colt revolvers and were blasting away into the trees. The popping from the forest increased. More smoke sifted lazily up through the branches. The meadow was now littered with trooper bodies.

Major Reno sat on his horse thirty yards behind the skirmish line. He was waving his saber and shouting. Beside him, a young blond lieutenant fired into the woods with his pistol. Suddenly Reno dropped his saber and threw his hand over his eyes. I thought he was shot, but he wasn't. Reno wiped his face, examined his hand, smacked his lips twice, and spat a piece of gray ooze out onto his saddle pommel. Puzzled, he leaned over to examine it. His eyes blew open in horror. He turned his eyes to the young lieutenant. The top of the lieutenant's head was gone. His exposed brain looked like a raw meatloaf. A small geyser of blood spurted up out of it.

"Oh, God," I said, and looked away.

When I looked back, Reno was screaming and gesticulating. "Major Reno has lost his nerve," Bernie said. "The great god Pan has him in his grip." I saw troopers running for their horses.

At last, I saw the warriors. A dense mass of horsemen thundered around the left-hand corner of the woods, thousands of them, shrieking and shooting. The entire Native American army of two thousand was charging Reno's two hundred-fifty men.

"Hmmm," Bernie said. "I suppose this is the signal for us to relocate, Lex." He let out a "giddyup" and we trotted away from the killing zone, across the Little Bighorn, and up the side of the bluff, me clinging to Wildfire's mane all the while.

From the heights, we watched Reno and his men fleeing for their lives. They had mounted their horses and waded across the river and were straggling up the bluff. Behind them came the enemy, shooting, whooping in approved Native American fashion, and performing all sorts of fancy horseback acrobatics. I saw one warrior wearing a fancy eagle headdress stand on his pony's back with the reins in his teeth, pump the lever on his Henry, and knock three troopers out of their saddles. Reno finally drew a bead on him with his Colt and blasted a .45 slug into his guts. He rolled over and over in the dust clutching his stomach and screaming, bringing the curtain down on his show. I felt kind of disappointed.

Reno and his troopers reached the summit of the bluff and threw themselves down on the ground in a ragged circle. With knives, bayonets, tin bowls, cups, and anything at hand, they set to scratching out shallow little holes in the dirt. It was pathetic. Once the Indians made up their minds to stop showing off, it was clear that they would charge in a mass and turn the troopers into roadkill.

"Bernie, where's Custer?" I asked.

"Off chasing women and children," he said. "Trouble is, they decamped an hour ago and are long gone. He'll be back shortly when he figures that out."

"He's got to come back and help right now! Doesn't he hear the shooting?"

"The woods muffle the sound. Anyway, if he hears it, he figures Reno is giving the savages a good thrashing. Don't you know that his troopers cannot be beaten by savages?"

"What they need is for the cavalry to arrive."

And the cavalry did arrive. A bugle toot-tooted the charge in the distance. That small troop Bernie had said was lagging behind the main column appeared over a rise.

"There's Captain Benteen," Bernie said. "On cue."

The little troop galloped hell for leather with guidons flapping, horses foaming, sabers slashing, and revolvers blasting right into the redskin army. You could not deny Benteen had courage.

The Indians parted—more out of surprise than anything else, I think—and Benteen's boys rode right into Reno's lines and leapt from their horses. Reno's men threw their hats into the air, slapped their saviors' backs in hearty fashion, and hip-hip-hurrahed. Reno, hatless with a bloody bandage wrapped around his head, rushed up to Benteen and gave him a manly handshake. I could swear that tears were running down Reno's cheeks. The cavalry had arrived, and he and his men were saved.

Not.

I watched Reno look around at Benteen's troopers with increasing panic. He asked, "Is this all of you?"

Benteen's men had arrived to save the day and were now just as surrounded, outnumbered, and thoroughly screwed as Reno's. In a moment, Benteen realized his predicament and started screaming commands. His men threw themselves down to the ground and set to work scratching out their own pathetic little hidey-holes.

Meanwhile, every Plains Indian in North America was riding in circles around the crest of the bluff, screeching holy terror and blasting away with everything they had. The troopers blasted back from their little circle—and effectively too. Plenty of riderless Indian ponies, maddened by fear, galloped around and around in tandem with the mounted warriors. The troopers had kept their nerve, so far, but it was just a matter of time before the great god Pan took charge. They were all going to die!

Suddenly, I was back in our kitchen. Max showed his food to Polly. Polly complained to Mom. Mom admonished Max. A floorboard creaked. Dad looked up again. "Can I help you?" he said.

And I heard the cock of a pistol.

"Bernie, we have to help them," I screamed. "You can do things, Bernie. I know you can. Stop this, Bernie! Stop this!"

"I can't."

"Yes, you can! Help them, for God's sake, Bernie!"

"It's not allowed."

"What do you mean? Not allowed by who?"

"We don't allow it. The Wargods will not allow it. We don't meddle with your past, except under approved circumstances. Those are the rules."

I burst into tears. "Please. Please. Please. We have to help them. Please."

Bernie threw a heavy arm across my shoulders. "I know what you want me to do, Lex, and I can't do it. I can't bring them back. Poor boy, I can't bring them back."

So, we sat there on our horses at a safe distance from the battle and watched them die. A pall of dust and smoke hung over the little knoll where the troopers huddled. Out of it flashed ripples of gunfire like lightning in a thundercloud; the air was full of the firecracker pop-pop of gunfire and the shrieks and cries of the wounded. Around the pall, the warriors rode, firing their rifles, shooting their arrows, and hurling their spears into the murk. With every circuit, one or two of the braver ones would peel off from the rest and charge into the smoke, hoping to break through the troopers' pathetic little defensive circle and begin the hand-to-hand massacre. Each time, one or two riderless ponies would gallop out. The troopers were holding on, but it was just a matter of time.

I couldn't watch any more. "Let's go, Bernie," I said. "That's enough. Let's go home."

"All right!"

"Sergeant, where did all those redskins come from?" a voice behind us squeaked. Custer's troop had returned from their wild-goose chase after the villagers, straggled up the bluff, and were drawn up a few yards behind us. Custer was seated on his horse amidst his little group of aides and flunkies. He peered through a pair of binoculars at the battle. "Hell and damnation, there are thousands of them!"

"Yes, sir," said Bernie.

"Wherever did they come from? Why didn't you warn me they were so many?"

Bernie didn't answer.

"They are attacking Reno and Benteen," Custer blustered. "Reno and Benteen appear to be quite beset with savages, do they not, Chief Scout?"

"Yes, sir," agreed Bernie, looking smug. "Quite beset."

"This is my fault." Custer sighed dramatically.

"No, no," the aides and flunkies murmured. "Never. Never."

"Yes, it is," Custer insisted. "There is only one thing for it. Lieutenant Smith!"

A formerly dashing young lieutenant—he had lost his hat, scratched his face, torn his trousers, and was looking less dashing after an hour thrashing through the woods and across the prairie after the Indian women and children—yelled, "Your orders, sir?"

"Lieutenant, we will draw off the savages attacking Reno and Benteen. We will draw them to that hilltop over there where we will make a stand." He pointed north to another knoll a mile away.

"Yes, sir!"

"Bugler, sound the charge!"

The bugler was too dry to manage it at first. He finally generated enough spit and sounded the charge.

"Come on, boys!" shouted Custer. "A ten-dollar gold piece to the man who brings me Sitting Bull's head!"

And so, in a cloud of dust and clanking of equipment, the Seventh Cavalry under the command of Colonel George Armstrong Custer "galloped off into immortality," as they say. The Indians attacking Reno and Benteen followed.

You have seen the Romantic paintings that are always being reproduced in history books. Or maybe you've seen old, black-and-white movies of Custer's last stand. The image is always the same. The Seventh Cavalry has made its last stand on the little knoll. Gorgeous George—hatless with blond hair flying, a bloody bandage wrapped around his forehead—stands in a tiny circle of dead and dying men and horses, a saber in one hand and horse pistol in the other.

"He was an idiot," I said.

"Yes," Bernie said.

"But he was brave."

"Yes. He was brave. And he saved Reno, Benteen, and their troopers. The Indians chased Custer over to that knoll. When they finished wiping him and his men out, they attacked Reno and Benteen again. But Reno and Benteen fought them off for a night and another day until a relief column arrived."

"So, Custer sacrificed himself."

"Yes. Your wars are squalid, stupid, and horrible, but they often have moments when you humans surpass yourselves. In war, men show their very worst sides and their very best. Humans are strange."

"We're strange? You Wargods travel in time, shape change, and have disgusting taste in clothes. You call humans strange!"

Bernie looked hurt. It was my crack about his clothes. "Let's ditch these horses," he said. "Kitty's not likely to take kindly to a pair of big, smelly beasts showing up in her house."

We dismounted, and he slapped me on the back. "I'm starved. How about some nice leftover squirrel stew, boy?" He grabbed my hand.

CHAPTER 13

The next morning, Bernie surpassed himself by serving me a nice, clean bowl of Count Chocula with fresh milk. "You've earned it," he said.

Count Chocula used to be my favorite cereal. Today, it was disgusting. I guess my tastes had changed. I pushed the bowl away. "Got any of that nice porridge the Romans conquered the world on?" I asked.

While I slopped down two bowls of his swill, Bernie commenced with his lecturing. Bernie was a very pretentious lecturer. He struck a Roman pose: back straight, chin up, chest out, right hand over his heart. "Yesterday we studied some of the many ways commanders lose battles," he said as I wolfed down my slop. "The first subject of today's class will be *plans*. Are you listening?"

"Yes, Bernie."

"Every commander, from the lowly lieutenant to the great general of an army, makes a battle plan. If he's a lieutenant, he scratches a plan out on a scrap of paper or just announces it to his platoon: 'This is what we're going to do.'

"If he's a general, he and his staff draw lines and boxes and arrows on maps, make long lists and time schedules down to the minute and tear them up and make new lists and schedules. The general sends messengers carrying vital orders this way and that and then changes his mind and sends messengers out with orders contradicting the first orders. Lieutenant or general, the result of all this fuss is always a brilliant plan in which victory is guaranteed. Got it?"

"Yes, Bernie. Commanders make perfect plans. I get it."

"Okay. So, today, we're going to see how one battle plan worked out."

Kitty purred and licked my hand in the darkness. Her tongue was the size of a large mop but scratchy like the coarsest sandpaper. Kitty and I had become besties since I had begun my evening ritual of putting her out. I would lay a raw leg of lamb in front of the Rubbermaid door, scramble up on the shed roof with a rake, pry open the door, and watch her creep out. In the dark, she appeared to be brown, covered with shaggy hair, about three times the size of the Rubbermaid, and had at least two heads. She would emerge, snap up her dinner, and purr contentedly. Then she would shamble off to her night's lair under the front porch.

Back in the Rubbermaid, Bernie warbled, "Au revoir, Kitty."

A minute later, we found ourselves at the base of a hill in the woods. They were normal woods like the woods in Vermont. No strange tropical trees. No gigantic prehistoric beasts. It was hot and muggy. No breeze. Beside us was a narrow forest road.

Bernie had changed again. Today he was a modest six foot three, ramrod erect, with a massive chest and a well-groomed black beard. He was decked out in a high-collared dark blue, thigh-length frock jacket with a double row of brass buttons and gold epaulettes, light blue pants with a yellow stripe, and a floppy hat with one side rakishly turned up. A silly little short sword and a gigantic holstered pistol were strapped on his belt. I sniffed cologne.

"Something die in your shorts, Bernie?" I inquired.

"I beg your pardon," he said, looking rather hurt.

"You stink to high heaven."

"I have merely adopted the fashion of the era—by way of camouflage. As matter of fact, I think I smell rather elegant." He puffed up.

"Sure you do, Berns."

"Please address me as Colonel."

"Sure, Colonel Berns."

"You are Lieutenant Lex, my aide. You, too, are dressed appropriately for the era."

I was in a blue uniform too, with the silly little sword, but I didn't have the hand howitzer. I liked Bernie's hat better than mine too. Mine was a cap—a kepi, as they're called. I felt like a Mouseketeer.

"We are federal officers of artillery on a reconnaissance mission for General Hancock," he said.

"That's a nice pistol you've got there, Colonel. How come I don't get one?"

"You don't get a sidearm because you'd only blow your foot off with it. Or shoot me."

"Mind if I take a look?"

"Look, but don't touch," he said sternly and pulled the pistol out of its holster.

"What sort of pistol would that be, Colonel?" I asked.

"This sidearm is a Remington Model 1858. It's a single-action, six-shot, .44 caliber percussion revolver," he said.

"Cool. How about letting me just hold it?"

"Absolutely not! This weapon is extremely dangerous. It's not a toy for a child, Lex." He re-holstered the Remington.

"Come on, Berns. I'm not a child."

"To be honest, Lex, you are a sixteen-year-old human male, which makes you emotionally and intellectually backward." He placed his hand on my shoulder to console me. "Lex, it's not your fault. Your brain won't be fully developed for another ten years. Basically, you suffer from a temporary cerebral handicap. No offense."

"None taken, Colonel."

"As well as making you plain stupid, your handicap makes young men of your age highly suggestible. You can be easily trained to take suicidal risks and commit acts of extreme violence. This makes you a perfect recruit for military service. Young males of your age are very useful for stopping bullets that might otherwise hit somebody important—like me."

"Thank you, Colonel."

"However, I would rather not have you stop a bullet today."

"Thanks again, Colonel."

"Time to go. It's a short walk, Lieutenant. Follow me." He turned on his heel, and we began trudging up the hill on the little dirt road. The air was heavy and muggy. There was absolutely no breeze. I started to sweat right away. From the far side of the hill ahead of us, I heard the low rumble of thunder.

There was a storm coming—but little did I know how big and what kind.

We walked uphill for about fifteen minutes. The thunder got a little louder at every step.

Finally, we reached a clearing at the top of the hill and found ourselves face to face with an enormous balloon the size of a house. It was about thirty feet across and sixty feet high, and its side was painted in florid gold letters: "Intrepid." It resembled Bernie's butt in his tight running shorts—but on a very much larger scale.

The balloon was tethered ten feet from the ground by a big steel cable attached to a wheel. A wicker basket—just like the basket my mom kept her gardening tools in, only man-sized—hung under the balloon. Attached to the balloon by a maze of copper tubing were two big crates set on two wagons. A dozen men in blue uniforms and one man dressed in civilian clothes were fussing around the crates, turning valves and peering at gauges.

"Professor Lowe?" Bernie asked, marching up to the civilian.

"Yes. I am he," he replied. He was tall and thin and had discarded his jacket for shirtsleeves. Like everyone else in the clearing besides me, he had facial hair. In his case, it consisted of a ridiculously huge mustache and a disgusting soul patch under his lower lip. I wondered what was up with this beard thing. Bernie had a beard. All of the soldiers working around us had great, bushy beards. One old guy looked like Santa Claus. I figured all that foliage must itch like the dickens in this heat and cause all sorts of nasty rashes and skin diseases. I further calculated that there must be a lot of rotting food under that shrubbery and maybe some wildlife as well.

"Professor Lowe, I am Colonel Polemarchos, and this is my aide, Lieutenant Lex." Bernie removed his hat and bowed. "Lieutenant Lex, Professor Thaddeus Lowe, chief aeronaut of the Union Army."

I tried to bow and nearly toppled over on my face.

"Lieutenant Lex is feeling a bit off today," Bernie explained. "General Hancock sends his compliments. He requests that the lieutenant and I be permitted to go up in your fine balloon to observe for the artillery."

Lowe returned Bernie's bow. "My compliments to General Hancock," Lowe replied and bowed again. "And I would be happy to comply with his request. I am at your service, sir." He bowed once more.

Bernie bowed back, sweeping his hat.

I bowed.

All this bowing, sir-ing, and hat-sweeping was total BS, in my opinion, and made me dizzy.

"Please step this way, gentlemen." He escorted us over the balloon. "We are just filling the gas bag with hydrogen. Please embark, gentlemen. The *Intrepid* is ready to depart."

I am afraid of heights, I don't mind confessing. My fear is perfectly sensible. People are not supposed to be up in the air. We are land animals. I like birds, but I am not a bird. I placed one hand on the rope ladder and froze.

"Get going, Lieutenant," Bernie hissed.

I started up, carefully placing a hand, a foot, the other hand, the other foot—and never looking down. I reached the basket, took a deep breath, hurled myself over its side, and crashed into the bottom. I lay there panting and pouring sweat. Bernie followed close behind.

The two soldiers took a hold on the cable wheel and began to turn. The balloon began to rise.

The rumble of thunder grew louder.

"So, hydrogen, is it?" Bernie said.

"But isn't hydrogen flammable?"

"It certainly is. On Thursday, May 6, 1937, I watched the German dirigible *Hindenburg* landing in Lakehurst, New Jersey. A crewman flipped his cigarette into the wrong corner and blew the Hindenburg sky high. I hope you're not planning to light up."

"I don't smoke, Bernie," I protested.

"Of course you do," he said.

It was true. I kept a pack of Marlboro Lights in a shoe in my closet and smoked one from time to time, blowing the smoke up Bernie's chimney. *What's the harm in that?*

"So, I smoke a little. Shoot me," I muttered.

"No need," Bernie said, looking at me sideways. "Someone will do that very soon now."

We rose slowly up through the trees. The rumbling grew louder and louder.

"This hill is called Big Round Top," Bernie said. "That smaller hill beside us is called Little Round Top."

We cleared the treetops. The rumbling became a roar.

CHAPTER 14

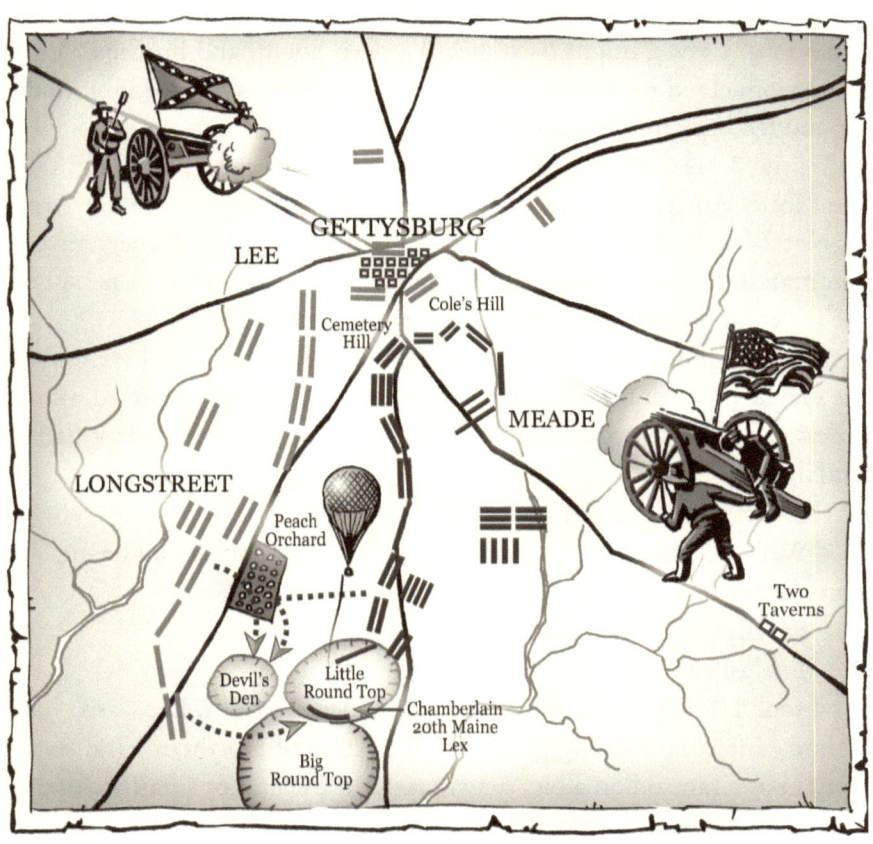

"Welcome to Gettysburg," Bernie said.

It was breathtaking, epic, a spectacle. This was war at its most spectacular and at a safe distance. I was awestruck.

A few hundred feet below us, two enormous armies were drawn up, facing each other on parallel grassy ridges divided by a pretty green valley lined with fields, fences, and stone walls. The two armies were engaged in a hot artillery duel. Down below on my left—to the west—little toy cannons serviced by tiny soldiers in gray belched and barked away, shrouded in clouds of white smoke. On my right, to the east, little toy cannons serviced by tiny soldiers in blue blasted back. Each ridge was spotted with shell explosions. I saw a bright flash, heard a deep boom, and flinched. A low mushroom cloud rose on the right ridge. Tiny figures hurtled up into the air and fell back into the smoke.

"July 2, 1863," Bernie said. "The greatest battle ever fought on the North American continent. On our left is the Confederate Army of Northern Virginia, seventy thousand men, General Robert E. Lee commanding. Their ridge is called Seminary Ridge. Look for General Lee. He's over on our left near that little grove of trees."

Bernie handed me a beautiful shiny brass telescope. "Lord Nelson's— the one he put over his blind eye whenever he wanted to ignore admiralty orders. I picked it up off the deck of the *Victory* after he was killed at Trafalgar."

"You stole it?" I asked, shocked.

"Well, someone would have taken it. Right? Might as well be me," he stammered.

"I'm disappointed in you, Bernie," I said.

He blushed.

I took Lord Nelson's telescope and scanned the ridge. Lee wasn't hard to find. The commanding general of the Army of Northern Virginia sat straight as a ramrod on a big, gray horse in the center of a flashy cloud of aides and officers. His gray uniform was immaculate. He wore a neatly-trimmed, salt-and-pepper beard, perfectly groomed. No scurrying fauna under that shrub. Lee was a very fine-looking, older gentleman, a man you would respect and revere. He reminded me of my grandfather. Lee was looking in our direction through a pair of binoculars. He lowered them.

He leaned to an exquisite aide with long waxed mustaches and long black ringlets and gave him an order. The aide saluted and galloped off.

"A beloved leader and a great commander, probably the greatest your nation has ever produced," Bernie said. "A man of enormous dignity and honor, respected by both sides. He owns no slaves, you know. Doesn't believe in it. He doesn't fight for slavery. He fights for his friends, family, and his home state, Virginia. Excellent poker player too, I must add. Took my shirt drawing to an inside straight. 'Better to be lucky than good,' as I always say."

I scanned the Confederate line with the telescope. The line began immediately to our left and below us, extended about three miles north, and then took a sharp right-hand turn to pass in front of a little town, Gettysburg itself. A thick pall of smoke lay over the town.

"To our right is the Union Army of the Potomac: ninety thousand men, commanded by General George Gordon Meade on Cemetery Ridge," Bernie went on. "General Lee has commanded his army for years and won many victories. General Meade has been in command of his army for just five days. He has never led such a large force before. He is a competent soldier, but he is cranky, hot-tempered, and not loved. His officers call him the Snapping Turtle. There he is." Bernie pointed.

I spotted him in the center point of the Union line seated on a black horse amidst tombstones and monuments and surrounded by his own staff of coat-holders and bootlicks. Meade was no match for Lee in manly beauty. He had a bald dome, a scraggly, unkempt forest of facial hair that doubtless hid a menagerie of vermin, and great black bags under his buggy eyes. Lee was noble. Meade looked like a grumpy old iguana in need of a powerful stool-softener.

"My money's on Lee," I said.

"Everyone's is," Bernie said.

The Union line began just below us at the base of Little Round Top, ran due north paralleling the Confederate line, then hooked to the right— the east—and ended on a pair of woody hills, Cemetery Hill and Culp's Hill, then on a creek and a swamp.

"The Union line looks like a standing fishhook," Bernie pointed out, "with the barb up there. Do you see?"

"Looks like an upside-down J to me."

"All the historians will say *fishhook*."

"I don't care what the historians say."

"Lex, have you no respect for authority?"

"It depends," I answered.

"A sensible answer. All right, then, listen." Bernie sighed. "Class is in session. This is the textbook military history version of how the Union and Confederate armies came to Gettysburg."

"I know the history. I've read Shelby Foote's *The Civil War: A Narrative* twice." I knew everything. I really was an arrogant little brat in those days.

"Mr. Foote wrote a fine book. But Mr. Foote was not there. We are. So, listen."

"Okay, Bernie."

"Your Civil War is now a bloodbath in its third year. Hundreds of thousands have already died. General Lee has come to believe the South cannot win a long war, so he has decided to risk everything in one great battle. He's decided to throw all his money on the table and roll the cards."

"Don't you mean roll the dice? You cut cards. You roll dice."

"Dice, then damn it!" he barked. "Shut up and listen, smartass, or I swear I'll have you shot at dawn! I can do it, you know."

Wham! He was interrupted by an artillery shell exploding in midair a few yards from us. I dove to the floor of the basket. Bernie didn't budge or flinch. The basket bucked and a thousand angry bees buzzed around us.

"What's that noise?" I whimpered.

"Henry Shrapnel's invention," he said. "Hundreds of little lead balls. Take your head right off."

"Were they shooting at us?"

"Of course they were shooting at us. Who else? We're as big as a house up here. They can't miss. Get up."

"Terrific." I curled up in a ball.

"Get up!" he roared. My ears rang. "Get up—or I'll throw you over the side!"

I pulled myself to my feet and stood with my eyes tightly shut, clutching the sides of the basket with white knuckles.

"Listen to me: an officer must never show fear. If you show your men that you're scared, they won't follow you. They must think you are unafraid. Then they will be unafraid. So, it is your duty to stand upright at the hottest portion of the battle and be killed if necessary."

"Sorry."

"As I was saying, Lee has decided to attack. Where would you attack, Lex?"

I pried my eyes open and looked over the Union line: hundreds of cannons and thousands of infantry and cavalry waiting to slaughter any Confederates who dared expose themselves to their fire on that long walk across the valley floor from Seminary Ridge to Cemetery Ridge. It was suicide.

"Nowhere," I answered. "If I were Lee, I'd go home."

"That's what Lee's favorite general, General Longstreet, told him. But Lee insists on attacking. So, Longstreet advised him not to attack directly across the valley. He suggested that Lee sweep around those two hills just below us, the Round Tops, and attack the Federals from the left flank and rear. Soldiers don't like to be attacked from the side and rear. It makes them nervous. They run away. Then you can shoot them or stab them in the back. Much safer and easier then shooting them or stabbing them in the front when they can shoot or stab you back."

"So, will Lee do it?"

"No."

"Why not?"

"I don't know why not."

"I thought you knew everything."

"Most everything, but not this. But I do want you to believe that I know everything. If a leader convinces his soldiers that he is invincible and omnipotent, they will follow him cheerfully to their deaths."

"You can count on me, Bernie." I had recovered my nerve and was a smartass again.

"There are theories why Lee insists on attacking despite Longstreet's best advice. One is that he is suffering from the heart disease that finally killed him. He is in pain. His mind is not clear. Napoleon was feeling poorly at Waterloo and lost the battle. History can turn on such a little thing as a commander's indigestion or a flare-up of his hemorrhoids. You are all human, after all."

Boom. Boom! Two more explosions, nearer this time—more angry bees. I ducked my head.

"Don't duck. Don't flinch. Teach yourself to show nothing," Bernie said. "Control your fear!"

"Yes, Colonel, sir. I'll try."

Boom! Zing! I flinched, but I didn't duck.

"Better," said Bernie. "Lee's plan is to decoy General Meade into moving most of his forces to the south of his line here just below us. Then Lee will attack him in the north and break the Union line. It's what you call a feint. You know what a feint is?"

"Sure. It's like when the quarterback fakes the run up the middle and then runs the ball around the end."

"If you say so. I know nothing about baseball," Bernie said. "In any event, Lee's plan is this: Longstreet's corps—it's the one just below us at the extreme south of the Confederate line—will start the battle by attacking diagonally northeast up that little dirt road. The other troops will follow at intervals, also attacking diagonally northeast. The whole attack is timed to lure Meade into withdrawing his forces from the north to reinforce the south. When Meade has weakened the north, Lee will climax the battle by attacking on the fishhook there in the far north and break through. Brilliant, don't you think?"

"I guess."

"Can you see any reason Lee's plan should fail?"

"Not a one."

"Okeydokey." Bernie shrugged. "Here's an important law of war: No plan survives first contact with the enemy. My good friend General von Moltke said that."

"General who?"

"German General who conquered France in the War of 1870."

"Why don't plans survive, Berns?'

"In part because war is an enormously complicated machine with thousands and thousands of moving parts that must all work together or the machine will break down and a lot of people will get killed. We learned that at Little Bighorn, didn't we?"

I guessed we had.

"But mostly because your enemy doesn't want your smart little plan to work and will do all sorts of unpredictable things to mess you up. That's his job." He looked at his watch again. "'Bout time for Dangerous Dan to prove Von Moltke right. Look down there, just in front of us: the big flag and the cluster of blue soldiers around it just to the north of little Round Top. That's General 'Dangerous Dan' Sickles."

I focused my telescope on a goggle-eyed little runt wearing a floppy hat with a jaunty peacock feather stuck in its band. He was haranguing a flock of cringing underlings, gesturing wildly and pointing toward the Confederate lines.

"The little dude with the feather?"

"That's your man. Dangerous Dan is a powerful New York congressman. He achieved his lofty military rank solely by calling in political debts and by blackmail: 'Senator, I know all about that fourteen-year-old girl. Does your wife?' He has no military training, experience, or talent whatsoever and a very excitable temperament. Two years ago, he shot his wife's lover to death on the street in front of the White House."

"How comes he's not in jail?"

"Your American democracy at work, which is to say by jury tampering and bribery. He pleaded temporary insanity and got acquitted. There is nothing temporary about Sickles's insanity."

Over the boom of artillery fire, I heard the rumble of drums beating time and the music of a military band echoing in the valley.

"Ah, see? Sickles is marching his two divisions forward. He's decided he doesn't like the spot Meade assigned him on the ridge. He prefers that pretty little orchard just ahead. Heaven only knows why."

"He likes apples?"

"It's a peach orchard, actually. Sickles didn't trouble to tell Meade he was going to occupy the orchard. At this minute, Meade is seeing what Dan's doing and is horrified. Dan is overturning Meade's whole plan. Meade is now sending riders—gallopers—carrying frantic messages telling Sickles to get back in line."

"I see them." Sure enough, I saw one rider after another galloping away from Meade's headquarters toward the peach orchard.

Preceded by the band, drumming and tooting away, two divisions of infantry, ten thousand of the Union's finest, rifles at their shoulders, bayonets fixed, flags flying, marched into the peach orchard. Sickles and his aides rode behind on horseback, sticking out their chests as puffed up as toads. The whole ensemble marched forward in in perfect parade ground formation. Sickles was swinging his saber over his head and exhorting his boys.

"Cool," I said.

"Oh, it will be much hotter in just a minute," Bernie replied.

Sickles, his tooting band and his ten thousand stopped amidst the trees. The drums beat. The horns blew and Sickles's troops reordered themselves into tidy lines.

"Impressive, isn't it?" asked Bernie. "Beautiful marching. Unfortunately, they've marched beautifully into a slaughterhouse. They are now all alone and unprotected several hundred yards from the rest of the Union army. Dangerous Dan has formed what we call a salient, a sort of military peninsula exposed to enemy fire from three sides," Bernie explained. "Putting your troops into a salient is about like putting your testicles into the garbage grinder. Watch."

Sickles's band, which now stood just behind the center of his new line, played a jolly, martial air while Sickles, beaming with joy, directed the bandsmen with his sword like a maestro.

"You will now see the pee hit the fan," Bernie said.

I had given up on correcting Bernie's idioms.

The Confederate lines on Seminary Ridge exploded fire and smoke from one end to the other. An instant later, the gigantic crash hit us. A gust of hot wind shook our basket. Every cannon in the Confederate army had cut loose on Dangerous Dan.

Bernie pulled out his golden pocket watch and popped it open. "Oh my," he tut-tutted. "Too early for the barrage. The Confederate artillery is wasting all their ammunition on Dangerous Dan and won't have enough left to soften up the rest of the Union line for the attack."

Explosions crashed in, above and all around the orchard. I saw one cannonball cut a furrow through the band's bass section, sending tubas and musicians—and pieces of musicians—turning somersaults in the air. I saw another cannonball remove the head and whole left side of Sickles's young aide riding beside him. Something hit Sickles too. He flinched, grimaced, gripped his right leg, and toppled from his horse.

"The surgeons will amputate that leg," Bernie said. "Then Sickles will have it displayed in a glass case in a Washington museum."

"Yikes. Why?"

"So he can visit it every year on the anniversary of this day. I believe it's still there for the public to admire. You should take a look the next time you are in Washington for the cherry blossoms."

The Confederate barrage roared on. In a moment Sickles's ten thousand had vanished in thick smoke. The cloud billowed and swirled as explosions flashed and thundered inside it.

Finally, the deep thunder of the cannon ceased and was superseded by the higher-pitched crack of rifle volleys. "Here comes Longstreet's attack, also early, before the Confederate units to the north are ready. Lee's plan depended on timing and coordination. Now it's wrecked because of Dangerous Dan."

Thousands of ghostly blue figures came running out of the smoke toward the Union lines.

"Pan has spoken, and they have broken," Bernie said poetically. He looked pleased with himself.

Some of the Federals still carried their rifles. Many did not. All were half-crazy with terror. I saw an officer battering a cringing private over the back with the flat of his sword. I saw another officer level his revolver at a fleeing soldier and drop him in his tracks with a shot between the shoulder blades. The officer turned his piece on another man and cocked it.

The soldier drove his bayonet into the officer's chest, yanked it out again, and ran on.

"You liked my Pan statue, didn't you?"

"Yes, Berns. You asked me that already."

The running men were soon followed out of the smoke by limping and staggering men, some supported by friends, others using their rifles as crutches. Last came the crawlers. Many were without arms or legs. Most of those who had advanced into the orchard never emerged from the smoke at all.

As the Union refugees retreated up Cemetery Ridge and scrambled over the rocky ground just below us, their officers screaming at them to rally, I heard a tremendous, high-pitched shriek rising from the smoke. It was bloodcurdling. I nearly jumped out of the basket.

"What's that?" I quaked.

"The rebel yell, of course," answered Bernie. "The falsetto is quite good, isn't it? The Zulu's battle cry is baritone and very good too, but I think I prefer the falsetto. Sounds like a thousand rabid weasels tearing each other's eyes out in a squash court. The best armies have the best war cries. A good war cry lifts morale, puts air in the lungs, accelerates the heart, puts lead in a soldier's pencil, warms up the legs, and terrorizes the enemy."

A bugle sounded.

"Here they come!" cried Bernie. "Remember: Longstreet was supposed to attack northeast, not due east, but his men just can't resist chasing those frightened Union boys."

A mass of Confederate infantry sprinted out of the smoke, charging hell for leather at the Union line just below us, intending to drive the boys in blue off Little Round Top, flank the whole Union position on Cemetery Ridge, win the battle, and even end the war.

But the Union officers had finally managed to rally their men. The soldiers were back in the trenches where they had been before they began their advance into the peach orchard. Their officers were waving their swords and jumping up and down in hysterics, screaming at them to reload their rifles. The soldiers were cramming in the powder and bullets. The officers raised their swords overhead. The soldiers leveled their rifles. The swords dropped. The whole Union line burst into flame with a gigantic crack. The front rank of the Confederate mass went down head over heels like it had tripped over a single wire. There was screaming, a lot of screaming. Then both Federals and Confederates were lost again in the billowing smoke cloud.

Bernie popped his watch. This time, it played Dixie: "I wish I was in the Land of Cotton, Old times there are not forgotten."

"That's 1,200 men killed in just eight minutes. You Americans have a real talent for murder, don't you?" He punched me a friendly noogie on the upper arm. "But the real significance of what you're just seen is not the slaughter. It's the fact that Sickles's advance screwed Lee's plan completely. This kind of thing happens all the time in war. But ... but."

"But what, Bernie?"

"But by a delicious irony, while Sickles's idiocy ruined Lee's plan, it actually enabled Longstreet's much better plan, which was … do you remember?"

"To attack to the right and roll up the whole Union line from south to north."

"Exactly. Now take a peek. What do you see?"

I looked down, taking care to cling to the edge of the basket with all my might. Sure enough, Confederate soldiers were swarming to our right and starting up Little Round Top. The attack Longstreet wanted but Lee had rejected had begun courtesy of Dangerous Dan Sickles.

CHAPTER 15

I didn't have a chance to examine the Confederate attack for more than thirty seconds before a cannonball whistled through our balloon a foot over my head.

"Oops," Bernie said.

The basket lurched. The gas bag whooshed. I grabbed hold of a rope and hung on for dear life. It was a wonder we didn't squirt away like a birthday balloon toward Washington or explode in a fireball like the *Hindenburg*. Happily, the bag simply collapsed. Down we went, tumbling straight into the trees covering Little Round Top and crashing through limbs and boughs. I shut my eyes tight, gritted my teeth, hung on and prayed: "God, don't take me. Take Bernie. He's not even human."

At last, we came to a stop. The basket swayed gently back and forth. I shook twigs out of my hair and spat out a pound of pine needles. A quick body inventory showed that I had no broken bones sticking through the skin, no brains leaking out of my skull, no arterial bleeding, and my essential parts were still intact. I was scratched and bruised, but in one piece. The thunder of the battle was muffled by the hill and the forest. I was in a little oasis of peace. I considered resting in the basket for the duration of the battle. I felt a twinge of guilt about wishing Bernie ill, but it was only a twinge.

I needn't have. I popped my head over the edge of the basket to make a visual reconnaissance. Just below me, Bernie was on the ground, chatting cheerfully with a tall, slender walrus-mustached Union officer.

"Lieutenant!" he yelled up to me. "What are you doing up there? Napping? Get down here and meet Colonel Chamberlain."

Busted. I clambered out of the basket, down the tree, hopped on to the ground, and did my best to salute Colonel Chamberlain without making a complete fool of myself. I'd never saluted anyone before in my life. Do you hold your hand flat over your eyebrow or at a slant? Do you snap it off? Or just lower your hand slowly? Was I supposed to stamp my feet? Click my heels? This was the nineteenth century, after all.

I tried all of the above. Chamberlain noted my embarrassment and offered his hand for a shake. "Good to meet you, Lieutenant," he said. "Glad you dropped in." His eyes twinkled.

It wasn't much of a joke, but a joke it was, and it showed he wasn't a pompous jerk, an idiot, or a homicidal maniac like most of the officers in the Union Army. He had a very slight Maine accent, nothing like a Maine potato farmer's or lobsterman's, just a touch of rural unpretentiousness mixed with something elegant and educated.

"Colonel Chamberlain commands the Twentieth Maine. He is also a Bowdoin College professor," Bernie said.

"Of rhetoric," Chamberlain added. Observing my blank expression, he added, "I'm not sure what it is either, but I do know it's not much use here." He chuckled.

"Tell us about your situation, Colonel," Bernie said.

"We just got here. They call this place Little Round Top. We're setting up a firing line there," he said, pointing down the hill a few yards to where his men were picking up rocks, stones, and logs and stacking them for cover. Some were digging shallow firing holes with their bayonets. Others were positioning themselves behind the thicker trees. They were working quickly and efficiently. "We're linked up tight with the Eighty-Third Pennsylvania boys on the right, but over on the left, there's nobody. I've sent my B Company over there into the woods a ways to keep an eye on things in case the Rebs try to sneak around. We are the end of the whole Union line here. Can't have 'em turning our flank, rolling up our line, and driving us right off the ridge, can we?"

"No, Colonel. We cannot." Bernie replied.

"What did you see from up there in your balloon, Colonel?" Chamberlain asked.

Just then, a Confederate shrapnel shell burst in the treetops over our heads, scattering us with leaves and twigs. It was followed by that bloodcurdling rebel yell echoing out of the woods below us and the sharp crack of a rifle volley from the Eighty-Third Pennsylvania.

"The Rebels appear to be attacking your hill, Colonel," said Bernie.

"My observation, exactly, Colonel," remarked Chamberlain, cool as a cucumber.

A young captain ran over to us, very distraught. "Lawrence," he cried. "They're in the woods below forming to attack. Hundreds of them!"

Chamberlain said, "Tom, please allow me to introduce Colonel Polemarchos and Lieutenant Lex. Gentlemen, my brother, Thomas Chamberlain."

We bowed and shook hands and all that other nonsense while half a dozen more shrapnel shells exploded in the treetops. I heard that awful buzzing sound. Neither Chamberlain nor Bernie flinched. I cannot say the same for Tom or myself. Tom ducked. I did too, but less than him. A little less, anyway.

"The Rebs are coming!" someone shouted.

The Chamberlain brothers stepped over to the line their men had formed, drew their revolvers, and took what cover they could find behind the trunk of a maple tree. Bernie and I joined them. The four of us formed a little Indian file behind that tree. The older Chamberlain came first, then the younger, then Bernie, then finally me. I sucked in my stomach to make myself as thin as possible. I wished I hadn't had two helpings of gruel that morning.

"Hold your fire, men, until I give the command!" shouted Chamberlain Senior. He turned back to Tom, Bernie, and me. "I was thinking of saying 'Don't fire until you see the whites of their eyes,' but then I realized we lost the Battle of Bunker Hill."

I leaned my head a little to the side around the trunk and peeked down the hill. Hunched figures were struggling toward us among the trees, rocks, and brush, carrying rifles across their chests. I saw one gray-clad officer waving his sword and brandishing his pistol. He was a big man, much bigger than the rest, but amazingly agile. He wore a long red feather in his hat as if to say, "Here I am. Try and shoot me." He was the leader. Just beside him, I glimpsed a soldier carrying the battle flag, the Confederate Stars and Bars, hanging limp in the heavy air. I yanked my head back.

"You are about to witness, Lex, the turning point of the War between the States," Bernie whispered. "If those Confederates drive this little band of soldiers off this hill, the Confederacy will win the war. If they fail, the Union will win. Aren't you thrilled to be here?"

"No!" I yelped as a rifle ball thunked into my favorite tree. "Bernie, when can I use this?" I asked, patting my sidearm.

"Never!" he growled. "Leave it in your holster."

Colonel Chamberlain and his brother stepped from the cover of the trunk—ill advisedly, in my opinion—and joined the firing line. I snuggled up to Bernie, whose shoulder rested against the trunk. Now that I had a closer look at my tree, I saw we had made a poor choice. It was not as stout as I had thought: only about one foot wide. Even if I sucked them in with all my might, parts of me stuck into the line of fire.

"We shouldn't be here," Bernie whispered.

"You're right about that," I replied, my voice shaking. "Let's run for it."

"Nah. We're here now. Let's enjoy ourselves." He drew his horse pistol and cocked his piece. "I won't use this unless it's absolutely necessary."

Something told me that "absolutely necessary" was coming pretty soon. Bernie's blood was up.

"Keep an eye on this Chamberlain fellow," he added. "He's a real leader."

I watched Chamberlain. He was standing tall, no more than six feet from us, straight as a ramrod, fully exposed. He raised his sword. "Twentieth Maine! Come to the ready!"

Every man on the line raised his rifle to his shoulder. "Aim low, boys! Nice and low. Every man pick a target." The rebels, a dense mass of them struggling up the steep slope, were now less than a hundred feet away. They let out their demon shriek and started to run, as best as they were able, up the steep slope, around trees and over rocks and fallen limbs. The hairs on my neck stood up straight. My stomach knotted.

"On my command." Chamberlain dropped his sword. "Fire!"

Four hundred .58 caliber Springfield rifles blasted a few yards from my head. I clapped my hands over my ears. My nose was bleeding. Bernie laid his hand on my shoulder. "Get down!" he yelled.

"What?" I screamed. My head was stuffed with cotton.

"Down!" Bernie pushed me to my knees. At that moment, the whole Rebel line answered with their volley. My tree shook. Chunks and splinters flew. A splinter cut my cheek.

I leaned out and peeked down the firing line. I was in the middle of a dense cloud of gun smoke so thick I couldn't see a yard in front of me. The air reeked of gunpowder and the metallic tang of blood. Beside me, still on his feet, Chamberlain was blasting away with his pistol. He ejected an empty cylinder and inserted a fresh one. To my right and left, every soldier of the Twentieth Maine was firing, reloading, firing, and reloading as fast as he was able. The air was filled with bees. The bullets made a pzzz-zip sound. Men were down. I saw one slumped over a rock, the back of his head a bloody mush. Another was sitting against a tree with his legs outstretched, a glazed look in his eyes and a great bloodstain on his chest. A private staggered backward from the line and fell onto his back inches from my face. There was a bloody hole where his lower jaw had been. A fat gorge of blood spouted out of the hole, and he died.

"They're running!" someone shouted. "Those fu**ing Rebs are running!"

The firing slackened, and I peeked further around my tree trunk. The Confederate soldiers weren't exactly running, but they were backing down the hill, firing as they went. They gradually disappeared into the woods. Behind them, on the forest floor, they left dozens of gray bodies. Some twitched and writhed. Some cried, "Mama, Mama." Some were still.

Colonel Chamberlain backed off the firing line and reloaded another cylinder. "Well, Colonel, we gave them a fine little welcome, didn't we?"

"Yes, very fine," Bernie said.

I whispered, "Bernie, does this guy have steel balls—or is he just faking it?"

"What's the difference?" Bernie asked.

"They'll be back any minute, of course," added Chamberlain. "As soon as they muster up the courage."

A sergeant ran up to us. "They're coming 'round our left, sir. Hundreds of them!"

"Thank you, Sergeant," Chamberlain replied as cool as if the man had just told him that tea was served in the library.

Bernie whispered in my ear, "This is the crisis. The Alabamians under Colonel Oates are coming around the left flank. Oates is a fire-eater and a smart soldier. He knows that the Union line ends here. He plans to flank us to the left, drive us away, and take Little Round Top. Then he'll drag artillery up here and blast the whole Federal Army off Cemetery Ridge from one end to the other. Then Lee marches on to Philadelphia—or even New York."

"Colonel, what are your orders?" screamed the sergeant. "Fall back?"

"Can't do that," Chamberlain replied. He just stood there, cool enough, thinking it over. Then—and I couldn't believe this—he stepped up on a rock to take a look. He was visible to every Confederate sharpshooter on Little Round Top. Immediately, rifles cracked from below in the woods. Bullets whizzed and whistled all around him and ricocheted off the rocks. Some of the bullets almost hit me!

"Sir, get down!" shouted the sergeant.

If it had been me, I would have knocked his legs right out from under him and sat on his chest. The crazy bastard was drawing fire from every Confederate rifle in the state of Pennsylvania.

"Jeez, Bernie. Get him down from there," I whispered.

"No, Lex. He's got to do it," Bernie whispered back. "His men know they are about to be flanked. They could crack and run at any moment. Before the god Pan takes them in his grip, Chamberlain must show his men that they have nothing to fear by showing that he has no fear. He knows this. You are seeing a born leader of men."

He didn't step down. He pulled out his binoculars and peered into the woods like he was some crazy bird-watcher searching for the last surviving red-crested, horn-billed, white-throated Alabama barn woodpecker. "Hmm," he said. "I think I see them. Yes, there they are. Looks like a full regiment. Hmm." He scratched his chin like he was ruminating on a thorny question in rhetoric—whatever rhetoric was.

Bullets thudded into my tree, spraying my face with more wood chips. My little tree looked like it had been gnawed by a million hungry termites and would crumble into sawdust at any moment.

Bullets whizzed overhead and pinged off the rocks. How the Confederate sharpshooters were managing to miss Chamberlain I could not imagine. A bullet took his hat and then snapped off his pistol holster. Still, Chamberlain stood there pondering. He made his decision. "Sergeant, we'll refuse the left flank!"

"Damn, he's got it," Bernie whispered and slammed his fist into his palm. "He's got it! Goddamn, he got it!"

"Sir?" asked the sergeant very puzzled. "We'll do what, sir?"

Chamberlain jumped down from his rock. "Sergeant, go over there to the left and tell Companies G, C, and H that they are to withdraw just far enough to form a line perpendicular to ours here. Like this." Chamberlain held his hands out horizontally with his fingertips touching, then bent his left hand down to form a right angle with his right. "They are to take whatever cover they can find and give the Rebels a nice volley when they appear. I wager they'll run like rabbits."

"Yes, sir." The sergeant hurried off, mumbling, "Refuse the flank. Refuse the flank. What the fu**?"

"Refusing the flank," Chamberlain said to Bernie. "I read about it just the other day in the officer's manual." He winked.

Bernie grunted. "Brilliant!" He whispered in my ear, "Those Alabamians will think they've got a clear run into our rear, then, boom, blasted from the flank! Won't they be surprised?" He forgot himself and rapped me sharply on the top of my kepi with the barrel of his Remington. It was still cold. He hadn't fired … yet. "When a great commander's plans go to hell in a handbasket, he adapts and acts! Never forget that! Never!"

"Here they come!" someone shouted. I saw them, but this time, they weren't yelling or running. They were gliding from tree to tree and from rock to rock in the smoke, sneaking up the hill instead of charging blindly. They too had adapted. I glimpsed that same big Confederate officer with the red feather, the leader. His hat was riddled. His uniform was torn. His sword was gone, but he still held his big pistol. The Stars and Bars were wrapped around his waist. Relentless, he moved up the hill toward us with that remarkable agility.

"Pick your targets!" Chamberlain shouted. "Fire at will, boys!"

The Twentieth Maine opened up, and so did the Rebels. We were back in the middle of the horrendous storm. Bullets were zinging overhead and thumping into my tree. Our line was blasting away, and the Rebels were blasting back—smoke, fire, screams, and moans.

A high-pitched voice, very young, shrieked, "Oh, God. Oh, God!"

I huddled behind my pathetic tree, shaking with terror.

The noise was titanic, insufferable.

God, make them stop!

I had no sense of time, just of the immense noise and the smell of gunpowder, smoke, and a hint of blood tickling my nostrils. I was lost in an insane world of black chaos. Suddenly, I heard a voice out of the fog.

"Lex?" the voice shouted. "Are you Lex?"

I looked up. The huge Confederate officer with the red feather was standing over me. His face was black with dirt and gunpowder. His eyes were wild.

I nodded.

He raised his pistol and cocked it. "Then die!"

It happened again. My pistol leapt out of my holster, cocked itself, and pointed at the big Confederate's forehead. I pulled the trigger. The big gun exploded and kicked upward in my hand. The top of his head went away, and the rest of him disappeared in the smoke.

The fire slackened. Somebody shouted, "They're done! They're backing off!" I heard a few scattered cheers: "Huzzah! Huzzah!"

I leaped up on the stone wall, lifted my head, and howled like a wolf at the sky. I felt wonderful. Strong. Mighty. Like a young god.

"Are you two all right?" Chamberlain asked. He was a dirty mess, but his voice was as calm as if he was discussing Aristotle's *Poetics* in the Bowdoin faculty lounge.

"Quite all right, thank you, Colonel," said Bernie. "Lex?"

"Great!" I answered. "Wonderful!"

Bernie looked at the smoking revolver in my hand and scowled.

The great battle still thundered just over the hill. All around me, I heard the ghastly wounded animal sounds—the whimpers, the gasping, the moans, the weeping, and the hideous bubbling shrieks. All were music to my ears.

"Is it over?" I asked.

"I don't think so," Bernie answered.

"Good," I said.

I heard a shout along the line: "I'm out!" and "Me too." And "Two rounds here" and "One here."

The sergeant whom Chamberlain had ordered to "refuse the flank" scrambled over. His head was filthy and hatless, and his left arm hung bloody and limp at his side. "We're about out of ammunition, Colonel. A lot of the men are already out. A few have one or two rounds."

Chamberlain's uniform was torn and stained with someone else's blood. He threw the lever on his pistol and caught the empty cylinder in his hand. He fished in his pocket for a loaded one. "I'm out too," he said.

"Here, Colonel." Bernie handed Chamberlain a fresh cylinder.

"Much obliged, Colonel." Chamberlain bowed, inserted the cylinder in his pistol, and locked it in. He climbed up on his rock again and took a look down the hill. "They're forming up for another charge. Stubborn fellows." He climbed back down again.

"What we gonna do, Colonel?" asked the sergeant. "Retreat now?"

Chamberlain said, "They've taken a beating. They've been climbing up this hill, running back, and climbing up again all day. They must be about played out. I wonder if they have any water down there … I doubt it. I think they're about done with this fight. All they need is a little persuasion, and I think they'll quit."

"Yes, sir."

"So, let's fix bayonets and charge."

"Sir?"

"Pass the order to fix bayonets, Sergeant."

Bernie beamed at me. The bloodthirsty maniac loved it. "Insane! Utterly insane!" he whispered. "But exactly the right thing to do!"

I loved it too.

The sergeant scrambled away. I heard the scattered cry: "Fix bayonets!" echo down the line. I heard far fewer voices than I had heard before.

Chamberlain said, "Why, Lieutenant, you have no rifle. He pulled the rifle from the dead hands of a private lying sprawled beside us. He yanked the bayonet from the private's belt, fixed it to the rifle, and handed the thing to me. The rifle was almost too hot to hold. "Have you ever been in a bayonet charge, Lieutenant?" he asked.

"Not lately, sir."

"Well, I haven't ever. Thank God we'll be running downhill. I'm fagged out. Bugler, sound the charge!"

"I'm afraid the bugler's dead," Bernie remarked. A severed head with most of a crumpled, blood-soaked bugle jammed deep into its mouth lay at Bernie's feet.

"Ah, I see." Chamberlain jumped up on his wall and pulled out his sword. "Men!" His voice was a little hoarse but amazingly strong and resonant considering how he had spent his afternoon. "This is the

Twentieth Maine's hill. Those people want to take it from us. When I give the word, we will teach them that no man can take what belongs to the Twentieth Maine."

There was a thin, but strong, cheer. I cheered too.

"Twentieth Maine, are you ready to drive those people off our hill?"

"Yes!" we shouted, stronger this time.

"Twentieth Maine, give them our steel! Charge! He jumped down off his wall and began trotting down the slope. Every last man who was still able staggered after him, screaming like a lunatic.

I screamed too, and I took one step.

Bernie seized me by my shoulders and held me back. "Not you, young Ares. We're saving you to get killed later."

So, with these inspiring words, Bernie and I did not make the famous charge at Little Round Top. Instead, we watched Colonel Joshua Chamberlain and the few survivors of the Twentieth Maine run screeching down the hill to disappear into the woods. There were a few scattered shots and then silence.

"What happened?" I asked.

"The Confederates ran away," Bernie said. "The unplanned Confederate flanking attack that would have won the war for the Confederacy failed after all. The next day, the Union won the Battle of Gettysburg—and two years later, the Civil War."

"Wow. That charge took balls."

"Chamberlain was a great leader. He received the Medal of Honor for this action."

Beethoven's "Song of Joy" tinkled from Bernie's pocket. He pulled out his gold watch, popped it open, and held the watch to his ear. "Hello?" he said into the watch face. "Polemarchos here. Yes, sir. I understand, sir. Right away, sir." He shut the watch. "Guess what, Lex?"

"What, Bernie?"

"We are called to action."

Yikes! What did that mean? Nobody had told me anything!

He grabbed my hand.

CHAPTER 16

When we stepped out of the Rubbermaid, we found two human heads, three and a half feet, and one hand stacked in a tidy little pile at the door.

"Ah," Bernie cooed. "A little present from Kitty. Good girl! Told you she was a good watch cat."

I stared at the grisly pile. "Bernie, who are … who were these people?"

"Why, Lex. Don't you know? These are people who came to kill us."

"Does this happen often?"

"Once or twice a month, I'd say."

I'd had more than enough mayhem for one day. Bernie half-carried me to his kitchen and gave me a basin to heave into while he cooked up some nice chicken soup. I was slurping up the last drops when the doorbell rang.

"That's the car," he said. "Run to your room, take a shower, and put on some decent clothes. We have an important appointment. Be sure to brush your hair and use deodorant and mouthwash."

"Jeez, Bernie," I protested. "I'm not three years old. I know how to wash myself."

"Hmmph. All teenagers are filthy."

When I got to my room, a beautiful Saville Row charcoal gray pinstriped suit was laid neatly out on my bed along with an off-white button-down shirt with French cuffs, gold cufflinks inscribed with my initials, a silk tie, silk undies, silk socks, a pair of shimmering brown wing tips, and a bright red pocket square handkerchief. I took my shower, careful to wash off all the battle grime, brushed my hair, used pit-spray, and changed.

I looked fabulous. *Something very important must be up*, I thought.

Bernie met me at the front door. He was wearing a Versailles-era diplomat's outfit: high starched collar, frock coat, and top hat. He carried a walking stick with which he poked me in the stomach. "You are on your best behavior," he said. "Correct?"

"Yes, Berns."

We jumped into the car. "Big doings at the house," the chauffeur announced, sending a waft of cheap rye into the back seat.

Half a dozen black limousines were drawn up in my grandfather's driveway when we arrived. From the dozen well-tailored thugs with sunglasses, earpieces, and submachine guns, I drew the conclusion that important people were gathered inside. Certainly, they were not there to guard just Bernie and me.

John answered the door. "You grandfather is waiting for you in his study," he said. In passing, I noted that he was now wearing two pistols under his morning suit.

"You will stand up straight," Bernie whispered. "You will not slouch or scratch yourself—and no playing pocket pool."

"Pocket pool? Who says I play pocket pool?"

"I say. When you're nervous, you touch yourself. And, sometimes, you pick your nose. You will not speak unless spoken to—and you will restrict your answers to 'yes, sir' and 'no, sir' if at all possible. If asked to elaborate, you will be exceedingly brief and concise. No rambling on. And no cursing."

"Fuck yeah, Bernie," I said to annoy him.

Two enormous bodyguards holding pump shotguns and wearing body armor stood on either side of the library door. They looked us over and patted us down before they opened the door and let us in.

Four people sat around a conference table looking very serious. My grandfather sat at one end. I hadn't kept up much on current events since starting with Bernie, but I did recognize the tall, skinny guy at the other end of the table as the president of the United States. The short woman in the middle was the secretary of state. Opposite her was some general, probably the chairman of the Joint Chiefs. His chest dripped with ribbons.

They all stood up when we entered. I was impressed. Imagine all of these famous people standing up for me!

I was wrong. They stood up for Bernie.

"Welcome, Dr. Polemarchos," my grandfather said. "Good to see you again. I believe you know everyone here."

Bernie walked around the room and shook hands with everyone. The general pushed out his chest and scowled. The president and secretary of state smiled.

"Gentlemen, Madame Secretary, this is my grandson, Alexius. We call him Lex." Bernie nudged me, and I made the rounds, pressing the flesh.

The president grabbed my fingers before I could take his whole hand. Politicians shake that way to save their hands from being crushed by the hundreds of people they have to shake hands with every day, but I think it's kind of unfriendly.

"I was sorry to hear about your father," he said. His voice was deep and musical. He had a nice smile. "I know you will make him proud."

"Thank you, Mr. President."

The secretary of state gave me the full, firm grip and piercing look in the eye. "So, you're the new one, are you?" she asked.

"Yes, ma'am."

The general grabbed my hand, held it, and crushed it. "You up to the job, boy?" he asked, clearly not looking for an answer. "You damn well better be," he declared and crushed my hand some more. He stared into my face to see if I flinched. What a jerk. I didn't give him the satisfaction. Anyway, I was much stronger than he was. I amped up my grip to half power and made him let go.

"He's doing very well," Bernie said.

I am?

The general grunted.

"He's well ahead of where his grandfather was at the same stage," Bernie said.

"Doesn't surprise me," Grandfather replied. "Look at what a big fellow he is. I was 140 pounds soaking wet at his age. You almost killed me with that vest of yours."

"It made a man of you," said Bernie, looking satisfied.

"How was Gettysburg?" asked the president. "Lincoln and I both come from Illinois. Did you know that?"

"No, sir."

"So, young man, are you ready?" the secretary of state asked.

"I'm sure I am, ma'am." Faking confidence, I added, "But ready for what exactly?"

"He doesn't know," Grandfather said.

The SOS turned to Bernie. "He doesn't know ... anything?"

"Just a little. He knows something about the Wargods and their time travel, of course, and he knows we are training to fight a battle. But we just began. We didn't expect the call so soon."

"He's dead meat," the general said with a casual certainty that froze my blood. "Roadkill. You're dead, kid. Sorry." He turned to Bernie. "When's the funeral? Won't be able to bury him in Arlington. He's not military. Don't know what he is. Do we have a backup?"

"He'll survive," said Bernie, ignoring the question. "He's not ready to command, of course, but he's fit, intelligent, and brave and quite able to take care of himself as a private soldier. Or as a junior officer, perhaps. Very junior."

"I thank him for his service," said the president.

"Tell me, young man, do you think you're ready to fight in a real battle?" asked the SOS.

"Fight in a real battle, ma'am? But I already have."

"No, you haven't," said Bernie, sounding impatient. "Not really."

"I think it's time for Lex to know everything, don't you, gentlemen?" said Madame Secretary. They all agreed. "Dr. Polemarchos, please explain."

Bernie struck his silly lecturer pose. "We Wargods are a race of policemen. We patrol the galaxy keeping an eye out for civilizations that are about to blow themselves up with nuclear weapons."

"None of your damn business what we do," the general grumbled under his breath. "It's our constitutional right to blow ourselves up."

"In 1945, when our instruments detected that you had used nuclear weapons at Hiroshima and Nagasaki, we came here to stop your mischief."

Bernie explained that at first the world leaders hadn't listened to the Wargods. They just went on building bigger and better weapons, threatening each other and making what was then known as the Cold War hotter and hotter.

"So, we had to make a demonstration and concentrate your minds."

"How?"

"Remember Pluto?"

I had read some books about astronomy at home. "Yes. It used to be a planet, but astronomers studied it more carefully, realized it was smaller than they had thought, and downgraded it to a dwarf planet."

"They downgraded it because we blew it in half. It was a demonstration to make you people stop your naughtiness."

I looked at Bernie with new eyes. If Bernie and his fellows could blow a planet in half, could he throw green fire from his fingertips, turn me into a toad, and control my mind? Would he transform into his true self—a disembodied brain and squirming tentacles in a fishbowl?

But, no, he was still just Ol' Berns, standing there, puffing out his chest, posturing like some pompous old Roman, and grinning.

Bernie said, "So, then we generously offered you people the opportunity to resolve your conflicts without destroying yourselves."

"How?" I asked.

"By refighting the great battles of the past instead of fighting nuclear war in the present."

Yikes! There was the answer. That was why we'd been training, traveling in time, playing with ape men, and getting shot at.

The clock went thunk, thunk, thunk. Everyone in the room stared at me, wondering how I would react to this insane, impossible idea. Would the kid laugh? Would he run screaming from the room? Would the top of his head explode?

But I kept my head. I was *so* cool. Nothing Bernie could do could surprise me now. I looked up at the big painting. "Like Waterloo?"

"Yes, Lex, like Waterloo. We refought Waterloo at the time of the Cuban Missile Crisis—1963. Your father and I beat the Frenchies so the Russians took their missiles out of Cuba, and there was no nuclear war."

Thunk. Thunk. Thunk.

Bernie got a dreamy look in his eye. "We Wargods, love your battles." He sighed. "It's our little hobby."

"Whatever floats your boat, Bernie," I said.

He gave me a very black look. I dropped the adolescent sarcasm.

"The North Koreans are acting up," the secretary of state said. "They are about to launch missiles at us. We are about to launch missiles at them."

"So, you and I will go fight our battle to resolve this argument without missiles," Bernie said.

I played cool, but my mind was racing with a hundred—a thousand—questions. "What battle?" I asked.

"You'll soon find out."

"And this will be a real battle?"

"The real battle. The real Battle of Waterloo, for instance, with a few modifications. For instance, I would be commanding instead of the duke of Wellington."

"And someone else than Napoleon would be commanding the French?"

"Yes.

"Who?"

"One of the Others."

"The Others?"

"The other Wargods."

"Other Wargods?"

"Yes, Lex. The Wargods who killed your family and tried to kill you."

Now I will meet them face to face, I thought. *And kill them.*

PART II

THE BATTLE

CHAPTER 17

It was hot, and I was again on the back of some beast bouncing and bumping along. The beast was brown like a horse, and it had stick-up ears like a horse. It smelled like a horse.

"My feet are dragging on the ground, Bernie," I complained. "Why is this horse so short?"

"Because he's a donkey," Bernie said. His voice was deep and rumbling again.

The donkey turned his head and looked at me. He had big, compassionate, brown eyes. He seemed to feel sorry for me.

"What's his name?" I asked.

"I don't know. You name him."

"I'll call him, Buster."

I turned to look at Bernie. He was huge again. He was mounted on a beautiful, tall black stallion.

"Bernie, how come you're riding a big, beautiful horse, and I'm riding this silly little ass?" I inquired. Far from being happy that I was closer to the ground, I was jealous.

"Because you are a slave, and I am your master," he replied. "The master gets the horse, and the slave gets the ass. That's the way things are done around here. And do not call me Bernie. You shall address me as *Lord, Lord Polemarchos,* or *Master.*"

I was cranky from the trip. "I'm no slave," I muttered.

"Oh? Is that so? Look at yourself," Bernie demanded.

I checked myself out. I wore ratty sandals smeared with dry donkey droppings and a short tunic made out of scratchy fabric like a potato sack. I wore a piece of frayed rope around my waist for a belt. From this rope hung a filthy table knife and a wooden spoon encrusted with last week's dinners.

"Now look at me," he demanded.

Bernie—I mean Lord Polemarchos—wore a tunic (I later learned this was called a *chiton*) spun from silk embossed with threads of solid gold. Around his waist, he wore a heavy leather belt studded with jewels. From the belt hung a long dagger dripping with rubies. Over his tunic, he wore a longer cloak/toga sort of thing (called a *himation*) also made of silk, decorated with a rich pattern in red, yellow and purple, and elaborately folded and secured with golden pins and silver brooches. Bernie wore gold earrings and rings on his fingers. His black hair and black beard glistened with some sort of perfumed greasy gel. Bernie was obviously a big shot.

"That's my stuff behind you," Bernie said. "You have no stuff because you are a miserable slave."

A huge pile of baggage was stacked high over the hindquarters of my little steed: sacks and chests, a tent, a suit of armor, a metal helmet, two long spears, several swords and daggers, and a big round shield. Bernie's precious compound bow from Troy and a quiver of arrows hung from the saddle. Beside it hung a passel of small dead mammals.

"Your job is to take care of my stuff," he said. "That's what slaves do. I don't lift a finger. You do all the work. You are my labor-saving device—the low-tech, ancient version."

We were riding up a steep hill on a deeply rutted, dusty dirt road lined with boulders, scrub bushes, cactus, and clumps of dried-up old fir trees.

"Where are we, Ber ... Master?"

"Greece. Attica, Mount Pendelikon," said Bernie. "It's where the Athenians quarry the marble for their temples."

"When are we, Master?"

"263 ab urbe condita."

"Huh?"

"My mistake. I'm getting too old for all this time travel. 'Two hundred sixty-three years from the founding of the city' by the ancient Roman calendar. 490 BCE by yours."

I was miserable. My butt was chafed. My legs were sore. It was blazing hot. My hair was soaked with sweat. I was thirsty. Buster smelled gamey and attracted clouds of flies. I could smell myself. I reeked. The flies liked me as much as Buster.

A simple little song kept going through my head and made me feel much better: "I will kill them. I will kill them. I will kill them all."

When we came to the summit, Bernie reined us in and pointed. "Behold the famed Acropolis of Athens."

Stretched out below us was a green plain. Rising out of it far in the distance, I saw a great, blue-gray rock outcropping surrounded by a defensive wall made of enormous stone blocks. The wall reminded me of the one around Troy. It must have been very ancient. Spotted all around the Acropolis were little white buildings. They were temples, I guessed. Clustered around the Acropolis like a litter of kittens nestled up against their mother was a vast, messy sprawl of dusty, nondescript little buildings— the city of Athens.

"That's not the Acropolis, Master," I said. "There's no Parthenon." I knew that the Parthenon, Athens's great temple dedicated to the city's patron goddess, Athena, and one of the Seven Wonders of the Ancient World, topped the Acropolis of Athens. No Parthenon, no Acropolis. No Athens.

Bernie had screwed up. We were probably outside of Cleveland.

"The Athenians built the Parthenon after this battle we're going to win," Bernie explained. "Athens's golden age is still ahead of her. If we don't win, Athens won't have a golden age at all. In fact, people in our day will probably have never even heard of Athens."

"Why?"

"Oh, the usual: massacre, rape, fire, pillage, not a stone standing upon a stone, salt sown in the ruins, etcetera, etcetera."

I raised my hand. "A little question, Lord."

"Yes, lowly slave. Shoot."

"Are you saying that if we lose this battle, history will be changed, Lord?"

"Probably," he said. "The Others hate how history has turned out— civilization, democracy, science, medicine, art, religion, hospitals, grocery stores, iPhones, computers, cheeseburgers and fries, baseball, football, pretty women in shirt skirts, streaming video, pug puppies—everything good you can name, the Others hate. They want history to all turn out in famine, disease, barbarism, war, slaughter, and a perpetual Dark Age. Black chaos is what the Others want.

"Why?"

"How should I know? I'm not an Other. I'm a good guy."

"I thought you know everything, Master."

"Only everything worth knowing. Of course, you needn't trouble yourself about all this. If the Others change history, we won't know it because the world as it is would seem perfectly normal and unchanged to us. Right?"

This was a bit too deep for me. "Huh?"

"Anyway, what do you think of Athens, the cradle of Western civilization?"

"It stinks. Maybe it's better close up."

"No, closer up, it looks and smells even worse. I hope you're up to date on your booster shots: diphtheria, tetanus, yellow fever, plague? Bubonic plague is as common as the sniffles in Athens this season."

"Plague!"

"No plague shots? Oh, well, if you get it, you get it. Don't pet the rats and keep an eye out for a high fever and big, black putrid lumps in your armpits and groin."

We rode on over the crest of the hill and down into the valley. Soon we were in hardscrabble farm country: stone walls, parched fields of maize, a few stunted olive trees, and miserable, tumble-down hovels.

A filthy urchin was herding six sickly goats down the side of the road. "Yo, Lord Polemarchos," he squeaked. "Been hunting? Have any luck?"

"Plenty," Bernie shouted back. "Here, for your dinner." He pulled a couple of dead vermin off his saddle and threw them to the ground in front of the kid. They plopped into a horse muffin.

"Wow! Thanks, Lord," the kid said, hurrying to pick up the corpses and dusting off the dung. "I love chipmunk. My mom will whip us up a nice pie. Today's my tenth birthday."

"Many happy returns and bon appétit!" Bernie cried. As we rode away, Bernie whispered. "He'll be dead of plague before he's eleven."

We rode around a bend right into a small procession of travelers, men and women old and young carrying their children and all their worldly possessions on their backs or pushing them in carts. Clearly, they were running away from something.

A dirty old farmer and his wizened crone of a wife were trudging along. He carried only a staff. His old lady was bent beneath a huge pack.

"Where are you going, farmer?" Bernie asked.

"To find safety in the city," the geezer replied. "Haven't you heard the news?"

"What news, Grandfather?"

"By Hades's big black dick, the barbarians are coming!" the geezer croaked.

"Where are the barbarians now?" Bernie asked.

"There are quad-zillions of them," said the farmer, widening his eyes. "They are more numerous than the grains of sand on the shores of the River Lethe. They are more numerous than the stars in the dome of heaven—"

"They are no more numerous than your nightly risings to pee," added his wife.

"Their ships cover the eastern ocean from horizon to horizon," the farmer droned on. "There are so many that their horsemen walk dry-shod from Asia to Athens in a single file a hundred miles long."

"They have giants from a place far to the East called India marching among them!" shrieked his wife. "Monsters as tall as the Acropolis with six heads. They eat men by the fistful. When they spit out the bones, the splinters strike men down like clouds of arrows."

"But where are they now?" asked Bernie patiently.

"They hold Eritrea under siege," the farmer answered. "They batter down the city walls with machines that hurl boulders the size of houses."

"They have a monstrous bird called a Roc," added his missus. "It drops giant turds on the heads of the poor Eritreans."

"Ah, an air force too," Bernie whispered to me. "Good to know."

"All is lost!" The crone threw herself to her knees. "Help us, Lord Polemarchos. Protect us from the barbarians." She wept, pulled her thin hair out in knots, and poured roadkill on her head.

"Don't worry, Mother," said Bernie. "I and my disgusting slave here, Lex, will kick those barbarians' hairy butts back to where they came from."

"Praise to Lord Polemarchos! Praise to his donkey! Praise even to his disgusting slave."

"Good luck to you, farmer," Bernie said, and we rode on.

I smelled Athens miles before we entered it. The outer suburbs were a rats' nest of filthy, twisting dirt streets, dark alleys, and one-story hovels. A drunk rolled out of a wine shop followed by two bouncers beating him mercilessly with cudgels. Garbage rotted in the streets. An old man squatted and took a dump on what would have been the sidewalk—if there had been a sidewalk. Passersby held their noses and stepped over a corpse sprawled in the road. He was turning black in the sun and was covered with fat green flies.

I covered my mouth with my tunic.

"The city of Socrates, Plato, and Aristotle," Bernie remarked. "How they managed to think all their deep thoughts in this stink, I can't imagine."

The street turned from dirt to cobblestone as we entered downtown. The thoroughfare was clogged with every kind of traffic: horses, wagons, carts, a herd of cattle, six pigs driven by a swineherd, and a sedan chair, its curtains discreetly drawn so the aristocratic lady within would not be offended by the stink and bustle outside. Male and female slaves carried just about anything on their heads from big sacks of grain to great jugs of wine to racks of bricks, boxes, trunks, and even a coffin. Bernie was right. Slaves did all the work here.

We rode on. People called to Bernie all along the way: "Welcome back, Lord Polemarchos! We love you, Lord Polemarchos!" Also: "Go to Hell, Polemarchos!"

A brick whistled past my ear.

"I'm a bit dry," Bernie said. "Care for a cold one?"

Without waiting for me to answer, he pulled his horse up in front of a disreputable-looking dive. Over this establishment's door hung a faded wooden sign showing an enormous serpent coiled around a sleeping infant. The serpent's jaws were opened wide to swallow the baby's head. The sign read "The Snake and Baby Inn."

Bernie and I dismounted. Bernie flipped a coin to a street urchin and told him to mind our rides. The urchin tugged his forelock.

We entered. The place smelled like sour wine and urine with a delicate background scent of aged vomit. There were no tables, chairs, or stools—just a bar with giant wine jars lined up behind it. People here did their drinking standing up.

The place was empty except for a burly bartender mopping up spilt wine from the floor. "We're closed," he growled, still mopping. He looked up, saw Bernie, and nodded toward a greasy bead curtain in the back.

We passed through the curtain into a back room lit by a single smoking candle. An enormous shaggy man was sitting at a rickety table nursing a filthy bowl of wine and muttering obscenities to himself. He had a livid scar across his forehead, black, oily hair down to the middle of his back and was dressed in stinking rags. Bernie walked right up to this monster and sat down.

"Polemarchos. How was your trip, old boy?" the man said in a rich Oxford accent.

"Tolerable. At least this one didn't vomit all over himself," Bernie said, looking at me. "Say hello to Lex, my new apprentice."

"Nice to meet you, Lex," said the horrible man.

"So, what's the situation in our cradle of democracy?" Bernie asked.

"The workers, when they are drunk—which is always—are gripped with martial ardor. They want to march out and fight the Persians today. The merchants want to flee into the Acropolis and pull the covers over their heads. The aristocrats are whispering treason and secretly negotiating a surrender. They are all at each other's throats. Six square blocks of the Illissos district were burned down last night, and sixty people were killed in the rioting. The Assembly has declared martial law and a curfew."

"Ah, Athens." Bernie sighed. "Peaceful democratic discourse and the free exchange of ideas …"

"God bless Democracy: 'The worst mode of government … except for all the others.' Winston Churchill will say that in two and a half thousand years."

"And our counterparts? What are they up to?" Bernie asked.

"They're conspiring with the aristocrats, bribing, assassinating, spreading rumors, and doing their very utmost to ruin city morale. They're succeeding. At this rate, the Athenians won't fight."

"We'll see that they do," said Bernie. "Who's my opponent this time?"

"This time, he poses as Hippias, the tyrant the Athenians booted out twenty years ago. He fled to the Persian court, and this Other has taken his identity."

"And Lex's opposite number?"

"Apollonius is the name he's taken. Mid-thirties. He's been with their outfit for five years. He's Iraqi, ex-Mukhabarat. Likes to torture and rape very young girls on his days off."

So, Hippias and Apollonius are their names! These are the ones who killed my family!

I flushed bright red and gripped the table top so tightly I felt my fingertips must be driving into the wood.

"What do you think of that, Lex?" Bernie asked.

"I look forward to meeting them," I said as coolly as I could.

"That's a stout fellow," remarked the horrible man. "Polemarchos, you must go to the Assembly now. There you must give the most stirring oration of your career and convince the Athenians to fight. Otherwise, we lose without even having a nice battle to enjoy."

"I'm on it," Bernie said, looking ready for the challenge.

"Good luck," said the beast man. "Oh, and one other thing."

"Yes?"

"We've counted six two-man assassination teams trying to track you down. We've eliminated two of them, which leaves …"

"Four."

"Plus the others we don't know about," added Mr. Horrible.

We remounted our steeds and set forth for the center of the city, the Agora, Athens's marketplace. Everyone knew Bernie. As we passed from the slums into more prosperous, residential neighborhoods, the citizens greeted us: "Lord Polemarchos, have you heard the news? The barbarians are coming."

"General Polemarchos, the Strategoi are meeting in the Agora in an hour. Are we goin' to fight or not?"

"General, what you doin' here? Get down to the Agora and tell those fools what to do."

And: "Get screwed, Polemarchos!" accompanied by excrement—canine, I think—flying past my head.

CHAPTER 18

The Athenian Agora, I knew from my reading, was a serene white marble courtyard shaded by stately cypress trees where bearded philosophers like Socrates exchanged high-minded thoughts on the nature of the soul and other worthy topics with their rapt students.

What the Agora really was, I found, was a tumultuous mob of filthy Athenians buying, selling, haggling, bickering, bargaining, boozing, arguing, fighting, screwing, stealing, shoplifting, and picking pockets in a huge, filthy outdoor market packed with hundreds of stalls selling everything from aardvark steaks to zebra throw rugs.

We dismounted and led our animals into the mob. We were headed toward the Strategeion, the building on the far side of the Agora where the city's generals met. It was slow going through the throng. Several times, we were blocked. Luckily, everyone loved Bernie and wanted to help. The cry went up: "Make way for Lord Polemarchos!" and "Stand aside for General Polemarchos!" and the crowd parted.

We were about halfway across the Agora and passing through an area specializing in wine stalls, gambling dens, and houses of ill repute, when I heard a shout: "Yo, Poly, where you going?"

Two dandies, brothers by their family resemblance, stepped out of the crowd. Each had one hand squeezing the bottom of a strumpet and the other squeezing a brimming wine bowl.

"Aeschylus, old fellow! Cynegeirus!" Bernie shouted. "Here to see us go to war, are you?"

"War? What war?" answered Aeschylus, the older of the two.

"We're lovers—not fighters, Lord," declared Cynegeirus, giving his girl's rump a friendly pinch. She giggled.

"We are artists, tragedians," added Aeschylus. "We have come to garner life experience in the flesh pots of the Agora."

"Oh, I see—research on life experience, is it?" Bernie noted. "Have you boys actually written any tragedies?"

"Well, not exactly," Aeschylus admitted.

"We are looking for good plots," said Cynegeirus. "We believe in art. We don't believe in war."

"Ah, Cynegeirus, but war believes in you," Bernie quipped.

The two brothers looked puzzled. At that moment a scrawny herald emerged out on to the marble steps of the Strategeion and roared, "Hear ye, hear ye! The meeting of the Strategoi is now in session. Let all persons with business to put before the generals gather here now. May Ares bless this city."

At that, the entire Athenian electorate stampeded toward the Strategeion, and we were swept across the cobblestones, up the steps, and into the building. We managed to find a spot safe from trampling under a large statue of some naked hero holding a shield and spear. Did Athenians fight naked? No way would I fight naked.

The mob was packed in shoulder to shoulder and stunk to high heaven. They were still pushing, shoving, and fidgeting when some old guy with a gray-specked beard stepped up to the podium and tried to make himself heard. Behind him sat eight other bearded worthies looking wise and serious.

"Citizens, citizens," pleaded the geezer. "Please settle down. The city is in dire peril. This assembly must decide what to do immediately. Can you boys hear me in the b-b-back?"

He was a distinguished-looking fellow, battle-scarred like an old soldier, but his high-pitched voice sounded like a girl.

"Ca-ca-Callimachus" some wag shouted, and everyone laughed at the poor old guy.

"Callimachus the Polemarch," said Bernie. "The War Archon. The equivalent of our commander in chief."

"To arms!" someone shouted. "Fight. Fight. Fight!"

And from the other side of the room, someone else said, "No! Negotiate! Talk-talk-talk."

Suddenly a band of a dozen howling thugs charged the podium

swinging cudgels. They were shoved back by armored soldiers holding shields and eight-foot spears across their chests.

"P-p-p-please," cried Callimachus. "Be calm."

"He doesn't seem to be much of a leader," I commented.

"The Athenians are suspicious of leaders. They have given the Polemarch no real power," Bernie explained. "He's really just the master of ceremonies."

"So, who's the real boss: the leader, the president, the king, the big kahuna, or whatever they have here?"

"The people—or should I say the *rabble*. Twenty years ago, they had that dictator, Hippias, but they threw him out and haven't trusted a leader since. Their democracy here is the first ever in history. Instead of one commander in chief, the people elect ten generals and make them vote on every little decision. Callimachus acts only as the tiebreaker."

"They'll never decide to go to war that way," I said. "They'll never make up their minds to do anything."

Bernie chuckled. "Watch me work my magic. I'll have 'em screaming for Persian blood in no time." He began shoving his way through the mob to the podium.

When they saw him coming, the hoi polloi began to chant: "Pol-e-march-os! Pol-e-march-os!" Bernie flashed them a two-handed v for victory sign and skipped up the stone steps like a twenty-year-old.

"Ah, ci-ci-citizens," said Callimachus. "Here is General Polemarchos, the only man here who has fought, and beaten, the P-P-Persians. Let's hear what he has to say."

The crowd gave Bernie the standing O—mixed with a few rocks, fruits, and obscenities.

Bernie dodged the rocks, ignored the obscenities, and struck a heroic posture with his arms folded across his chest.

I didn't catch the first part of Bernie's oration. I was too busy keeping an eye on our stuff. It seemed to me that all Athenians were thieves. They would have carried Buster off on their backs if I hadn't stopped them. Also, speeches bore me. Athenians didn't have TV, Xbox or smartphones. Their chief source of entertainment was working out naked, listening to long, tedious speeches, politics, and making war on neighboring cities.

Folks told me later that Bernie delivered a real barn burner. I tuned back in at the climax when a tall, very skinny, dark-skinned guy, pouring sweat and half-dead from exhaustion, limped up the stairs to the podium.

The mob shouted, "Philippides. Philippides!"

He whispered in Bernie's ear.

"News from Eritrea!" Bernie cried. "The Eritreans retired to their Acropolis and fought like men. But they were betrayed! Traitors opened the gates by night."

"Betrayed! Betrayed!" the mob howled.

"The barbarians have burned Eritrea to the ground, put the men to the sword, raped and enslaved the women and girls, and ..."

Not a sound from the crowd.

"They have castrated every boy in the city and sent them to the boy brothels of Babylon."

"The boy brothels of Babylon!" A great moan from the crowd.

A chill went up my spine too.

"Such is the fate of Athens and the Athenians if we do not fight these barbarians!" Bernie roared. "Will we wait to be betrayed? Or will we fight like men?"

I'm sure the Persians heard the Athenian mob shrieking for their blood all the way to Eritrea. I saw Bernie talking to the Philippides guy for a moment. Then Phil took off in a jog.

Bernie said, "I have dispatched Philippides to Sparta to seek their aid. Soon ten thousand Lacedemonian hoplites will stand shoulder to shoulder with us!"

The good citizens of Athens let loose another bloodcurdling howl. Half a hundred wharf rats, back-alley cutthroats, pickpockets, pimps, plug-uglies, and other upstanding Athenian citizens surrounded Bernie. I thought he was done for, but they hoisted him up on their shoulders and paraded him out into the Agora and into the streets. Men, women, and children poured out of their houses and joined the mob. They reached to touch Bernie's sandals. Women threw their underclothes at him. The mob grew to thousands.

I fetched Buster and Bernie's horse and joined the fun. Every time the crowd passed a wine shop, buxom serving girls wearing mini-chitons rushed out with wine jugs and poured their rotgut directly down the throats of us parched patriots. Thus inspired, we stopped from time to time to loot shops and homes owned by traitors—who all just happened to be wealthy aristocrats. I picked up a few items myself, including a nice gold ring in the shape of intertwined snakes, which I wear to this day.

Finally, we arrived at Bernie's house. The footpads and throat-slitters let Bernie down from their shoulders, gave him a rousing cheer, and pressed on for a bit more raping and pillaging before the booze got the better of them.

CHAPTER 19

I began my career as a slave in Bernie's house, a two-story place built of whitewashed, sun-dried brick with a red tile roof. I guessed that the Athens PD wasn't on the job because it was built like a fortress. All the windows—narrow slits too small for a man to crawl through and sealed up tight with heavy wooden shutters—were on the second story. The double front door was a massive hunk of oak studded with big iron bolts. A couple of bald-headed bruisers with Ps monogrammed on their tunics stood on either side of the door glaring at the crowd and slapping wooden truncheons into their palms. The bruisers opened the double doors, and Bernie strode inside. I handed the horse and Buster's reins to the bruisers and followed Bernie to begin my new life.

Bernie's house slaves, a dozen ancient family retainers, were lined up to greet their master. Standing before them was a ferocious, coal-black woman with arms folded across her ample bosom. She must have tipped the scales at least three hundred minas.

"This is Gorga," said Bernie, "my housekeeper. Gorga is a former queen of Nubia. She will inform you of your duties."

Gorga's biceps were as thick around as my waist. She wore her hair in dreadlocks beaded with human finger bones. She gave me the once-over. "You call yourself a slave, slave?" she said with disgust.

"Well, yes," I replied. "I guess."

She whacked me a good one on the top of my head. I saw stars and staggered.

"You guess? Slaves do not guess, slave!" she thundered.

"Yes, ma'am."

She rammed her face six inches from mine. "Do you guess that your job is to unload the master's belongings from that stupid ugly donkey of yours?"

"Yes, ma'am. But Buster's not stupid. He's a very bright donk—"

She whacked me again.

"Then do it, by Zeus! Now!" She grabbed me by the arm and flipped me into the street. I landed at Buster's feet. He looked down at me with his big brown sad eyes as if to say: "You and I are in this together, Lex."

Gorga kept me going until well after dark. I unloaded Buster, carried all of Bernie's stuff inside, and put it away in its appropriate shelves and cupboards.

Gorga pulled everything down from the shelves and cupboards, screamed that everything was in the wrong place, and made me put it back again. Next, I did all the dishes in the kitchen and scrubbed the floor—three times until I got it right. Then, I swept the whole house. Next, I collected all the house's chamber pots—the reeking urns that passed for toilets in fifth-century Athens—and emptied them into the street. Next Gorga made me mop up all the piss and shit that had sloshed on the floor. Then she had me do the wash for the whole household in a big cauldron of water boiling over an open fire in the courtyard. Judging by the yellow-stained and brown-tracked underwear, the Athenians changed their boxers about once every other year and wiped none too carefully between changes either. Finally, Gorga gave me a break for dinner—a jug of water and half a loaf of coarse bread.

When I had finished my feast, she said, "Now go serve your master his wine in the dining room. Do not speak a single word. And do not listen to a single word either. Remember, you are a slave, and slaves are pieces of furniture."

"Yes, Gorga."

"The master has important guests. Take the Lycian there." She pointed to a rack of purple amphorae. "It's the master's finest vintage, a thousand drachma an amphora. If you spill a single drop, I shall beat you as you have never been beaten in your life, and then I will tear off your head and shit down your neck hole."

"Yes, ma'am." I meekly took an amphora of the Lycian from the wine shelf and lugged it up the stairs to the dining room.

Bernie was reclining on a couch in his party robes with three fancy-dressed worthies. One was Callimachus, the red-faced and jolly general in chief. The other two I didn't recognize. I assumed they were generals. Judging by the empties littering the floor and tables, they were well on their way to blackout time. When I stepped into the room, they stopped their conversation.

"He can be trusted," said Bernie. "Can't speak a word of any civilized language, can you, Lex?" he asked me in English.

"No, master," I replied in English.

"By Zeus!" said Callimachus. "What hideous gobbledygook is that he speaks, Polemarchos?"

"The monkey babble of a nasty little island to the far, far north that will never amount to anything," Bernie replied in Greek.

"Sounds like a pig being slaughtered," muttered the older of the two other generals as he wiped his chin with his white beard.

"Pour the wine, Lex, pour the wine," Bernie commanded.

I passed around the table refilling each cup. The old general drained his and uttered an enormous, wet belch. His head crashed down on the table knocking plates and cups every which way. He began to snore. Two slaves entered silently, picked him up, and carried him out the door.

"I'm ready for bed, myself." Callimachus pulled himself to his feet, wavering and collapsing back again. "Is our business done, Polemarchos?"

"The Spartans have been notified, as have the Plataeans," Bernie replied. "We can certainly count on them at least, if not those Spartan pricks. The infantry will muster tomorrow and march as soon as the Persians land. We have men watching the beach at Marathon. They have built a warning fire."

"My cavalry is ready," said the young general.

"You'll have your work cut out for you against the Persian horse, Alcibiades. They're the best in the world. And there'll be thousands of them."

"Every one of us is willing to die for our city," said Alcibiades.

"I know you are," Bernie responded with a hint of sadness.

"Come on, Alcibiades," cried Callimachus. "Let's walk home. Shall we stop for a quickie at Madame Deinomache's House of Aphrodite? It's on the way. Polemarchos's excellent wine has made me randy as a stallion."

"Capital idea, my friend! The good madam has a pair of Macedonian twin sisters who adore me," Alcibiades replied, perking up substantially.

Arm in arm, the two staggered out, roaring an obscene drinking song recounting the amorous misadventures of a lecherous donkey, two well-hung dwarfs, and Helen of Troy.

"Where exactly is this Madame Deinomache's House of Aphrodite?" I asked after they left.

"Control yourself, Lex," Bernie said. "Our business here is war, not debauchery. And Madame Deinomache doesn't allow lowly slaves in her establishment."

"Yes, Master."

"I have a mission for you. Your first solo mission. The Persians are about to land at the village of Marathon, about twenty-five miles north of here. I want you to take Buster there tomorrow morning and scout the ground."

"I'm a spy now?"

"Yes. You are my spy. Remember what you learned about reconnaissance at Little Bighorn?"

"Yes, Lord."

"I want you to report back to me within twenty-four hours with a map: a good, detailed map. I've never been to Marathon myself, and the ancient sources are unreliable. Herodotus was more novelist than historian. He liked to make things up."

"Okay."

"And I want you to include in your report the dispositions, numbers, and regiments of the Persian force."

"Sure, Lord Berns," I said.

"Lastly, I want you to be very careful," he said, looking at me like he was watching a stupid puppy getting set to step onto an interstate highway. "I sent six scouts to Marathon yesterday. None returned."

"I'll be careful."

"I want you to find a safe hiding place with a good view of the Persian camp and make your recon from there. Climb a good high tree. Take notes in this." He flipped me a small roll of something like paper and a little packet of quill and small bottle of ink. "It's papyrus. For heaven's sake, don't get caught with it."

"If they find it, does it burst into flame? Does it melt in water? Can I eat it?"

"No and no and no. We're not allowed twentieth-century equipment. Don't get caught with it. Take no chances."

"Do not enter the Persian camp under any circumstances. Find that tree. Do you understand?"

"Yes, Bernie."

"Leave at dawn with Buster."

"Yes, Berns."

"Remember: Do not enter the Persian camp," he repeated.

"I won't. I promise. Wouldn't think of it. Not me. I'm no fool. Too dangerous."

"Hmm," said Bernie.

CHAPTER 20

I lied. I had decided even before I left the room that I would ride to Marathon, sneak into the Persian camp, find Hippias and Apollonius, and butcher them.

But before I left, I needed to get a good night's sleep. Gorga was kind enough to bed me down just outside Bernie's bedroom door on a filthy rug swarming with bedbugs. I lay there on the floor all night planning my vengeance.

My plan was to pretend to be a wine sutler, a civilian seller of supplies. All armies have them. If the Persians boozed half as much as the Greeks, I figured they'd welcome a load of Bernie's best rotgut with open arms. I'd walk right into the Persian camp, find Hippias and Apollonius, kill them, drop their bloody heads into Buster's saddlebags, and return to Bernie with all the intelligence he needed to win the upcoming battle in a walk.

Once I had conceived this foolproof plan, I spent the rest of the night itching and mulling over just how I would slay Hippias and Apollonius. Would it would be by bludgeon, blade, or fire? Fire was good. Those two had burned my house and my family. Would it be quickly or slowly? Slowly on a spit like a roast pig was best. I nodded off stripping the skin off Hippias's face in my mind's eye. He was screaming most musically.

I woke up before dawn. The house was still. I pulled myself to my feet, groaning with lower back pain and covered with bites. I staggered out to the stables and loaded up Buster with a change of clothes, a few crusts of bread, a bottle of water, and twelve amphorae: six of Bernie's fanciest Lycian red and six of some paint remover swill.

Buster turned to look at me with those big, sad, brown eyes. Buster had to sleep standing up ankle deep in his own crap. He had to carry me on his back. And Buster was not a donkey in his first dewy blush of youth. A donkey's life is one of ceaseless toil and misery. And yet, Buster felt sorry for me.

I almost forgot that I had no weapon. I pulled a heavy sickle down from the stable wall. It had a razor edge. I stashed it in Buster's saddlebag, climbed up on Buster's old sway back, and started on our journey. The sun had not yet risen. The city was asleep except for a few delivery carts. Buster's hooves echoed on the cobblestones. As we left the city and started across the plain, my mind turned back to revenge.

Revenge, I know, has acquired a bad reputation in recent times. Revenge has become "inappropriate." People say, "The best revenge is moving on and getting over it," "Forgive and forget," and the one that really makes me heave: "Smile. It's the best revenge of all."

All this is total BS, in my opinion. My personal philosophy is that, yes, we should forgive our enemies, but not before they are dead—and preferably disemboweled and beheaded too. I felt exactly that way in 490 BC, and I feel the same way today.

As we knocked off mile after mile and the sun began to rise and take the chill off the night air, Buster's gentle, swaying gait lulled me into even more delicious fantasies of vengeful violence. Exactly how would I kill Hippias and Apollonius? Would I simply slash their throats or drive a sword into their hearts? Was that enough to satisfy justice? Should I begin by submitting them to unspeakable tortures? Skinning them alive with a fish-scaling knife? Tearing their skin with red-hot pliers? Crushing their private parts with white-hot walnut-crackers? Hammering roofing nails under their fingernails? Burying them alive? I smiled to myself when I thought of burying them alive.

As a practical matter, I wondered how exactly one kills a Wargod. Bernie had commented that he was not really immortal. What did that mean? I assumed that Wargods were harder to kill than humans. Would stabbing them through the heart like a vampire do the job? Would more extreme measures—beheading, burning, submerging them in a vat of acid, chopping them into small bits, or blowing them up—be necessary? Blowing them up presented a problem. There were no explosives in ancient Greece. As Buster and I plodded across the Attic plain, I mused over all these delights.

We began to pass small, armed bands of peasants and farmers walking toward Marathon. In one of the bands was the same ancient farmer and his old wife we had met on our way to Athens. The farmer carried a splintery spear and wore a rusty old helmet. His wife trudged along a few steps behind him bent beneath his battle-scarred old wooden shield.

"Yo, farmer," I called. "Where you going?"

"By Ares's golden love sword, I go to slaughter barbarians and drink their blood," he boasted, sticking out his scrawny chest and then abruptly yakking up a slimy clam loogie.

"And I go to strip their bloody corpses of their gold and jewels," croaked his wife. "And cut off their man parts to make a nice necklace for my adorable little great-granddaughter, Iona. It's her sixth birthday, you know."

"Good luck, guys," I cried, feeling slightly queasy even though I had been fantasizing about doing worse to Hippias only moments before.

"Look there!" The farmer pointed up to the summit of the mountain and jumped up and down as best he was able. "The barbarians have landed!"

A great plume of black smoke rose from the summit of Mount Pendelikon. The Persian invasion had begun. The warning bonfire had been lit. I gave poor Buster a gentle prod with my heels, and he broke like a thoroughbred into a slow walk.

An hour later, I arrived at the summit and the smoldering remnants of the beacon. Two guards loafed around the coals, their arms and armor stacked beside them. They were roasting a plump rat for their supper. I had had no breakfast, and the fragrant aroma of rat fat sizzling on the open fire made my mouth water. The two guards were passing around a wineskin and lying to each other about women.

"She said she'd worked in Madame Deinomache's for thirty years and never seen a bigger," the bigger guard said.

"Meathead, they say that to everyone," replied the smaller. "For the tip, you fool."

"No way! She said she loves me!"

"Humpin' Hades, Keos, you are the stupidest man who ever lived."

"You there, stop!" Keos, the big guard, seized his spear, jumped up and shouted as I rode up. He was a rough customer with a great diagonal scar that ran across his forehead, down over his nose, under his left eye, and all the way to his jaw. "Where do you and that ugly donkey think you're going?"

Keos seized Buster's bridle with one hand and poked his spearpoint at my face with the other. Theos, the shorter soldier, was also on his feet, sword in hand. Like his colleague, he was battle-scarred. He was missing his left ear. The two of them were not the elegant heroes illustrated in picture histories of Athenian hoplites. They were ugly, muscular brutes. They looked like tough farmers, used to a lifetime of dawn to dusk hard physical labor. Both looked to be about sixty, but they were probably thirty. They were hairy too, and dirty, and they smelled like shit, piss, and old sweat, like all Greeks.

"He looks like a Persian spy," said Keos. "I think I'll stick him."

"Hold off, Keos. He doesn't look like a Persian to me."

"There's only one way to be sure." Keos waved his nasty spear in my face. "Everyone knows that Persians bleed purple."

"He asked you a question," said Theos. "Where do you think you're going?"

I explained my business. When I showed them my wine amphora, they invited me to sit down and share their rat. I opened one of the inferior vintages and poured cups for all of us.

They were a jolly, honest pair. They drank, sang filthy songs and talked about their farms. Mostly they boasted about their gorgeous wives, their precocious kids, all the whores they had bedded, their exploits in battle, all the barbarians they would slay, and all the fabulous loot they were going to steal.

Keos said "Lex, did you know that the barbarians wear trousers in battle? How unmanly is that?"

"Unmanly but sensible." Theos was clearly the more intelligent of the two. "Look at these." He showed us his bare legs. They were crisscrossed with jagged scars.

My feeling was that trousers made a lot more sense than their little short skirts and bare legs. Letting your junk swing freely in the breeze for someone to hack off struck me as a very poor idea indeed.

"I still say the Persians are girls," Keos insisted.

They told many lies and laughed a lot. They were good guys, typical professional soldiers, I guess.

After a couple of hours, I excused myself and went on my way. I wanted to enter the Persian camp before it got dark or I got too drunk.

After a half-mile climb to the summit of the mountain, Buster and I saw the enemy army and fleet spread out across the plain and Bay of Marathon. Thousands of toy ships were drawn up on the beach, unloading thousands of toy men and toy horses. Behind the beached ships, thousands more ships awaited their turn. On the shore, hordes of brightly uniformed soldiers and cavalry, flags and banners waving, formed, reformed, ran, and galloped this way and that in a milling anthill of colorful disorder.

CHAPTER 21

I rode Buster down the mountain and through the old olive and pine trees at its base and emerged out of the wood onto the Marathon plain about a mile and a half from the camp gate.

I immediately saw the Saka galloping toward us. There were two of them, squat little fellows wearing high pointy caps and mounted on shaggy little steppe ponies. Each carried a compound bow and a nasty battle ax for close work. The leading Saka was waving his hand over his head. I thought he was saying hello. Seeking to be friendly, I waved back. Then I realized that the little brute was twirling a lasso over his head like a rodeo cowboy. He let loose, and the lasso dropped neatly over my shoulders, fell to my waist, and yanked tight. In an instant, I found myself lying on my back on the ground.

Lasso Man sat on his pony glaring down at me. His skin was dark brown. He wore a scraggly Fu Manchu mustache and had squinty central Asian eyes. His cheeks were covered with hideous ritual scars.

"My, my," he growled. "What do we have here?"

"A purveyor of fine wines to the world-conquering soldiers of Darius the Great," I croaked in perfect Sakese. Sakese is a barbaric, dissonant language. It sounds like a toad being run over by a road roller.

"He speaks our language!" exclaimed his colleague.

"It so happens that my dear mother is Saka," I improvised. "I learned your beautiful language at her breast. As a child, mama lulled me to sleep with stories of her beloved homeland, its noble people, and its heroic soldiers, much like you. Probably we are cousins."

"I hope not," said Lasso Man. "For I plan to reduce my extended family by one in a moment or two with my ax."

The other Saka tapped on an amphora with his knuckles. "He's not lying. He is a wine merchant. These amphorae are full."

"Good. We'll kill him, take the wine, and get blasted," Lasso Man said.

The colleague uncorked one amphora, poured himself a cup, and drained it. "Not bad," he said, smacking his lips. "Goes down smooth."

"Very good. Slit his throat, and we'll go," said Lasso Man.

The colleague drew his dagger.

I wasn't frightened. I was too dumb to realize that I was in mortal danger. So, instead of pleading for mercy, I took the high road. "By all means, help yourself, gentlemen. That will be one half siglos for the small cup and one siglos for the large," I said.

"One half siglos for this thimble?" The colleague held up the smaller cup. "It's highway robbery!"

"Not for my superb vintages," I replied. "Why that one there was laid down in the year 470 in oaken casks of the finest quality."

"Kill him and be done with it," Lasso Man insisted. "And let's head back to camp with the goods."

The colleague raised his dagger.

I thought fast and talked faster: "Of course, I would not advise you to sample that one." I pointed to an amphora of the Lycian. "That one is headed to your commander's tent, by special order."

He believed me. People say I have an honest face. "Datis's wine?" gasped Lasso Man. "Stay your hand, Attila."

"Go ahead. Drink your fill. I'm sure Lord Datis will relish watching you being rent into quarters by wild horses or nailed upside down to a pole outside his tent with your head in a bowl of venomous serpents."

"Come to think of it, we will escort this worthy merchant to Lord Datis's tent," Lasso Man said.

And so, I got a police escort right into the barbarian camp.

Lasso Man cried, "Open the gates and make way for Lord Datis's personal wine merchant!"

The guards scurried to comply.

I played the spy as we passed through the camp. I noted that the Persians had situated their camp intelligently. Guarded by the sea on the left and a swampy lake on the right, it blocked the road from Athens and protected their precious fleet.

The Persians had certainly been busy little barbarian beavers, I noted. In only forty-eight hours, they had raised an earthen rampart ten feet tall, enclosing an area at least half a mile square, pitched thousands of gaily colored tents, laid out broad boulevards, and paved them with white gravel. They had even pitched latrine tents surrounded by incense braziers to kill the stink. These barbarians were efficient and organized. They were pros.

In the exact center of the camp, I saw the biggest and gaudiest tent of all, a monster the size of a Barnum and Bailey circus three-ringer covered with the biggest and flashiest flags and banners. Lasso Man led me and Buster to the tent's service entrance.

"Lord Datis's wine has arrived!" Lasso Man bellowed to the two guards. "Summon the wine steward!"

One guard scurried away and returned after a few moments with the steward, a bald-headed little eunuch wearing rouge and heavy eye makeup. As the tent flap flew back and the steward emerged, I peeked inside. My fingers touched the handle of the scythe hidden under my chiton. Hippias or Apollonius might be standing right there, and I could hack one of those bastards' heads off and make a run for it.

Instead of the Others, I saw a girl peeking out from behind a silk curtain. I only saw her for an instant, but the memory will stay with me for the rest of my life. Her dark eyes were shaped like almonds. Her hair was black and lustrous. Her skin was a deep, rich mahogany. I saw her as she saw me. I gaped.

She gave me a knowing look that set my soul aflame. Then, with a silken swish, she vanished behind her curtain.

"Who was that?" I choked.

The steward said, "That was Lord Datis's favorite, Lady Yasmine, and if you stare at her like that again, I shall have your eyes scooped out with white-hot spoons."

I bowed. "Yes, Lord."

The steward sneered and said, "So, you bring wine for Lord Datis?"

I snapped out of it. "Yes, lord."

"I would taste your wine," he announced. "If it is not the very finest, I shall have your nose and tongue removed and served to you stir-fried with vegetables … in season."

"By Dionysus's most horrendous hangover, you will not be disappointed, sir," I replied, silently praying that Bernie's taste in wine was good and that my nose and tongue might remain where God had put them.

He pulled a bejeweled cup from under his robe, popped the cork of an amphora, and poured himself a sip. He sloshed it around and inhaled its bouquet. He tasted it.

"Satisfactory," he pronounced. He poured himself a brimful and slugged it back. "In fact, quite tasty. One golden daric for the two amphorae."

"Lord, you would ruin a poor wine monger!" I pleaded. "In Sardis, this vintage sells for ten golden darics an amphora wholesale."

"Two. It is my final offer. Perhaps I shall slit your miserable throat and just take the wine? Guards!"

"No! No, lord! It is a fair price. The fairest!"

I saved my throat and made out like a bandit. I still have the three golden darics in my safety-deposit box. In 2010, their gold value was approximately one thousand dollars. Their numismatic value, in absolutely mint condition, was over one million.

There is profit to be made in war.

After a couple of complimentary cups, the Saka set me free to sell my remaining wares around the camp. Everyone was very happy to see me, and I made a pretty penny as well. I went from tent to tent pitching my wares in proper wine-monger form: "Wine here! Get ya wine here. Babylonian Brain-Blaster, Tyrian Tangle-Foot. Drown your sorrows! Forget that 'Dear Zarathustra" letter from your faithless slut of a girlfriend—the bitch. All my fine vintages guaranteed hangover-free. Only one little siglos for a gigantic cupful like a bucket! Get ya wine here!"

Meanwhile, I spied. I estimated the size of the Persian force at between thirty-five thousand and forty-five thousand men. About two-thirds seemed to be infantry, and one-third were cavalry. I jotted down descriptions of the Persian regimental uniforms. There were dozens and dozens of them, all tastelessly gaudy in Oriental fashion. King Darius's empire stretched from Turkey to India, and he had summoned his soldiers from every corner of it.

I wrote everything down in my little papyrus notebook. I rode Buster over to the beach and sold wine to the sailors. They were especially enthusiastic drinkers. While they boozed, I counted the ships and asked questions. There were 612 ships drawn up on the beach or anchored just offshore. I jotted it all down. Once I was pouring wine for a pair of Egyptian marines, big men with big thirsts, and I heard a ghastly shriek from a black tent a few yards away.

"What's that?" I asked—in perfect Egyptian, of course. "Are they slaughtering animals in there?"

One laughed. "Nah, brother—not animals."

"Then what?"

"Men. And sometimes women too, young, pretty ones." He leered. "That's the "Pavilion of Joy," as it is called. It accompanies the army wherever we go."

"The what?"

"The torture tent, ignorant savage! Wanna see it? Cost you one drachma to see the show."

I declined his invitation. Little did I know that I would see the Pavilion of Joy later free of charge.

Just as the sun was setting, I ran out of wine. I no longer had an excuse for being in the Persian camp and had a decision to make. Should I leave now and bring my precious intelligence upon which the future of Greece, and all history depended, back to Bernie?

Or should I say to hell with saving Greece, the world, and history and stay in the camp to slaughter Hippias and Apollonius and fulfill my dreams of personal vengeance?

To hell with my duty to history. I was down with the slaying and the slaughtering.

But there was a problem. I had no idea what Hippias and Apollonius looked like. Nor did I know where they were. Probably they were in the big command tent, guarded by a regiment of royal guardsmen, armed to the teeth, and on the lookout for assassins like me night and day. I could break into the tent and start killing everyone, hoping to hack my way through to my targets. On second thought, that seemed like suicide.

I decided I must postpone my dreams of bloody vengeance for the time being. I decided to do my duty, sacrifice my own interests, and feel plenty noble and selfless in the process. I would leave the camp, take my intel back to Bernie, and save Greece, history, and the world. I was sorry

I'd never see the girl in the tent again, but I put my chin up, pushed out my chest, stood up ramrod straight, slipped my papyrus notebook into an empty amphora, climbed aboard Buster, and headed for the gate.

CHAPTER 22

"No good deed shall go unpunished," some wise soul once said.

"Get down off that stupid donkey," demanded the captain of *Median Sparabara* at the camp gate.

"Why, sir?" I asked innocently.

"To be searched. Every civilian must be searched leaving the camp. Orders."

"Sir, I am only an honest wine monger who has sold all his wares and must now return to his cellar and replenish his stock so he can return to quench you heroes' thirst on the morrow after your great victory."

"Get down off that f*cking ass. Now!"

Another *Sparabara* guard was poking around the amphorae, knocking them with his knuckles, popping the corks, and peering inside. It would be only a matter of seconds until he discovered my papyrus and busted me as a spy. Then off to the Pavilion of Joy I'd go.

I acted decisively as Bernie had taught me at Little Round Top. I swatted Buster across the rump with the reins and cried, "High-ho, Buster, away!"

Buster had many admirable qualities, but lightning speed was not one of them. He yelped, lurched forward one yard, stopped dead, and looked back at me disapprovingly.

The captain swung his spear. The handle whacked me full in the chest, and I tumbled backward. I landed flat on my back.

Buster, finally alarmed, was trotting out the gate in a cloud of dust with the precious intelligence report on his back.

"Go, Buster, go!" I gasped.

The captain swung his spear again, and the lights went out.

"Wake up," said a voice in Persian.

I was back on the floor outside of Bernie's bedroom door under that dirty old blanket, and a flea was biting my cheek. I swatted the flea away. It bit me again. I swatted it away again, but it came back and bit me again. I tried to swat it away a third time, but my wrist wouldn't move.

"Wake up," said a stern voice.

I had a terrible headache. I opened my eyes, but they wouldn't focus. I squinted hard and made out a face inches away from my own. In the dim torchlight, I saw that it was an old woman's face with deep wrinkles, rheumy brown eyes, a big nose, yellow teeth, and bad breath like rotting meat. The old woman was holding my wrist with one hand and pinching my cheek hard with the other. It hurt.

"Wake up, spy!"

"Stop pinching me!" I barked in English. I tried to pull my hand away, but her grip was like iron.

"What tongue is that, Grandmother?" a gruff male voice asked.

"Greek," said the old woman and let my wrist go. "He's a dirty Greek spy."

"Not Greek," I said in Persian. "Sogdian." I named an obscure language spoken by a few thousand miserable nomads in the far northeastern corner of the empire. "I am a poor Sogdian wine-seller."

"Lying Greek spy!" spat the old woman. "Get him up."

A pair of guards, big hairy brutes wearing spiked helmets, pulled me to my feet and pinioned my arms. The old lady was a dwarf less than four feet tall. The steel cap on her head came up only to the middle of my chest. She wore a leather butcher's apron and leather trousers both stained with blood.

"Where am I?" I asked.

She cackled. "In the Pavilion of Joy—from whence none return. Confess you are a spy, and we will kill you quickly."

That sounded like a bad deal to me. "Thank you so much, but I'm not a spy." I thought of the guilty evidence galloping away on Buster's back. "I'm a Sogdian wine—"

"Show him the instruments of torture!" she shrieked.

The two brutes dragged me over to a long wooden table. It was encrusted with dried blood and vomit and fixed with four rusty iron shackles from which hung tendrils of rotten flesh. On this grisly table, dozens of surgical-looking instruments were laid out in tidy rows. By contrast to the filthy table and the shackles, the instruments were spotlessly clean and freshly honed. Their edges glimmered in the torchlight. The old hag took good care of her tools.

The old lady picked up one. The brutes pushed my head close for a good look. The instrument looked very much like a vegetable peeler. She giggled. "For peeling your carrot."

She picked up an instrument that looked just like a garlic press. "For nut cracking," she cackled.

She showed me knives and scalpels, hacksaws and hammers, several different sizes of vises, a meat grinder, some clamps, a set of wrenches, and a tool that looked just like a cheese grater. My stomach churned as I viewed hell's kitchen.

Beside the instrument table was a hole in the dirt floor. Overhanging the hole was a wooden crane. By the flickering torchlight I saw a man, or what had once been a man, hanging on the wall in an iron cage beside the hole. His face was unrecognizable as human. His nose and ears were gone. His eye sockets were black and empty. His mouth hung open. There was only a bloody, black stump where his tongue had been. To my astonishment, I saw his chest rise and fall. The poor wretch was still alive.

"That is what you will be when I'm through with you," she said. "Now are you ready to confess?"

"I'd like to," I admitted. And I meant it. I didn't like the look of that cheese grater. "But I can't. I'm not a spy."

"Bag him!" she shrieked.

The brutes threw me to the ground and turned me over on my stomach. They threw a sack over my head and down to my waist, tied my wrists behind my back, and tied my ankles. The sack was so tight around my face that, every time I inhaled, I sucked it against my mouth and nose. I couldn't take a full breath. I immediately began to pour sweat and pant.

"Haul him up!" commanded the horrible old lady.

They seized my ankles. My feet flew out, and I was upside down, dangling from the hook over the hole.

"Lower him!"

I was descending. The blackness grew even blacker. The old lady's voice dimmed. "A little more, a little more. Stop!"

The top of my head thumped against the bottom of the hole.

"Now fill it in," the old bitch's faraway voice said.

Buried alive!

Clods of earth began to fall around my face and thump against my shoulders. Dust sifted through the gaps in the burlap and filled my mouth and nose. I struggled to take a breath, inhaled the thick dust, gagged, and choked. I was upside down, bewildered, confused, and staring out into pitch darkness.

I felt pure, raw terror and panic. I thrashed and kicked, trying to loosen the ropes that bound my wrists and ankles. My shoulders and head crashed back and forth against the sides of the hole. The clods continued to fall. The level of the earth on the floor of the hole continued to rise. The dirt reached my forehead, covered my forehead, crept to the bridge of my nose and over my nose, clogging my nostrils. I tried to inhale through my mouth but couldn't. My head was exploding. A red mist covered my eyes. I heard myself screaming.

Then I stopped struggling.

Mom, Dad, Max, Polly, I love you. I'll see you soon.

But I was to be saved to suffer worse horrors. I felt the rope yank on my ankles again, and I began to rise. The dirt poured away from my face, nostrils, and mouth. I gagged, spat, and vomited. Finally, I managed to take a deep breath. Light showed dimly through the gaps in the burlap.

"Get him out of there and clean him up," the old witch ordered.

I lurched upward, swung clear of the hole, and crashed to the ground. One brute whipped the bag off my head. The other brute threw a bucket of water in my face. I sputtered and gasped and sucked in clear air. They pulled me to my feet. I heard a bell clanging outside.

"New orders from the command tent" said the crone. "You are not to be buried alive after all. Congratulations. You are to be impaled! But, first, you will see what you are in for."

As the bell continued ringing, the two brutes dragged me out through the tent flap into the open air. A happy crowd of soldiers was gathered just ahead of us. Civilian sutlers, just like me, were circulating through the crowd selling cold drinks and snacks. It was a party atmosphere. The brutes cleared a way through the crowd to the front and held me there.

Before me was an open, grassy space. Lying on his stomach on the grass was the naked, half-dead wretch from the tent, apparently unconscious.

Beside him lay a wooden pole about seven feet long and the thickness of a baseball bat. One end was sharpened to a point. Three soldiers stood over the poor prisoner. One was clanging the bell. The other was brushing the pole with some gooey substance from a pot. The third was slapping the prisoner in the face to wake him up.

"Have you ever seen an impalement?" asked Brute One.

I gulped. "Uh, no."

"They're using grease this time," said Brute Two.

"That'll make it quicker," his partner replied. "They won't use grease for you, spy."

"For me?"

The prisoner groaned and twitched.

"He's ready," said the soldier who had been slapping the poor wretch to wake him up.

The bell-ringer gave off clanging. Together, he and the slapper seized the prisoner around the waist and pulled him up to all fours like an animal. The bell-ringer held him up. The other two picked the sharp end of the pole up off the ground and held it aimed at the prisoner's backside.

The crowd counted. "One … two …"

"Three!" They thrust the pole home. The prisoner screamed.

"Four," the crowd howled.

The soldiers pulled the pole upright.

That's when I fainted.

CHAPTER 23

It was night. I was lying facedown on filthy straw. It reeked of pee. I inhaled the fragrance of a fresh black turd one inch from my nostrils. I winced and sat up. My head crashed against the ceiling.

"They threw you into my lavatory," a voice said. "Very sorry." He spoke some sing-song language I couldn't identify, but of course, I understood it perfectly.

I was in a wicker version of the cages in which affluent American suburbanites keep their Labrador retrievers. Outside the cage, a couple of large, hairy guards slouched, chewed, and spat.

I had a litter mate, crouching at the far end of our cage. He was about my age, much shorter and so scrawny that his ribs poked through the skin on his bare stomach. He wore nothing but a grimy loincloth. His skin was dark brown, and his eyes were black. His tangled black hair hung to his shoulders.

"Where am I?" I asked.

"In a cage, Sahib," he said.

"I see that," I barked. I was feeling sick and cranky.

"They threw you in at sunrise. I thought you were dead."

"I wish I was dead."

"No, no, Sahib. Where's there's life, there's hope—as the holy books teach us." He picked up a cracked wooden bowl and handed it to me. "Would you like some cooling refreshment? I'm afraid it's all I have to offer. I was selfish and already ate my miserable crust of moldy, bug-infested bread. I should have anticipated your arrival."

I skimmed the film of dead bugs off and drank. The water was hot and stank. "Much obliged," I said, spitting out a roach.

"Sorry about the lavatory," he repeated. "I begged them not to throw you over there, but they just beat me mercilessly and went ahead and did what they wanted." He massaged his jaw. "The Medes are an unpleasant people. They do not know that cleanliness is next to godliness."

"Not your fault."

"I apologize for my miserable need to answer the call of nature, Sahib," he said. "In the future, I shall try to hold it."

"If you gotta go, you gotta go," I replied.

"Thank you, Sahib. You are most forgiving. Please allow me to introduce myself." He straightened up—as much as he was able—placing his palms together in front of his face and bowing his head. "I am Ramesh Ramajaputra, bowman third class, army of the southern Punjab."

"Pleased to meet you, Ramesh," I replied. "I'm Lex, a wine merchant. What brings you to this lovely cage?"

"I am a miserable deserter," he announced, hanging his head in shame.

Ramesh told his story. Nine months ago, he was a happy farmer on the banks of the Indus River in love with his girlfriend, Aditya, to whom he was betrothed. One day as he was out tilling his father's fields, a squadron of the king's cavalry kidnapped him and put him in the army. They gave him a uniform, a bow, and quiver and trained him to use them.

"Master Sergeant Narendra says I am the finest marksman he has ever commanded," he said proudly. "He says I can shoot the balls off a flea at the distance of one whole yojana, Sahib."

Then four months ago, Ramesh's king signed a treaty with the Persian king, Darius, agreeing to send troops to assist Darius in his conquest of some place on the far side of the world.

Ramesh had heard stories of Greece. It was a hellish place inhabited by ferocious demons made of bronze. He didn't want to leave his beautiful Aditya. He didn't want to leave his Indus Valley. And he certainly didn't want to go to this hell called Greece to fight metal demons whose bodies were proof against even his perfectly aimed arrows. But Ramesh had no choice. His regiment of archers left the Indus Valley and marched west for three months along the King's Road until they finally came to the sea.

Ramesh had never seen the sea before, and he was terrified. "If the God Vishnu had meant men to travel on the sea, he would have given us scales and gills. Don't you think, Sahib?"

"Absolutely," I said.

The cruel Persian soldiers whipped Ramesh and his regiment aboard the ships. By the grace of Vishnu, sea monsters did not devour them, giant whirlpools did not suck them down, and storms did not cast them upon razor-sharp reefs. In time, they arrived at the Bay of Marathon.

Ramesh began to sob. "I miss my darling Aditya. I miss my home. I do not want to fight demons of bronze. So, I ran away and hid in the forest. I am a coward. I deserve to die a most horrible death."

"Die? Who said you're going to die, Ramesh?"

"The Persians. I will be impaled tomorrow."

All of a sudden, the nightmare came rushing back to me. "I can see why you are so upset," I said.

He placed his hand on mine. "I did not mean to alarm you, Sahib, but impalement is also the Medes's favorite method of executing spies."

"I'm not a spy!" I protested.

"I know that, Sahib, but the Medes who brought you here said you are a spy, and it is their opinion that counts—not mine."

"I'm a wine monger!" I protested.

"Of course you are, Sahib. But the guards did happen to mention that you are scheduled to be impaled tomorrow at the noon execution." His eyes brightened. "Perhaps we will be impaled side by side. Wouldn't that be congenial?"

"Terrific," I said without much conviction.

"Ah, Yasmine brings our supper, praise Vishnu."

In an instant, all thoughts of death and disembowelment fled from my mind as I beheld, for the second time, the most beautiful girl in all the world. Standing only a foot or two away on the other side of the wicker bars was the beauty from Datis's tent. I was struck mute by the burning thunderbolt of love. My head spun. My knees went weak—or at least they would have if I had room to stand up. I beheld the face of an angel, her skin the color of rich mahogany, enormous black, almond-shaped eyes, high cheekbones, and full lips. She was very tall and slender, and her thick black hair cascaded to her waist. She wore a spotless, white, ankle-length dress tied around the waist with a red silk sash, trimmed with a silver border and slit up one side to display one gloriously long, elegant brown leg. She carried a water jug.

"This is my sister, Yasmine, Sahib."

I gaped, speechless.

"Yasmine, this is my new friend, Lex Sahib."

Yasmine placed her palms together before her face and bowed. She peeked at me through her fingers and smiled. "Hello, Lex Sahib," she said. Her voice was husky.

My neck tingled. I blushed and gaped some more.

"Is your friend a mute?" asked Yasmine. "Or a dimwit?"

"Neither, my sister," Ramesh replied. "But he is a little upset. He just learned that he is to be impaled tomorrow. Having my new friend beside me as we both die in excruciating agony will be much consolation, don't you think?"

"Ramesh! Hush. You will not be impaled." She lowered her voice to a whisper. "I will get you out of here. I promise."

"You will?" I gasped. "How?"

"Yasmine has much influence over General Datis," said Ramesh. "She is the general's favorite."

"Favorite what?" I blurted.

"Our king saw Yasmine working in the fields one day and took her."

"You were kidnapped?"

"Not exactly," she replied. "My father sold me to the king for three copper tamrarupa."

"Our king then sold her to King Darius. Darius gave her to General Datis as a birthday gift," her brother explained.

"You're a slave!" I swore to myself that I would devote my life to freeing my true love from the shackles of slavery!

"Oh, no, Sahib. Not a slave. Yasmine is the general's favorite concubine. Aren't you, sister?"

"Yes," she replied, throwing a smoldering glance my way. Her black eyes burned through mine, turned my brain to a gelatinous pudding, and burned smoking out the back of my skull. "Lord Datis likes me very much."

I blushed to my toes and looked away.

"Yasmine has means of persuading General Datis to be merciful," said Ramesh.

"What means?" I gasped and instantly regretted I had asked.

"Why, by the means all beautiful women use to have their way with men, Sahib."

"You don't mean?"

"Yes, young Sahib, he does mean." Yasmine laughed. She gazed at me with amused interest, the way you might look at a clumsy puppy stumbling over his feet and down the stairs while he pees on the floor. She leaned over to pick up her water jug. The top of her frock fell slightly away and showed me the edge of one perfect brown breast. I glued my eyes to her cleavage. I simply couldn't help myself. Am I made of stone? When I looked back up from her breast, she was looking me straight in the eye.

"May I refresh your water?" she asked.

I burned.

Ramesh handed me our cup. I dropped it through my trembling fingers. She did not stoop to pick it up.

"I brought you dinner," she said, producing two green-tinged pieces of bread from beneath her sash. "And this too." She pulled out a wrapped parcel.

Ramesh seized it and tore it open. A great shank of meat was dripping delicious fat. "Lamb, from the general's table," she said proudly. "I pinched it while he was snoring away like an old hog after we ..."

After we what? I wanted to kill Datis. I wanted to kill him more than I wanted to kill Hippias and Apollonius.

Ramesh tore off half, handed the other half to me, and we dug in. It was delicious. Grease poured over our chins.

"You two eat like hogs." Lost in thought, she watched us dine. At last, she said, "As soon as the moment is right, I will ask Lord Datis to give you an audience. Perhaps if you grovel in just the right way, he will show you mercy."

She bid us goodnight and left. I watched her bottom sway under her dress as she walked away. It was a lovely, round, perfectly shaped bottom. I was sure it was the loveliest bottom in all the world of 490 BCE.

Darkness fell. Having no cable TV or video games on hand in the evening, people of the ancient world went to bed early. I tossed and turned on my filthy straw in a fever for my Yasmine.

Chapter 24

"The enemy! The enemy! The bronze demons are at the gates!"

It was the middle of the night, and soldiers were running with torches and shrieking. Trumpets were blasting. Gongs were clanging. Sergeants and officers bellowed orders. Sleepy soldiers poured out of their tents. A squadron of heavy lancers thundered past.

"The bronze demons have come!" Ramesh whimpered from his corner of our cage.

I placed a reassuring hand on his shoulder. He was trembling. "Don't worry, Ramesh," I said. "The demons are friends of mine. I won't let them hurt you."

"Friends of yours?" he asked. "I thought you were a wine monger, Sahib."

"Well, yes I am. Of course. But I …" I was still young and hadn't learned to lie very efficiently. "My brother is in the Greek army, you see."

He looked at me funny. "How is that you speak my language perfectly, Sahib? You even speak it with the accent of my village."

"I have a talent. I pick up languages easily."

"In seconds?" he asked incredulously.

"Sometimes. I'm actually Greek," I whispered.

"Ahh-eee! You are a bronze demon!"

"Sh, Ramesh. Keep your voice down. Of course, I'm not a bronze demon. Do I sound like I'm made of metal?" I tapped myself on the leg.

He poked my arm for reassurance. "No, Sahib. But only a god can speak all the languages of man as you do." He groveled and poured dirty straw over his head. "You must be Vishnu disguised in human form come to judge the sinful doings of mankind. I worship you!" He buried his head in his lavatory.

I rather liked the idea of being worshipped as a god, but Ramesh was making such a fuss I was afraid he might attract unwelcome attention from our guards. "Ramesh, stop!" I cried. "You're getting shit in your hair. Calm down, be quiet, and I will plan how we can escape and go to my friends."

"Yes, Vishnu Sahib," he replied and poured a handful of feces on his head.

The Persian army took its positions and stood ready to meet the Greek attack until dawn. But the attack never came. The sun rose to show that the Athenian army and its Platean allies had come no closer than the slope and olive wood through which I had passed on my way with Buster to the camp.

When my goddess Yasmine brought us our breakfast, which included two nice pieces of juicy chicken that told me loud and clear that she loved me as I loved her, Ramesh told her that I was the god Vishnu come to earth in human form.

Yasmine placed her elegant, ringed hand on one lovely hip, cocked her gold-braceleted elbow, and looked me up and down. She laughed, her perfect breasts shaking most deliciously. "You're such an idiot, brother. He's no god. He's just a stupid boy like you."

Yasmine then described what she had seen and heard while she had flirting shamelessly with the soldiers on the ramparts. "The Greeks are in the woods at the base of the mountain. They are cutting down trees and building a camp to block the road to Athens," she whispered.

"Are they many?" I asked.

"Thousands of them, but not nearly so many thousands as the Persians. Lord Datis said that he will sweep them aside like flies, put your city to the torch, and impale all its citizens. He ordered ten thousand impalement stakes to be prepared immediately."

This was not good news.

"But I know it's all bluster. He's worried. He confided to me in the bedroom that King Darius will cut off his ears, nose, hands, and other parts and cast him into his dungeon if he fails to conquer your city within one week. He sobbed like a baby and asked me to hold him. What a woman he is!" She spat.

"Did you happen to see a donkey?" I asked. I was worried that Buster might have become a Saka donkey-chop and my vital intelligence might not have reached the Bernster.

"Donkey? I saw thousands of donkeys. Your army is crawling with donkeys carrying all sorts of packs and things."

"Big brown eyes?" I said. "This donkey is a close personal friend of mine."

"At a time like this, you're worried about a donkey?"

Yasmine, I noted, was not a sentimental girl.

The day passed, and the Athenians still did not attack. Yasmine came with lunch. Before she arrived, I cleaned up. I shook the filth out of my hair and washed my face with the putrid water from our bowl. I tidied up my half of the cage by picking the worst tidbits up and throwing them outside. I fluffed up the reeking, flattened straw. I made Ramesh tidy his side too. He muttered that I was making a fool of myself talking about Yasmine night and day. To him, she was just his little brat sister, so I ought to clean up both sides of our cage. But he went ahead and helped tidy up, and we made our home nice for our guest.

When Yasmine came, I turned on my charm, such as it was. I complimented her on her dress and a new hairdo. I inquired if she had lost weight. This earned us two honey cakes stolen from Datis's table.

In addition to sweet cakes, my compliments earned us secrets. Hiding behind a curtain, Yasmine had overheard Datis's spies report that the Athenians were delaying their attack until the Spartan army arrived. The Spartans were a fanatically religious people who sacrificed newborn infants to their ferocious god of war, the spies reported. They would arrive in five or six days, when their supply of newborns was exhausted.

"I think my mighty Lord Datis is afraid of these Spartans," she whispered as we gulped our dinner. "If he is not afraid of them, why is he so desperate to destroy the other bronze men before these Spartan demons arrive?"

While Yasmine poured wine, served pretty treats off a golden platter, and spied, Datis sought battle counsel from his commanders. They bickered and argued like old ladies, she said, and finally agreed to entice the Greeks into battle tomorrow with harassing attacks. "Like poking a dog with a stick," one general had said. The Persian plan was for their infantry to hold the Greeks while the Persians' eight thousand armored cavalrymen, the best in the world, would sweep around the Greek flank and slaughter the demons.

The next morning at dawn, we were awakened by the pounding of drums and the blasts of bugles. Hordes of mounted archers thundered past us and out the gates, covering us with a layer of fine dust. In the late afternoon, they slunk back, dusty and exhausted. Their quivers were empty, but they had nothing to show for it.

I asked one guard what had happened.

"The bronze demons did not attack," he said. "Cowards, they hid in the woods. Our arrows fell among the trees and bounced off their bronze helmets. They had no more effect than if we had pissed on their sandals."

When Yasmine brought us our supper, her left eye was blackened. "The pig stuck me," she hissed. "I am through with him!" She told us that the Greeks had actually leapt up on their ramparts and displayed their rumps to the Persian archers. "Datis became beastly drunk and fell into a rage. His spies say the Spartan host is only a three-day march away. He threw a cup at me."

"I'll kill him!" I shouted.

"My hero," Yasmine said. I suspected she was being sarcastic. "Do not trouble yourself. I will take care of Lord Datis myself when the time comes—with this." She drew a tiny curved dagger from the sleeve of her gown. "I call her Kali's Tooth."

"Back home, Yasmine was in training to be a priestess of Kali the Destroyer," said Ramesh proudly. "That is her sacrificial instrument. It is dipped in the poison of the king cobra."

"How charming," I said, thinking that there was a good deal more to my sweet little Yasmine than first met the eye.

"I will slice off those parts of which he is so proud—without reason, I might add because he is equipped no better than a squirrel—and serve them to him for his supper," she announced with terrifying conviction.

"You go, girl," I said.

"But what about us, my sister?" asked Ramesh. "Would you leave us here to be impaled tomorrow while you slake your thirst for vengeance?"

"Typical! Do you see how he thinks only of himself, Sahib Lex? And yet I have selflessly sacrificed myself for him." She touched her blackened eye and winced. "Datis has ruined my looks."

"No, no," I said. "I didn't even notice it. Just a little touch of makeup …"

"But he felt guilty afterward and insisted on making it up to me. I could have asked for riches or for a kingdom. Instead, I spoke for you two. Datis has agreed to hear your case this evening. Prepare yourselves."

She hurried off. I watched her bottom wiggle until she was out of sight.

CHAPTER 25

Six Medes, ugly bearded thugs with gold nose rings, came for us after supper. One, I was alarmed to see, was the captain who had knocked me out at the camp gate. They hauled us out of our cage by our feet. They beat us with sticks until their arms got weary, manacled us together with enormous chains that would have restrained a bull elephant in rut, dragged us to Datis's command tent, and hurled us onto the floor of his throne room. I lay on my stomach with my nose pressed against a priceless Persian carpet.

We groveled. Ramesh had informed me that there were certain time-tested techniques for groveling before an ancient Oriental potentate, and we followed them to the letter.

First, we prostrated ourselves. Ramesh and I lay on our stomachs before Datis and repeatedly smashed our foreheads against the floor as hard as we could, just short of fracturing our skulls and losing consciousness.

Second, we kept our eyes downcast. You never raise your eyes to actually look at the potentate. To do so means instant death.

Third, we heaped filth upon our heads. Because Datis's floor was covered with a spotless Persian carpet and no actual filth was on hand, we pantomimed the filth-heaping.

Fourth, we stuffed the imaginary filth into our mouths and pretended to chew and swallow it.

Fifth, we tore our hair out in fistfuls. This we did not pantomime. It was excruciatingly painful and left me with four unsightly bald spots.

Sixth, we rent our garments into tatters, taking care to retain a vestige of modesty.

Seventh, we vocalized our abasement by wailing and keening for mercy: "Oh, Lord Datis, have mercy on our miserable selves! Oh, Lord Datis, most powerful and merciful, spare us, your most loyal slaves …"

After we had gone through each step, an enormous baritone voice boomed, "Enough!" Datis was apparently satisfied with our groveling.

I took a chance and peeked through my fingers. I saw a giant of a man seated upon a golden throne engraved with disturbing scenes of slaughter: Datis on a rearing stallion launching arrows at naked, cringing Indians, Datis holding on high the gory head of some defeated king, Datis standing on top of a mountain of skulls.

Datis, even while seated, was taller than me. He must have punished the bathroom scales at four hundred pounds. And yet, to my astonishment, this man mountain affected to be metrosexual. He wore black eye shadow and pink rouge. His jet-black hair hung in ringlets to his shoulders and was spotted with precious gems. His black beard, also coiffed into ringlets and glittering with jewels, hung to his waist. I guessed his age to be about fifty. His staff of hairdressers must have dyed his hair daily. Datis's banana-sized fingers were ablaze with golden rings. He wore a golden kaftan made of a heavy fabric that could have been torn from the curtain rods of a nineteenth-century Paris brothel. His slippers were scarlet with curled-up toes. He reeked of stale perfume. An attendant bustled over with a spray bottle and gave him a couple of refresher squirts. Eau de horse piss. My eyes watered.

Was this monster an Other Wargod?

I doubted it.

"What are the charges?" Datis thundered.

My Mede Captain said, "Lord, the little one is a deserter. The bigger one is a Greek spy. I captured him trying to sneak out of the camp."

"Who speaks in these men's defense?" bellowed Datis. The monster never spoke below an ear-shattering roar.

"I do," Yasmine purred.

Our adorable defense attorney was dressed to convert a ravenous lion to veganism. Stepping forward to address Datis, she shrugged off the virginal white gown that covered her from head to toe, and it crumpled to the floor at her feet. A hush fell over the room. Datis's eyes goggled, the disgusting old lecher. She was stark naked.

Stark naked except for her bells that is.

Hundreds and hundreds of tiny silver bells covered Yasmine's body.

They covered her arms from her wrists to just above her elbows, her legs from her ankles to tawny mid-thigh. A bell hung from each breast. A gauzy belt of bells hung low on her hips covering only her most intimate portions front and rear. Her long black hair hung in dreadlocks. From each lock hung a larger, golden bell.

She took three steps toward Datis, bent down on one knee and bowed her head. As she did, her bells chimed and tinkled. The melody was magical. I didn't merely hear it. I felt it. Every man in the room groaned as if he had been punched in the stomach.

"Lord Datis," she said huskily. "The deserter is my brother: a frightened little boy far from home. I plead for his life."

"Granted," Datis boomed, unable to take his eyes off of her. Only if he was made of stone could Datis have refused.

The bells jingled again. Datis sighed deeply as if Yasmine's melody had reminded him of the long-lost love of his life and consumed him with sorrow and longing.

"The other is a common wine merchant. I believe he is also a dimwit," she said dismissively.

"He's a Greek spy!" the Mede captain barked.

"Are you a spy, boy?" This was a new voice.

"No, sir," I said. "I am just a lowly wine seller."

And then I realized it: Oh my God. The voice had asked me in English! And I had answered in English!

I was busted! Ruined! Screwed! Or was I?

I figured I was dead anyway so I peeked. I saw a very old man, eighty at least, with white hair and a white beard, standing behind Datis's throne. By his clothes, I could see that he was Greek. Or at least posing as a Greek.

"Who's that?" I whispered to Ramesh.

"Hippias," Ramesh whispered back.

So, there he was! My enemy! The man I had come to slaughter. My entire body went rigid with hatred and blood lust. I could barely restrain myself from leaping up and tearing out his throat with my teeth.

A younger man beside Hippias whispered, "And that one?"

"His aide, Apollonius."

By his olive skin, hook nose, copiously overgrown with black nose hair, and squinty little, lizard-lidded eyes alight with reptilian cunning, I knew him instantly as Iraqi secret police. In a moment, he would out me. The guards would hustle me out into the yard and ram that stake where the sun don't shine!

But neither Apollonius nor Hippias said a word.

Why not?

It came to me. If Apollonius and Hippias showed that they spoke and understood a language that wouldn't exist for three thousand years, Datis would probably have them impaled.

Finally, Hippias said, "He's a spy, Lord Datis." He spoke without conviction, as if he didn't care whether Datis believed him or not.

"My lord ..." said Yasmine.

Datis's eyes flew from Hippias to her—though to which part of her I would rather not say.

She stepped toward Datis and smiled. She swayed. Her bells whispered their bewitching melody. "What evidence can Lord Hippias offer that this young man is actually a spy?"

"Well, Hippias?" Datis asked.

"Spy or not, Lord, why not execute him and be sure he is no danger to you?" asked Hippias.

"Because Lord Datis loves justice," replied Yasmine. "This boy is no spy and no Greek. He is our village idiot."

Village idiot? Who says! No way!

"He is devoted to my brother and followed him like a pet dog all the way from India. He snuck into our camp disguised as a wine merchant just to be with him."

Datis gave me a long, hard look. "The boy is obviously an imbecile," he concluded. "I give him his life."

"Thank you, lord." She bowed. Her bells whispered and teased.

"Return them to their cage," Datis commanded. "Let them be sent to our colony in Basra. There, they will live out the remainder of their days breaking big rocks into gravel for the royal roads."

"Lord!" Yasmine objected.

"I have spoken," thundered Datis.

The Saka dragged us by our heels out of the tent and beat us enthusiastically all the way back to our cage.

Lying bruised, battered, and bleeding on our vile straw, Ramesh and I reviewed our situation.

"At least we are not to be impaled, Sahib," he noted cheerfully.

"I see your point," I quipped.

"Sahib has made a most witty pun." He laughed. "Surely it will be some days or even weeks before they bind us in chains, hurl us into the stinking, rat-infested hold of some leaky ship, and sail us to the fever swamps of southern Mesopotamia where we will spend the rest of our miserably short lives in backbreaking toil under a blistering desert sun. But during that time, we should accept our fate and enjoy each other's company, don't you think, Sahib?"

"Not really," I growled.

"I'm sure you will feel better after a good night's sleep," Ramesh said.

"I will not."

"Good night, Sahib. Sweet dreams." With that, he sprinkled a few sticks of urine-soaked straw over his shoulders for a blanket and fell into a deep sleep.

I could not sleep. I did not share Ramesh's cheery optimism. I sat up with my back pressed against the bars of my cage and reviewed my misfortunes. *Why me? Why did I get mixed up with Bernie? Why did he send me on this suicidal spying mission? Why did I, obsessed with my lust for vengeance, disobey his orders and enter the Persian camp? Why was I, a twenty-first-century homeschooled nerd, doing in a cage in 490 BC Greece? Why was it my destiny to spend my few remaining days at hard labor in Basra while my high school friends played football and groped their pretty girlfriends in the back seats of their pickup trucks? And, most of all, why had Yasmine called me the village idiot? Did she really feel that way about me? And why had Mom, Dad, Polly, and Max had to die? I missed them terribly, and I missed our house and my room at home and our woods.*

I tried to distract myself with more pleasant thoughts, like sticking a dagger into Hippias's stomach, slicing upward, seeing his guts spill out onto the ground, and watching the light go out of his eyes. Even that didn't make me feel better. I had sunk as low as low can be.

Finally, I must have nodded off. I dreamed that Yasmine was dancing and jingling her little silver bells while Apollonius pawed her with one hand and greased a horrifying barbed stake with the other.

It was the blackest night of my life. The Dark Night of my Young Soul.

CHAPTER 26

"Shhh," Someone whispered.

"Wha—" I moaned back.

"You were talking in your sleep."

It was Yasmine. Her face was painted black. She was fiddling with the lock on the cage.

"What are ya doing?" I mumbled.

"I'm letting you out. Wake up, Ramesh."

"Where are the guards?" I asked.

"They are slumbering in the arms of Mother Kali," Jasmine whispered.

The cage door creaked open.

I kicked Ramesh. He moaned and said, "Thank you, Sahib." He rolled over. I kicked him again, harder. He sat up and blinked. "Is it time for breakfast? Eggs would be nice."

"Breakfast later. You two put these on," Yasmine whispered. She thrust a bundle of clothes into the cage. They were women's clothes.

"What are we doing?" I asked.

"You are about to be murdered. It's time to go," she said.

"Murdered?" Ramesh blurted. "Us? Why?"

"Hippias seems to have taken a dislike to Lex Sahib. He has demanded that Apollonius bring him your head. The assassins are on their way right now to harvest it."

Ramesh cried, "But Lord Datis promised!"

"Lord Datis doesn't know. He is at the beach secretly loading his cavalry and half of his infantry onto his ships to sail them to Athens. The other half of the infantry remains here to hold the Greek army at bay."

The Persian army divided? Half, including all the cavalry, on their way to attack Athens! This was life-and-death intelligence. Bernie had to know.

We scrambled into our clothes. Mine was a fetching cloak in dark blue slit high up my thighs with a gold hood. I looked fabulous.

"You are camp followers, and I am your procuress," Yasmine announced.

Camp followers?

"Army whores, little boy, and I'm your boss lady. Keep your hoods up and mouths shut. I will do the talking."

We slipped out of our cage and stepped over our two guards. They were sleeping soundly indeed, sprawled on their backs with their eyes wide open, their hands frozen clawing at their throats, and blood oozing from their ears and noses.

We padded silently through the moonless night. It was well past midnight, and Datis had ordered total silence in the camp so the Greeks would have no inkling that half his army was embarking to attack Athens. No one stirred. We hurried toward the main gate past a few hunched figures asleep around campfires that were little more than glowing embers. It was almost as if a sleeping spell had been cast over half of the Persian army.

We reached the front gate. Two Persian spearmen jumped out of the shadows. "Who goes there?" One held his spear to block our path.

"Just us girls out for an evening stroll, Corporal," cooed Yasmine.

"Done with work for the evening, ladies?" asked the second spearman.

"And exhausted," Yasmine said, yawning. "The second platoon of the first Hazarabam are studs." She winked.

"Not as studly as us members of the first," the spearman said.

"So true. All we harlots tremble when we hear that the first platoon is in camp."

"Perhaps you'd like to give these two soldiers of the first platoon of Hazarabam a freebie?" the second spearman suggested, licking his lips like an iguana.

"Alas, not tonight," Jasmine replied, almost managing to sound like she regretted turning them down. "Perhaps tomorrow. We are worn out. We thought we'd take a turn around the walls in the fresh air and then retire for the night. If you gentlemen would be so kind as to open the gate for us."

"Unfortunately, we have orders not to open the gate for anybody. Don't we, Bagoas?"

"Yes, Harpagus. It's worth our heads."

"Of course, we could make an exception," said Harpagus.

"For certain considerations … over there in our tent." Bagoas pointed to a little two-man tent pitched by the wall.

"Oh, you cheeky monkeys," Yasmine said. "But we really are tired, aren't we, girls?"

Ramesh and I murmured our soprano agreement.

"We have wine," Bagoas offered.

"Something to take the chill off?" asked Harpagus hopefully.

"We really shouldn't …" Yasmine cooed in coquettish indecision. "All right, boys. I'm sure that the girls and I can manage one more job."

Bagoas reached around and pinched my bottom. "By Ahriman, your butt is like a rock." He slobbered on my shoulder. "I choose you, big mama."

Harpagus seized Yasmine. "Come on, boys." She giggled, slipped out of his grasp, ran to the tent, and dove in. "Last one in gets sloppy seconds!" she cried from inside. The two Persians roared with lust and dove in after her.

We heard a thud from the tent, followed by a muffled shriek. The tent jumped and roiled, then silence. Yasmine emerged brushing dust off her gown. She tossed a handful of bloody meat into the darkness. Then my little Indus flower licked her fingers.

"The first platoon is not so studly now," she said. "Let's get the gate open." She wiped Kali's Tooth on her cloak and slid it back into her sleeve.

We swung the gate open and set out into the darkness toward the distant fires of the Greek camp. At first, we walked along the beach, taking care to avoid the Persian pickets and the treacherous marsh edging the sand to the north. Once we had to plunge into the sea and swim for a ways to skirt a party of Persian scouts singing bawdy songs around a fire.

A jellyfish stung me on the leg, and I whimpered.

Yasmine told me to be a man.

We swam around the scouts, regained the shore, and trotted north toward the swamp. When a squadron of Saka galloped by, we plunged up to our necks in the stinking water. It was warm as pee and smelled the same.

It was rough going through the surf, jellyfish and leeches, but in the end, I was rewarded. As soon as we reached firm ground again, Yasmine stripped off her waterlogged clothes and pressed on naked. It was pitch-black, but I was just able to follow her by gluing my eyes to the perfect round orb of her lovely bottom.

When we finally reached the Marathon plain, the no-man's land between the Greeks and the Persians, there was not even a leech-infested bog to hide in. We dodged from rock to rock and from stunted bush to stunted bush toward the Greek campfires. Finally, we reached the olive woods and threw ourselves down in the deep shadow of a giant old tree. The cicadas were clattering. My heart was pounding. Beside me, Yasmine's breath came fast, hot, and heavy. With salvation only a few hundred yards away, I felt a rush of adrenaline. I nudged up next to her and inhaled deeply of her sensual musk of sweat mixed with perfume. The night embraced us. Was this the moment I had been longing for? My hand crawled toward her dusky thigh.

"What's that?" she whispered and sat up.

"What?" I breathed. A twig snapped.

"That," she said.

"Demons!" Ramesh whispered.

All of us were on our feet. Kali's Tooth was in Yasmine's hand.

But it was only a black cat. It screeched, turning our blood cold. Then it scrambled up an olive tree and sat down on a branch, blinking its yellow eyes.

"Let's move on," Yasmine said.

Then they were three of them: two small men and one big man all dressed in black. Two leapt on Jasmine and Ramesh, dagger blades flashing. I didn't see the third until I felt his garrote digging into the soft flesh of my throat and his knee pressing hard into the small of my back.

"Die, infidel pig!" the hideous brute grunted in Arabic and exhaled hot garlic into my ear.

I struggled to push my right hand between the strangler's rope and my Adam's apple, but Apollonius was too strong. I reached behind me with my left hand and clawed at his eyes, searching for any way to hurt him and make him stop. His knee pressed harder. My spine would snap in at any moment. The garrote tightened. I couldn't breathe.

Then, suddenly, I could breathe again. I was flat on my back in the dirt. My eyes couldn't focus. My throat was shredded and sore, but I was still alive.

"Are you all right, young man?" asked a gruff voice. "Your assassin has fled. He's quick for a big man."

"Who are you?" I gasped.

"Why, don't you remember us, young sutler? It is I, Theos, from the mountain. And my comrade, Keos. We shared a rat supper."

"Thank you, Theos," I said.

"This one slumbers in the embrace of the mistress," Yasmine whispered from the darkness.

"Good work, miss," Theos said. "Now please take my cloak. You'll catch your death of cold, and your nudity inflames my associate's beastly appetites."

"This one sups with Lord Hades," Keos said. "He has little conversation for he lacks his tongue ... as well as his head."

"Who were those thugs?" Ramesh pulled himself up off the ground and rubbed his throat.

"The Azi Dahaka," replied Yasmine. "A cult of assassins devoted to Dahag, the three-headed Persian demon of sin, corruption, and unspeakable vice. They kill with the silken strangling cord. Datis gave Hippias two Azi Dahaka as bodyguards. They lie here. The one who escaped is Apollonius, Hippias's aide."

"Ah, Theos, we should take the assassins' heads to Lord Polemarchos. Surely he will reward us."

I said, "I *know* he will because I am no sutler. I am Lord Polemarchos's chief of espionage sent here to scout the Persians. He will reward you in gold if you take us to him immediately."

CHAPTER 27

When I used the magic word, gold, Keos and Theos couldn't escort us to Bernie fast enough.

"Make way for General Polemarchos's number one spy!"

They led us through the woods, knocked aside the sentries at the gate, and brought us safe and sound right into the Athenian camp.

The camp of the soldiers of democracy was a shithole, literally. There were no latrines. Men were defecating wherever they pleased, and the camp stank to high heaven. In contrast to the Persian camp with its hundreds of crisp, neatly laid-out tents, the Greek soldiers were sprawled randomly on the ground among the olive trees wherever they had happened to pass out from exhaustion or drink. These Greeks, I could see, were not professional soldiers. They were a citizen militia and a thoroughly unimpressive bunch: bearded, dirty cutthroats like Theos and Keos, short, stocky and bandy-legged. Compared to the tall, elegant Persians with their extravagantly colored uniforms and perfumed love locks, the Athenians were gorillas, I'm sorry to say. They did not fill me with confidence in victory.

We headed for the one tent in the camp: a ragged, patched affair. Bernie was standing outside it brushing his teeth dressed in a scarlet terry cloth bathrobe imprinted with a crest that read "The Ritz. Paris. 1940."

"Ah, there you are," he said to me in English. "You know, I really shouldn't be using this toothbrush. They haven't been invented. The ancients used twigs. But I don't want to lose my teeth. I floss too—after every meal. Do you take care of your teeth, Lex?"

"I guess."

"All of you should know that good teeth are the key to good health," he said, speaking in Greek, English, and the Indus Valley language simultaneously. "Do you want to spend a fortune on dentist's bills when you're older? I'm five uh … fifty years old next April, but I still have every one of my teeth." He showed us all his glimmering, pearly whites.

"Oh, sir, you can't be that old," piped Yasmine, who knew how to flatter a man of power. "I would take you for no more than thirty-nine."

You'll be sleeping with an alien next, you adorable little slut, I thought.

Bernie beamed. "What a charming young lady. Won't you introduce me to your friends, Lex?"

I introduced Bernie around. Yasmine curtsied prettily, this time, taking care that her cloak should not fall open. I had already seen her transform herself from a concubine to a witch to an assassin. Now she had become a debutante. My beloved Yasmine was a very adaptable girl.

Ramesh started to grovel, but Bernie motioned him back to his feet.

Theos and Keos knuckled their foreheads.

"So, Lex, what have you been up to?" Bernie asked, taking a scented baby wipe out of his leather toilet kit, tearing it open, and washing his face and hands. My friends stared at the wipe. "A little invention of mine," he explained. "What do you have to report?"

I told Bernie about my adventures: my capture, Datis, our escape, and our rescue from the Azi Dahaka by Keos and Theos.

Keos and Theos waited patiently. "I promised them a reward," I said.

"Of course. Of course. Of course." Bernie tossed each of them leather purses, which jingled invitingly.

"Thank you, General." They bobbed their heads and knuckled their foreheads again.

"Would you boys like to stay on here and help me out?" asked Bernie. "My friend Lex here could use two stouthearted lads like yourselves to show him and his friends the ropes."

Theos looked at Keos. Keos looked at Theos. They both snuck a look at Yasmine.

"Naturally, I'd make it worth your trouble," Bernie added.

"Oh, yes, lord." They knuckled.

"In that case, gentlemen, you may begin your duties by fetching this young lady some proper clothes and her brother a weapon. I suspect he'll soon need it."

"A bow, please, General Sahib," said Ramesh. "If it pleases you."

"You shall have the finest bow we have," Bernie said. "Now Lex and I must talk." He threw his arm over my shoulder and led me into his tent.

The inside of the Athenian command tent was as spare as Datis's tent was lavish. The floor was dirt. The only furnishings were half a dozen crude wooden stools. A pile of weapons and armor occupied one corner. Bernie's bed—a down sleeping bag on a king-sized air mattress—occupied another. Bernie was not about to deny himself certain comforts, however historically inaccurate they might be. I wondered how he explained his air mattress to the Greeks. Maybe only I could see it. You never knew what tricks old Berns might be up to.

We sat down.

"Did Buster get to you?" I asked.

"Who?"

"Buster, my donkey—gray, big brown eyes, loyal, hardworking, and true. He was carrying my notes."

"Nope. No donkey. You could check over there with the butcher. He might have your donkey." My heart sank. Buster did not deserve such a cruel fate. "So, what do you have for me?"

I told him my estimates of the size of the Persian army, the number of ships, the various regiments I had identified, the proportions of cavalry and infantry, and so forth, reciting from memory. I tend to have a good memory for everything that interests me. I forget everything else completely.

"Good job," he said. "And our counterparts? Did you meet them?"

"Hippias?"

"Yes. His real name is George."

"And his aide? An Iraqi. Calls himself Apollonius?"

"His real name is Mustafa."

"He tried to kill me."

"Naturally. He's a beast. I'm sure he wants to get his hands on your girlfriend."

"We're just friends," I said.

"Just friends, are you?" Bernie winked. "Don't tell me you've fallen into that dreaded friend zone already, Lex." I blushed. "All you modern boys are such snowflakes. Why, when I was your age, I ..."

I didn't want to know what Bernie was doing at my age, and I didn't want to know with whom—or with what—he was doing it. I hastened to change the subject. "Bernie, the most important thing is that Datis loaded all his cavalry and half his infantry onto his ships last night. And they sailed for Athens."

"Ah," he said. "That is important. Good work. The Strategoi must hear of it immediately. Congratulations, Lex. You are a first-class spy. You deserve a medal—but you will not get one because you went into the Persian camp against my orders. For that, you deserve to be rent into four quarters by wild stallions and your entrails scorched by a red-hot iron. Would you rather get the medal and then be disemboweled or disemboweled and then get the medal?" Bernie took one look at the horror on my face and added, "Okay. We'll just call it even and quits then. Okay?"

"Uh, okay."

A few minutes later, Athens's high command—the ten elected Strategoi, plus Callimachus, the war archon—shuffled into the tent. Most were middle-aged. Some were very old. All were seedy and red-eyed and smelled none too sweet. They sat down in a circle on the little stools, grunting and yawning and scratching their private parts. My heart sank. These fools were about to make a decision that would determine the future of the world and all history.

Not to mention the future of me.

Callimachus called on Bernie first.

He stood. "My agent has returned from reconnoitering the Persian camp and will now make his report." He motioned me to enter the circle and speak.

I hate public speaking. It terrifies me. My stomach knotted. My knees shook. Cold sweat formed on my brow.

The Strategoi squinted at me through rheumy eyes.

"Who the hell is this punk?" someone at the back of the room asked.

"Lord Polemarchos's bed-warmer probably," some wag joked.

I gulped and began, "The Persians have six hundred ships."

"By Apollo," someone said. "I am impressed. The boy can count up to six hundred." He was one of the younger generals, a tall, languid aristocrat with long golden locks. He was cleaner than the others. His chiton was spotless white and not stained with food.

"Their commander is General Datis."

"We already know that," said the young general, examining his perfect manicure. "Polemarchos, your little spy is pretty, but he bores me."

"Patience, Aristides," Bernie said. "The boy has more."

"Tonight, Datis will load all his cavalry and half his army aboard ships and sail to Athens," I continued.

That woke them up. They stopped scratching and started whispering and muttering.

"And Hippias is with him," I added.

That did it. Hippias was the magic word. At the mention of his name, the room exploded. The Strategoi on the right side of the tent shouted, "Treason! We are betrayed!"

The generals on the left side shrieked, "He has returned! We are saved!"

Two wizened ancients seized each other's throats, grappled, and fell to the dirt floor, clawing at each other's eyes and gasping with the exertion. Their friends separated them moments before both died of apoplexy.

Callimachus managed to restore order. He called on Aristides.

Aristides struck a noble pose with his chin in the air and his chest pushed out. "My fellow citizens, clearly we must march back to Athens," he said.

"Yes! To the city!" his supporters shouted.

"We were fools to come here," Aristides snickered, casting a haughty look at Bernie. "I always opposed such a reckless plan. The Persians have never been defeated in the field. We cannot defeat them here now."

"Massacred! Massacred!" shouted his bootlicks and lickspittles.

"We must return to the city and ask the great king for terms. Hippias is a loyal Athenian of noble blood. He wants only the best for Athens. He will speak for us."

"Hurray for Hippias, our savior!" Aristides's minions parroted.

"Hippias will persuade the Persians to let us pay them homage. We shall offer them bread and salt in their manner, and their army will then depart. We will have peace! To Athens now!"

"Peace! Peace! To Athens now!" As one man, the ten generals rushed for the door. Only Callimachus remained behind, looking shocked and dismayed.

So much for Western civilization, I thought. *So much for America. By this time tomorrow, the boys of America will be speaking Persian and wearing their hair in perfumed ringlets.*

"Democracy is a real bitch, isn't it, Lex?" Bernie whispered. "Now hear my battle speech." He rose to his feet and cleared his throat: "Ah-hum."

It was no ordinary throat clearing. It echoed in the tent like the growl of a very grumpy, very large, and very hungry lion who had just entered the tent looking for his breakfast. The generals stopped in their tracks, turned, and gaped at Bernie. Then, as one man, they fell back onto their stools and folded their hands in their laps like good little Strategoi.

I composed myself to hear Bernie work his magic. This would be the speech to end all speeches.

"Fellow citizens," he began. His tone was surprisingly mild and conversational. "The Persians are sending their cavalry away and will oppose us here only with their infantry. The Persian infantry with their cloth armor and their grass shields and their little toy bows cannot stand against our bronze-clad hoplites. If we attack them now, they will break—and we will destroy them."

Bernie paused. Total silence in the tent. It was so quiet I heard ants humming "Hi-Ho. Hi-Ho. It's Off to Work We Go" on the floor at my feet.

"I propose we should vote," Bernie said calmly.

Is that all? Where's the barn-burning Bernie? Where's the eloquent Bernie who could lift this tent off its pegs?

They voted with stones in a helmet. Plain for yes. Black for no. One by one, the stones rattled in. Callimachus did the count. It was a five-to-five tie.

Bernie stood up and said, "It lies with you, Callimachus, to see Athens enslaved or made free. And if you make her free, you will be remembered so long as there are men alive."

That was it. It was a great snooze. Bernie didn't bring his A game. I wondered how he could put the future of Western civilization in the hands of a third-rate stooge like Callimachus with such second-rate oratory. We were screwed.

To my astonishment, Callimachus pulled himself up to his full five foot three and rumbled, "We attack!" It sounded like it had been his idea all along.

The Battle of Marathon would be fought after all.

CHAPTER 28

The generals poured out from the tent and scattered to their units to carry the word. Last to leave were the three Plataeans, generals of the thousand loyal soldiers from that tiny city who had come to help Athens. They had not been allowed to speak and were looking forlorn as they shuffled toward the door.

"Uh-oh," Bernie said. "Need to do some fence-mending here." He jumped up and hurried over to the Plataeans. "Thanks, boys. Thanks for coming," he said, slapping a couple of backs and shaking some hands. "Don't worry, boys. We'll take care of you tomorrow. We've got your backs."

The Plataeans beamed and left, all jolly and smiling.

Bernie came back and sat down. "A minute ago, they thought they were to be lambs led to the slaughter tomorrow. I'm quite sure they were planning to sneak away during the night. A smile and handshake from the great Polemarchos, and they'll be happy lambs led to the slaughter."

"Berns, Master, what's with your speech? It sucked. You didn't try. Weren't you worried about the vote? I didn't know which way Callimachus would go."

"Nonsense, my boy. I knew exactly which way Callimachus would go. He would go for the hundred gold pieces I gave him the other night at my house. He'll get another four hundred today for voting according to his principles. Isn't democracy wonderful?"

"I guess."

"Now go. I have more hands to shake, backs to slap, babies to kiss, and cash incentives to distribute. Go find your friends. They'll prepare you for the battle tomorrow. Get busy. You have a lot to learn in a very short time."

The Athenian army had woken up, shaken off their hangovers, and begun preparing for battle. The slaves of the wealthier hoplites were busy burnishing their masters' elegant panoplies of armor to a high gleam while their masters boozed and breakfasted with their buddies. The poorer men were scuffing the rust off old family helmets and shields that a couple of days before had hung over their farms' fireplaces. Rich and poor alike were sharpening the heads of their double-ended eight-foot spears and grinding their sword blades on rocks. A few of the younger, fitter men were swinging swords to loosen up or even exchanging a few practice cuts with their friends—all stark naked, of course. Weirdos.

I found Theos, Keos, and Ramesh cooking a juicy frog from the marsh on the steps of the little marble temple in the woods.

"Greetings, Lex," cried Theos. "Join us for brunch. Its frogs' legs. My specialty. Is it true that we'll be taking bushel baskets of barbarian heads tomorrow?"

I sat down beside them.

Keos poured me a wooden cup of wine, cut it with water, and handed it to me. I took a swig. It made my head spin. Even cut, Athenian wine was a skull-blaster. It was more like grain alcohol and water than wine and water.

"Yes," I said. "Lord Polemarchos just now confided in me that we fight tomorrow." Not at all shy about making myself seem as important as possible.

Keos whacked me on the back. "Good news! Good news! Killing, maiming, and good clean fun! You have a bite to eat now. Then Theos and I will teach you how to fight like a Greek." He handed me a leg, and I took a bite. It wasn't so bad. It tasted like chicken.

Yasmine, still wrapped in Theos's cloak, sat alone sharpening Kali's Tooth on a marble step and singing a charming song to herself in Hindi. "The more blood that is shed, the more joyful is my Mistress Kali," she crooned.

"Her hymn to her mistress, the Destroyer," Ramesh explained. "She prays that she will be able to offer Kali much slaughter tomorrow."

"Blood to my ankles, blood to my knees, blood to my shoulders; blood, blood, blood, oceans of blood for my mistress, Kali."

This is the woman I love, I mused fondly.

"Lord Polemarchos sent me this bow," Ramesh announced, proudly holding Bernie's bow. "I have named him Silent Death. Tomorrow I shall place an arrow in each of Datis's eyes."

"You do that, boy," snarled Keos. "But take care you don't hit me as I shall be holding Datis's severed head on high by his curly ringlets."

"Nor me," said Theos. "My spear will already be buried in his guts, and his reeking bowels will be spilled out upon the ground at my feet."

"The Sahibs do not understand that they will find Lord Datis already dead," said Ramesh. "The reach of Silent Death is leagues beyond that of you bronze-footed monsters."

"Screw you, little twerp," Theos rebutted, glowering and fingering his sword hilt.

I didn't much like the direction this discussion was heading and decided to change the subject. "So, boys, weren't you going to show me how to fight like a Greek?"

"Like a Greek! Yes! Yes! Like a man—not a girl!" said Theos and Keos, leaping up. "Come with us." They each grabbed an arm.

They dragged me over to a nearby olive tree. Beside the tree, there was a tarp covering a man-sized shapeless lump. Theos drew the tarp away, and there I saw the famous Greek panoply: the array of weapons, armor, and equipment the Greeks wore to war.

There were three complete panoplies hung up on wooden frames. Standing upright in front of each was the three-foot diameter shield, the hoplon, after which the hoplite was named. "Yours is the one in the middle," Keos said.

I noticed two things right away. First, the equipment looked heavy, very heavy, especially that shield. I was supposed to carry all this around in the August heat? Second, Theos's and Keos's panoplies were shiny and clean, but my panoply was filthy and rusty.

"Why do I get the old stuff?" I asked.

"Your boss sent it over with that barbarian's toy bow," said Theos. "He said to tell you to clean it up."

"Yeah," said Keos. "'A soldier must care for his weapons,' Lord Polemarchos said."

"And after you've cleaned it all up, you can paint your own personal coat of arms on the shield," Keos said.

"Like what?" I asked.

"Anything you want."

Theos guffawed. "Yeah, like maybe a picture of your girlfriend's bottom."

I blushed and scowled. "Don't be gross," I muttered.

Theos laughed. "Oh, no! Our little tulip thinks I'm being disrespectful to his little Indian hellcat."

"While, by Ares's love hammer, he dreams of debauching her night and day," Keos said.

"I do not!" I cried and pouted.

"Never mind, Priapus. Strip down and put this on." Keos held up an article of clothing that looked like an ancient jockstrap. "We call this the ball-hugger. Can't have 'em dangling. Don't want 'em sliced off, do we?"

I agreed with that, so I stripped. Out of the corner of my eye, I saw Yasmine shamelessly ogling my sculpted physique. Or was she examining the edge on Kali's Tooth? Anyway, I blushed and turned my back when I pulled off my boxers.

"By Zeus!" Theos exclaimed so Yasmine heard. "He's colossal! That poor girl doesn't know what she's getting in for." Then he winked at me.

I pulled on the ball-hugger. Next came a linen T-shirt and a padded felt vest. After that came the bronze breastplate in two pieces hinged with leather straps, next felt padding for the greaves and the greaves themselves, like a baseball catcher's shin guards but made of solid bronze. I lifted one leg and almost toppled over on my face. Keos placed a little felt skull cap on my head. Then Theos placed the helmet. It was the Corinthian type: a cylinder of solid bronze with eye slits and a long nosepiece. On the top of the helmet was a crest with a fine, red horsehair plume a foot high. The helmet was very heavy and bit into my collarbones. It was dark and quiet inside. I felt like I was seeing the world through the tiny view slit in a tank. In fact, I had become a tank. Right away, I started to sweat.

Now for the great shield, the hoplon, the source of the Hoplite's power. A bronze sheet riveted to two inches of wood, it was shaped like shallow bowl curved inward. Two leather straps were fixed to the inside on opposite sides of the bowl. I slid my left arm through the leather grip on the left to the other on the right and closed my fingers around it. I took the shield's weight. It crashed to the ground.

Keos laughed. "No. You bear its weight on your shoulder not on your arms." He rested the bowl edge on my left shoulder. It cut into my flesh but balanced well. It covered my left side all the way from my shoulder to just below my knees. I snuggled up within the bowl. It made me feel safe.

"Your dory, mighty hoplite." Theos held out my spear. It was a foot taller than me. There was a big leaf-shaped spearhead on one end and a narrow spike on the other. "That spike's the lizard sticker. You use the spear like this." Theos hauled it overhead and plunged it downward. "Or like this." He placed it under his arm and thrust it straight forward.

Keos held up a straight-bladed sword two feet long. "The xiphos is for stabbing your enemy's nuts or his neck. Or, if you wish, the kipos." He held up a sort of curved-blade cleaver. "For chopping and lopping."

"I like the xiphos," Yasmine chimed in prettily. "More versatile. It can stab, slice, or hack."

"The little lady has a fine eye for a weapon. She says the xiphos." Keos fastened it around my waist with a belt and scabbard. "Done," he reported with some satisfaction.

I struck a heroic pose. "Behold! Our tulip is now Hercules!" cried Theos.

But I did not feel heroic. More like stuck in quicksand. The outfit was so heavy—it must have weighed eighty or a hundred pounds—that I felt that my feet must be sinking into the ground to my calves. I would never be able to handle the weight if I hadn't trained with Bernie's horrible vest. I never thought I'd admit that the vest had been useful.

"He looks like a big turtle," Yasmine said. "Can he fight in it?"

"Ah, the lady wants to see her hero fight, does she?" said Theos. "By Zeus, let's give her what she wants, Keos. Get into your gear and fight this young god of war."

"Oh, to the death, please!" Yasmine said, clapping her adorable little hands. "Oh, please, do fight to the death. Please!" She plopped down on the ground, crossed her legs demurely, and watched intently. All she lacked was a bowl of popcorn and her iPhone to send a few texts to her girlfriends.

Keos pulled on his armor, took up his shield and spear, and faced me. He crouched and raised his shield. Keos was nearly a full foot shorter than me, and his shield covered his entire left side from his ankles to his chin. His little eyes glared at me through the slits on his helmet like the eyes of a dragon peering out of his cave.

Keos raised his spear overhead and pointed it downward at my face. "Attack me," he said.

I copied his pose: knees bent in a crouch, poised, shield up, and spear overhead. "I don't want to hurt you," I said. I poked my spear lightly at his shield.

"You needn't worry about that," Theos said. "I said *attack* me," Keos growled, not moving an inch.

"Kill him!" shrieked Yasmine. "I want you to kill him!"

I poked again, a little harder. My spear point bounced off the face of his shield.

Keos lowered his shoulder, lunged forward, crashed his shield against mine, and drove his legs.

My helmet went flying one way, my spear went flying another, and I ended up flat on my back.

Keos stood with one foot on my chest and his lizard sticker tickling my throat. "You are dead," he said.

"Ooh," cooed Yasmine. "But aren't you really going to kill him?"

"I'm afraid not today, miss." Bernie was leaning over me and smiling. "Excellent, Lex! Your friend has just demonstrated what we call the *shock*, the first element of hoplite tactics."

"Thank you," I gasped.

Keos roared, "Imagine our ten thousand armored warriors crashing into the Persian line just as Keos crashed into you. The barbarians fight in pajamas and silken slippers. Our hoplites will crush them underfoot. And as they lie on their backs, holding their little dicks and whimpering for mercy, we will slaughter them like this!" He rammed his lizard sticker into the ground a millimeter from my left cheek.

I heard a whoosh passing overhead followed by a resounding thunk.

"Fine shooting, young Indian," Bernie said. "I see you have already mastered my steppe bow."

"With all due respect, Lord Polemarchos." Ramesh pointed at an olive tree twenty yards away. His arrow was buried six inches into the tree's trunk. "See how the storm of Persian arrows will pierce you bronze Sahibs as they lumber across the field to attack the men you call barbarians."

"You bronze men are too slow-footed in all that metal," added Yasmine.

"Your permission to arrest these two disrespectful barbarians, Lord

Polemarchos, hack them into tidbits, and feed them to the dogs," said Keos hopefully, raising his spear.

Theos drew his sword.

Ramesh nocked another arrow on his bow string.

Yasmine hefted Kali's Tooth lightly in her palm and crouched like a feral alley cat about to pounce on a mouse. She hissed.

Meanwhile, I lay on my back, suffocating under my spear. The sweat was pouring down my face and body, making a hot puddle around my butt cheeks. I was starting to itch down there too, but I couldn't reach to scratch. I was developing a major case of swamp ass.

Bernie chuckled. "No, no. No hacking to bits today. The young archer here makes sense. His way of war is different than ours, that's all. We Greeks prefer to close with our enemies and overwhelm them with sheer weight."

"Stupid brutes," Ramesh commented.

Yasmine hissed and spat.

"The Persians shoot from a distance and then scoot away."

"Women," growled Theos.

"Cowards," Keos added.

"No," said Bernie. "Just two different philosophies of war, each equally effective. Now, boys, pick this young man up off the ground. He has learned about the shock, now teach him the othismos, the push." Bernie turned and walked away.

Theos helped me up. As the sweat poured down from my butt down my legs and puddled at my feet, he changed into his armor and took up his shield and spear.

Keos positioned himself on Theos's right so the left side of his shield covered his friend's unprotected right side. "In this way, each hoplite protects his neighbor," Keos said.

"The phalanx fights as one man," Theos said proudly.

"The line must never be broken," said Keos.

They demonstrated the stance: crouched behind our shields, spear tucked into our elbows, legs bent like springs.

Then the one step forward—just one—at full force sending our shields crashing into the enemy.

The three of us, shoulder to shoulder, practiced the push over and over. Finally, we were a machine.

Theos positioned himself in front of us, and we practiced live. Soon, Keos and I were knocking him ass over teakettle every time. After about an hour of this—hard work in the heat—Keos said I had the push locked.

"Excellent," said Theos. "You are strong and agile ... and enormous." He winked at Yasmine. She replied with an obscene gesture. "You are a born hoplite. You've done this before?"

"Well, kind of," I replied. "Where I come from, it's called football."

Now you must learn the kill," Theos said.

Yasmine purred contentedly.

Theos demonstrated the overhand stroke. "This you will use when you are in a rear rank of the phalanx and must strike over the heads of your comrades. Aim toward your enemy's neck at the gap between his breastplate and his chin. Push and strike thus." He charged one step forward and thrust the spear downward. "This blow should either crush his larynx, drive your point through to sever his spine, or cut the veins and arteries of the neck. In either case, he will be dead in seconds."

"Careful," Yasmine pointed out. "Be sure to look away or his blood will spurt in your eyes and blind you."

"Excellent point, young lady," Keos commented.

Theos next showed me the savage underhand thrust. "If you are in the front rank, this stroke will disembowel your enemy."

"When your stricken enemy falls to the ground, step over him, and as you step, use the lizard sticker. Aim for the throat." Keos stepped and drove the spike into the ground. "One well-aimed stroke should do the job."

We drilled the shock, the push and the kill over and over for hours until we all dropped to the ground from exhaustion.

"Not bad. Not bad," Theos said.

We sprawled with our helmets tipped back on our heads, pouring sweat. Yasmine brought us a jar of ice-cold water from a nearby spring. When she poured it into my bowl, she caught my eye. She seemed actually to smile—to smile! Just a little. I gulped the water—and her love—down in deep draughts.

We drilled for hours more. As the sun was setting over Mount Parnassus, we quit for the night. Ramesh fed the fire to a merry blaze, and we all had a bite of nice leftover cold toad for dinner. All through the woods and up the hillside overlooking the plain, the marsh, and the Persian camp, cook fires began to twinkle, and I heard the voices of men setting down to get good and drunk.

Theos pulled out the wineskin and poured himself and Keos overflowing cups.

"Tomorrow, you will learn much more," said Keos.

I sipped the wine.

Theos and Keos drank and broke into filthy songs. My favorite was the one about the three-way between Juno, Athena, and yet another very well-equipped donkey. The wine made Theos and Keos bawdy, but it opened my heart. The amorous ass in their ballad reminded me of Buster. I missed my old friend terribly. I wondered what had become of him. Was he safe? Was he cold? Was he hungry? Was he lonely? I was lonely for Buster. A tear for my Buster dribbled down my cheek. In the next moment, I was sobbing my heart out for Mom, Dad, Polly, and Max.

Yasmine sat cross-legged by the fire, gravely watching the tears running down my cheeks. Without a word, she stood up. She took my hand and effortlessly pulled me to my feet. "Come." She led me out into the darkness beyond the firelight.

We sat down on the grass under an ancient olive tree. The night was hot and still. Nothing stirred. The Greek army had drunk itself into a stupor and gone to sleep. Cicadas chirped. A warm breeze stirred the olive leaves. An owl hooted twice over our heads.

"Tell me of your sorrow, Lex Sahib." Yasmine whispered. Her voice was deeper and throatier, like a cat purring—but not a little kitten, a big cat, a black panther.

I told her everything. It poured out of me. When I was done, she said, "The mistress teaches us that there is only one cure for your sorrow, Lex Sahib."

She placed her hand on the back of my neck and pulled her face to mine. She kissed me.

My lips burned. My head spun.

"The only cure is blood."

I heard the flapping of great wings above my head and then the piercing death shriek of some small animal.

Yasmine had disappeared into the night, leaving me burning.

PART III

THE DAY OF BATTLE

CHAPTER 29

RALLY OF GREEK CENTER

N

BATTLE OF MARATHON
GREEK DOUBLE ENVELOPMENT,
400 B.C.

Rosy-fingered dawn was spreading her painted fingertips over the wine-dark sea when I awakened. Yasmine was gone, but I felt terrific: strong as a bull, clearheaded, and focused with an awful intensity on what I would do this day. I was draining the snake against a rock when I heard a low murmur through the trees. The murmur became the trampling of thousands of feet. I peeked from behind an ancient olive tree.

"They're out! The barbarians are out!" I shouted.

Two miles across the plain, the entire Persian army—twenty thousand strong—was marching out of their camp. Leading the march were the first Hazarabam of Median elite spearmen. Datis's imperial guard were decked out in all their parade ground finery and furiously waved banners, some of them fifty feet long. They shrieked a battle cry at the top of their lungs that raised the hair on the back of my neck.

They also raised the Greek army. Within seconds, thousands of Greeks surrounded me. None had troubled to put on their armor. In fact, none had troubled to put on their clothes. They were crowded together in their birthday suits, gaping, smiling, waggling their junk at the Persians, and hurling obscenities. Very embarrassing.

Behind the imperial guard marched their regimental band, dressed all in scarlet with golden elf hats, belting out an ear-splitting din on drums, horns, bugles, cymbals, gongs, sticks, and cowbells. Persian music left a lot to be desired. It was apparently intended to drive us from the battlefield with busted eardrums.

While the band blasted, the guard arrayed themselves in a line ten ranks deep, and the rest of the army marched onto the field. One after another, Hazarabam from every corner of the Persian Empire marched out and formed up. Each regiment was led by two ranks of heavy spearmen carrying their tall wicker shields, but I noted that this was only a thin outer shell. The inner core of the army was composed of unarmored, half-naked bowmen. Each wore the particular uniform of their region: Babylonians dressed only in linen loincloths, Assyrians in fish-scale breastplates and conical bronze caps, Cypriots, Nubians with leopard skins slung over one shoulder, Phoenician marines, Egyptians wearing feathered caps, Parthians, slingers from the far mountains of Bactria dressed in the skins of beasts, wild Sogdians from the edge of the northern steppe, Scythians with necklaces of human finger bones around their necks, and Ramesh's colleagues, dark-skinned Ghandharians from the far Indus Valley at the very eastern edge of the Persian world. Each one of these regiments marched out and positioned itself.

At last, the entire Persian host was on the field. They formed a line ten men deep stretching all the way from the beach on our right to the foothills a mile away on our left.

"By the Myrmidons of Achilles, there are a lot of them," someone said.

The Persian host raised a mighty war cry.

"Oh, my, I'm *so* scared," remarked a hoplite beside me and scratched his bare ass.

"Me too," another said, yawning. "I think I just shit myself."

The Persian band fell silent, and a hush fell over their army. With a great stamp of feet and rattle of arms, the Persian army came to attention. "Hail, Datis!" roared from twenty-thousand throats. From out of the camp, Datis and his retinue of fifty gorgeously accoutered noble horsemen came galloping. Riding on Datis's right hand, I saw the Others, Hippias and Apollonius. My face flushed, and power surged through my body. My eyes misted with red. This was the mistress's blessing.

Datis was wearing a golden crown. His cuirass was made of solid gold chain links encrusted with precious gems. His chest-length braided black beard dripped with gold and pearls and blazed like fire in the morning sunlight. He was mounted on an enormous snow-white charger. Datis drew his sword, a fearsome golden scimitar, and raised it high. His giant steed neighed, reared, and pummeled the air with razor-sharp, silver-shod hooves.

Datis looked like a god!

I believe that there is a palpable moment in every battle when one army or the other trembles on the brink of disintegration. I remembered it from Troy when the Trojan army shivered, trembled, and then fled before the walls of their city. This was that moment for the Athenians. A tremor passed through the crowd as if a frigid north wind had blown over all of us. I shivered. My knees and legs weakened. I wanted to run away. I wasn't even sure I could run away.

It was the moment when the leader must step forward or the great god Pan will triumph.

Bernie's voice boomed out over the army. "By Zeus!" he roared.

The eyes of ten thousand turned toward the rock on which he was standing.

"What a beautiful man!" He paused to let us all muse on how Datis surpassed us all in manly gorgeousness a hundred times over. "I love him." He paused again to allow us all to consider our tender feelings for Datis. "After we fuck him, let's fuck his pretty horse."

Ten thousand Greeks exploded with laughter. The spell was broken.

"To arms, you drunken Greek perverts!" Bernie roared affectionately.

The army let out a giant roar and scattered back to their campsites to prepare for battle. I found Theos and Keos strapping on their breastplates.

My little Aphrodite sat on a rock, dipping Kali's Stinger in a small bottle of cobra venom. She flashed me a homicidal glare—my angel.

Ramesh was examining the shafts of his arrows for warps. "Allow me to help you, Sahib." Ramesh held up a greave.

I stripped. Yasmine pretended not to notice, but you can be sure she feasted her eyes secretly on my manly form. Ramesh assisted me into my armor. Finally, he handed me my shield and my spear and stepped back to admire the effect.

"A young god of war," Bernie said, standing a few yards away. Beside him stood Aeschylus and Cynegeirus. The two brothers were dressed in brilliant, gleaming panoplies that put mine to shame. Each had attached a peacock feather to his crest and hung a garland of posies around his neck.

"Lex, I have assigned these two stalwarts to fight beside you in the battle line," Bernie said.

"I thought you boys said you were lovers, not fighters," I piped in.

"As artists, it is our duty to seek out and experience all facets of life," Aeschylus pompously proclaimed.

"What'd he say?" Theos asked Keos.

"No idea," answered Theos.

Trumpets blasted. Drums thundered. The cry went out over the camp: "Form the battle line! Form the line!"

As your kindergarten teacher tried to line you up to go to the cafeteria at lunchtime alphabetically but Sammy White, the dumb kid, couldn't remember his last name and half of you didn't know your ABCs anyway. As nobody wanted to stand next to Sammy because he smelled like he'd just shit his pants, and all the boys wanted to stand next to Candy, the class cutie, and the whole class was yelling, pushing, and shoving, and the teacher was screaming, so everyone in the Greek army was pushing and shoving, and the Greek commanders were yelling and screaming and losing it.

So the Greek rabble formed up for the Battle of Marathon. It wasn't pretty.

In the middle of this chaos, Bernie stood like a serene island in a raging sea of discord, calmly directing men to the standards of their various regiments, helping others up who had fallen on their faces in their heavy armor, soothing a very young soldier, no more than thirteen, who was sitting on the ground and weeping with fear.

We Greeks lined up on the little slope overlooking the plain of Marathon. We were about a mile from the Persians. I was with the Antiochus regiment in the center of the army, the place of highest honor reserved for the finest troops. Theos stood beside me on my right, and Keos was on my left. I was glad to have these two tough veterans at my side. Aeschylus and his brother stood shoulder to shoulder on Keos's left. I was not overly confident of those two fancy boys. I didn't see Ramesh and Yasmine. They were somewhere behind us with the mob of irregulars: slaves and peasants armed with bows, slings, and farm implements hoping to pick up a bit of booty after a Greek victory.

I was taller than just about every man in the Greek army, so I was able to get a good look at our whole line from one end to the other. The sun was rising, and it was already getting hot, so every man had taken the rest position, his spear straight up, his shield resting on its rim on the ground, and his helmet tipped backward off his face. I stood on tiptoe and saw that Bernie had arranged us so that our line exactly matched the length of the Persian line even though the Persians had at least twice our number on the field.

"We're only four ranks deep," Theos whispered.

"The rest of the regiments are eight ranks," Keos pointed out.

"We are too weak," Theos added.

"What's the old fox up to?" asked Keos.

"I don't like it," said Theos. "I have a bad feeling about this battle."

"You have a bad feeling about every battle," Keos retorted.

"If I ... you know ... fall, will you make sure my wife is taken care of, old friend?" asked Theos.

"Damn right I'll take care of her," replied Theos, thrusting his hips in and out obscenely.

An eerie silence fell over the field. Aside from an occasional cough, the shuffle of a foot, or the metallic clunk of a greave, ten thousand Greeks had fallen still. Not a sound came from the Persians either. Thirty thousand men stood staring at each other.

Suddenly, every horn in the Persian army let out a single huge blast. The Persian infantry ranks parted, and a rider on a magnificent black charger galloped out onto the field. I recognized the horseman as one of the grandest noblemen of Datis's guard. Long black hair flying behind him, he galloped at full speed all the way to the far right of our line. When he reached the flank, he wheeled his steed on a dime and galloped at full speed all the way to our right flank. Back and forth, he galloped, zigzagging ever closer to us, performing all sorts of astounding tricks of horsemanship. He jumped off his horse, hit the ground with his feet, and bounced back up into the saddle again. He rode backward. He did a somersault and landed back in the saddle. He stood on his horse. He stood on one foot on his horse. He even stood on his hands on his horse. My personal opinion is that he couldn't hold a candle to our Native American horsemen at Little Bighorn, but he impressed the gullible Greeks.

He was hypnotizing us. Even Bernie fell under the horseman's spell. Bernie stepped a few yards in front of the line to get a better view. He applauded the horseman's fancier tricks. Back and forth, up and down the line, the horseman galloped, moving on every circuit a little closer to Bernie. I felt a quiver of apprehension. When the Persian was thundering by Bernie, no more than twenty yards away, I almost cried out a warning, but before I could, the Persian snatched a javelin from beneath his robes and hurled it. The army gasped. The javelin quivered in the exact center of Bernie's shield right where his heart would have been had he not raised it to cover himself.

We cheered. Then we gasped again. Bernie had fallen! Stepping backward to take the javelin on his shield, his foot had caught on a stone. He fell to one knee. His shield fell flat on the ground. The horseman drew his horse to a halt only a few feet away. At the horse's feet, Bernie scrambled for his shield. The Persian pulled out another javelin. He cocked his arm for the throw. Bernie was utterly defenseless.

I heard a whirring sound overhead and an arrow drove into the horseman's left eye. He tumbled from his horse into the dust on his face. The arrowhead, smeared with clots of brain, protruded from the back of his head. His feet kicked once, kicked twice, and he lay still. His riderless horse galloped away.

"Praise Apollo the bowman!" exclaimed Theos.

"No, Sahib, not your infidel god," said little Ramesh, standing just behind us. He lowered Bernie's compound bow, the weapon of horse kings.

Bernie stood, dusted himself up, and strode out to the corpse. He drew his sword, and with one stroke, he hacked off the champion's head. He seized it by the hair and tossed it at Ramesh's feet. "Good shot, bowman," he shouted so all the army could hear. "After we win this battle, I shall fill it with gold."

"Hurrah! Hurrah for Lord Polemarchos!" the army roared, pleased by Bernie's manly generosity—not to mention the prospect of rich booty for themselves in the near future.

"Hurrah! Hurrah for the little squirt bowman!"

The army cheered.

"Now make way for the high priest," Bernie cried.

A dirty old priest stepped out in front of the line with a tarnished bowl, a scrawny pigeon, and a knife. No golden bowl and white bull. Traditional values had declined in Greece since the Trojan War, I thought. The priest gutted the pigeon into the bowl and stuck his nose in the guts.

"The auguries are favorable!" the dirty old priest croaked.

"The gods smile on our victory!" Bernie cried. "We fight today!" The army roared and slammed their spears against their shields. "We will march toward the enemy line. When I raise my spear, we will run. Run! But only when I raise my spear. Do you understand?"

The army roared assent.

"Will you follow me?"

"Yes!" they roared.

The sun was well up by now, and I was baking like an Easter leg of lamb inside my armor. Under my Corinthian helmet, I could barely hear or see the outside world, but I could feel my brain simmering. The sweat soaked my hair. It poured down my brow and stung my eyes. It clogged my ears, poured down my neck, oozed down my torso under my chest plate, soaked my ball-hugger underwear, dribbled down my legs, and filled my sandals. I shifted one foot and felt the slosh.

It was the heat that made me pour sweat—not fear. I had been afraid at Little Bighorn, at Gettysburg, even when those ape men charged us, but I felt nothing now. I stood on my toes and looked down the Athenian line. Our ten thousand hoplites stood like statues. Not a cough. Not a shuffle. Not a clank or ping of metal on metal. Were they afraid? They must be. Why wasn't I?

A mile across the plain, the thirty thousand Persians also stood like statues. No more banner-waving and trumpet-blasting and drum-thumping for them. Certainly, they were terrified.

Bernie hoisted the bowl curve of his shield onto his left shoulder and raised his spear high overhead. I saw a brilliant flash as Bernie's spear point caught the sun. A fire spirit leapt from the tip of Bernie's spear and danced down the Greek line, touching each hoplite's spear point in turn. It leapt from one end of our line to the other. It was a miracle, and I saw it with my own eyes.

"Those people have come here to make you slaves," Bernie roared, his voice echoing off the hills and the mountains like a god's. He paused for a second and cried:

"For Greece! And for freedom!"

Yasmine's kiss burned my lips. Bernie's words seared my heart. I would have followed Bernie into the gates of hell.

CHAPTER 30

And that, God help us, is what we did. With one great crash of bronze on bronze, ten thousand helmets slammed down over the metal collars of ten thousand breastplates. With one giant grunt, ten thousand Greeks hoisted the bowl rims of ten thousand shields up onto their left shoulders, lowered their spear points, and stepped out down the gentle slope toward the Persian line.

All I could see through the tiny view slit of my helmet was the back of the man in front of me. At first, I felt very alone. I glanced at Theos and then at Keos, heads down, determined, good men, my friends. I felt reassured that they were beside me. Then I heard the sergeants calling out helpful hints and cheerful suggestions to the men:

"Theron, dress it up, you stupid bastard! Panes, get the fuck in step, you child molester! You, Pollio, catch up! Don't worry about the Persians. Catch up—or I'll kill you before they do!"

We began to sing. It was not really a song but a cadence chant to keep us all in step and maintain the unity of the phalanx. The chant told a story, a classic tale common to every war and every army in every time and place. A brave soldier goes off to war and leaves his lonely wife behind. The soldier's best buddy, a shirker, takes up with his wife. While the soldier is up to his neck in filth and slaughter, the buddy and the wife are going at it in ways that the song described in hilarious, obscene detail. The song cheered me up and took my mind off the mayhem that was just a few hundred yards ahead.

Down the slope we marched, singing about just what was going to happen to that buddy, and all our disloyal slacker buddies, when we got home again. From time to time, Theos on my left would remind me in no uncertain terms that my shield had the all-important role of protecting him and that I fucking well better not stray too far to my right to snuggle up under Keos's shield. Then Keos would advise me in no uncertain terms that I was nestling up to him too close and who did I think he was, that little Indian slut I'd been humping? That turned my mind to Yasmine, and I wondered whether, if I was a great hero in the battle, which I was going to be, she would, you know ... I decided that she would.

And so it went with all of us slogging, singing, throwing insults, and even daydreaming to keep up our spirits until we were about two or three hundred yards from the Persians. At this point, my curiosity got the better of me. I craned my neck, wiped the sweat from my eyes, and squinted through my eye slits to see what the enemy was doing.

He wasn't doing anything. To my astonishment, the Persian host was still just standing there, staring at us. The lords of the earth couldn't believe that this small army of farmers was going to attack them.

But they couldn't stand there gaping forever. Suddenly they woke up and began scurrying about like angry ants. The spearmen in the front line hoisted their wicker shields over their heads and rammed their bottom edges down into the earth, forming a neat but flimsy wall five feet tall. From the shelter of this wall, the Persian archers stepped forward, drew their bows, and let fly a huge cloud of arrows.

"Oh, shit," I said.

I lowered my head so the arrows would hit the top of my helmet and bounce off—I hoped. The whole Greek line raised their shields up off their shoulders and held them up against the rain of arrows.

But the rain never came. We were still out of range. The arrows thudded into the earth fifty yards ahead of us, forming a field of shafts topped with gaily colored feathers as thick as a field of poppies ready for the picking. At about two hundred yards from the Persian line, we waded into the arrows, knocking them over and crunching the shafts underfoot.

The Persian bowmen got the message: if they didn't start gunning us down with their arrows soon, ten thousand pissed-off bronze monsters were going to crash into them, crushing, hacking, spearing, and trampling them underfoot. They started furiously yanking fresh arrows from their quivers and nocking them to their bows.

We'd better hurry, I thought.

Then I saw Hippias and Apollonius. At that moment, it did not seem to me to be implausible that I should be able see them—two figures in a host of tens of thousands—or that they should be standing together just in front of the Persian first line exactly opposite me and only a hundred yards away. Nevertheless, that extraordinary clarity of vision that had first come upon me in football came to me again. Both men, I saw, wore no helmet or armor. Each was unarmed. At a hundred yards, I saw their faces as clearly as if they were just across Bernie's living room. Both were smiling. The teeth of both men, I saw, were filed to sharp points. I heard Yasmine's voice: "The only cure is blood!"

I would tear Hippias and Apollonius apart with my bare hands. My body heat soared. My heart pounded in my chest. Power surged into my arms and legs. A bloody red mist covered my eyes.

"Antiochus Regiment, follow me!" I shouted and lit out at a full sprint toward the Persian line.

"Lex, what the hell are you doing?" Theos shouted.

An instant later, Theos and Keos cried, "Antiochus, charge!"

I looked back over my shoulder, and the whole Antiochus regiment and the Leontis Regiment beside us—the entire center of the Greek line—was thundering along just ten yards behind me.

They were following me! I was the leader. Never mind Bernie's orders, I was the Wargod!

Seventy-five yards now. My legs churned. My shield bounced up and down on my shoulder. My armor clanked and bit into my flesh. The Persians let loose a flight of arrows, but I had fooled them. None touched us. They flew over our heads, making a sound like a million angry bees.

Fifty yards now. Inspired by my lust for revenge, I still felt fresh and strong, but my fellow soldiers were faltering. Their legs ached and cramped. Their shields felt unbearably heavy. They were blinded by sweat. They couldn't catch their breath.

I glanced to the right. Theos had fallen behind. He was breathing very hard. Dimly, I heard him gasp. "Tighten up! Goddamn it! Tighten up!"

I glanced to the right. Keos's breath was coming in sharp, rapid rasps. He stumbled. I thought he was going down, but he managed to recover.

Twenty-five yards, and I shouted to lower our spearheads from forty-five degrees to horizontal. Through my eye slit, I saw fear and horror contort the barbarians' faces.

At ten yards, we used our last breath to roar out the *paean*, our war cry. It was a high-pitched screech very much like the rebel yell. I saw Persians breaking away from their line and running away.

And I saw Hippias and Apollonius again. They were weaving their way through the Persian lines to the back where they would be safest from our onslaught. Apollonius stopped. He turned and caught my eye. Then he smirked and waved a cheerful goodbye. He and Hippias disappeared.

Then we struck.

The shock sounded like the crack of a lightning bolt splintering a tree. Metal on metal, metal on flesh, metal on bone, we drove into the very center of their line, the part occupied by the Persian so-called elite heavy spearmen. They were heavily armed and armored men by Persian standards, but they were lacey little girls by ours.

We hit them as an out-of-control truck jumps the curb, careens onto the sidewalk, and mows down a shrieking flock of kindergarten kids on a field trip to the museum. The Persians buckled. We crashed through one rank, two ranks, three ranks, tossing them aside, shattering their pathetic wicker shields, and stomping them, screaming, into the ground.

I knew exactly what to do. I knew exactly how to do it. Shoulder to shoulder, we began our push. I put my left shoulder to my shield, rammed it into the face of the Persian in front of me, and as I stepped, thrust my spear down over his shoulder. It struck something soft.

As I pushed, the Hoplite behind me drove his shield into my back and pushed me. The man behind him pushed him in turn, and our whole line took one step forward. A screaming Persian lost his footing, fell at my feet, and groped at my legs. I cursed and drove my lizard sticker into his mouth.

Theos, that bastard, might have warned me to aim for a softer part. The sticker caught in the back of the Persian's skull. I struggled to free it and nearly tripped, cursing all the more. I wiggled it out of the bone, raised my spear high, pushed, and thrust down again. Push-step-stroke. Push-step-stroke again. And again. And again.

We had become a death machine.

I felt no fear. I felt nothing but rage and an irresistible need to cut my way through the Persian army to murder Apollonius and Hippias. As loud as the battle raging around me was, I heard nothing. I smelled nothing: neither the sweat, nor the blood, nor the shit and piss pouring out of the bodies of the thirty thousand men fighting and dying within yards of me. I felt no fatigue. A Persian sword slashed my forearm. I saw the wound—it was deep—but I felt no pain. Every one of my senses was focused on the tiny area that I could reach with my spear: my kill zone.

Many years later, I learned that among the Vikings there was a cult of warriors called Berserkers. "Bearskin wearers" it means in the Old Norse language. The Berserkers were famous for falling into an invincible battle ecstasy. You could hack a Berserker's head off, it was said, and he would continue to snap his jaws at your ankles. I had become a Berserker.

Step by step, we pushed forward, killing all as we went. Then we weren't moving forward anymore. The man behind me pushed. The man behind him pushed. With all my might, I put my shoulder against my shield and tried to take a step, but I could not.

I glanced at Theos beside me. He was straining with every bit of strength he had remaining in his body to move just another inch forward. His helmet had been knocked back on his head, and I could see his sweat-stained, filthy face and the cords standing out on his neck. His bloodshot eyes met mine.

The message in his eyes was clear. The men of the Antiochus and Leontis regiments were done. They had exhausted their strength. They were spent.

For a moment, we hung frozen, straining every muscle to advance. Then our momentum collapsed. Both regiments recoiled half a step as a body. The hoplite in front of me tumbled backward, spraying arterial blood from a neck wound into my eyes. I wiped the blood away and saw I was face-to-face with Persians. A spearman rammed his shield against me, trying to push me back. I thrust my spear right through the wicker into his face. He shrieked and fell, dragging my spear out of my hand. I parried a Saka battle ax with my shield and drew my sword. The Saka aimed a roundhouse ax blow at my skull. I ducked, slashed at his midsection, and saw his intestines gushing out. All around me, man fought man to the death, hacking, piercing, clawing at one another's throats and eyes, screaming, gasping, groaning, crying for their mothers, roaring with rage. The bodies were piled three and four high. The ground was puddled with blood. I stumbled on a rolling head: long black hair, a Persian, eyes staring wide, mouth frozen in a howl. My feet slipped backward and out from under me. My helmet flew off. My forehead crashed into the ground.

Dazed, I lay on my stomach in the dust. I had a dim sense of many running footsteps all around me. A foot in a slipper kicked my head and then rushed on. Slowly I came to my senses. My vision cleared. I sat up and looked around me. Except for the many dead, I was alone inside a vast dust cloud raised by the churning feet of forty thousand soldiers. Inside the cloud, the sounds of battle were now muted. The battle had moved on. Theos and Keos, the whole regiment, had vanished. They had retreated.

The great god Pan had summoned them, and they had fled.

It wasn't a failure of courage. It was a failure of numbers. Our line, only four ranks deep, simply could not overcome ten ranks of Persians. It was not the regiment's fault.

The fault was mine. In my lust for revenge, I had ignored Bernie's orders to wait for his signal to run. I had known better than Bernie. I had led our regiments, men carrying nearly a hundred pounds of armor and weapons in blazing August heat, on a sprint that was beyond their strength. It was too far. I had exhausted them. It was my fault that they had been defeated and run away. They were right to leave me for dead.

I sat there on the ground all alone in my dust cloud feeling very sorry for myself.

With no particular interest, I noticed a figure emerging out of the cloud. Friend or enemy, I didn't care. As the figure came closer, I realized it was gigantic. It came closer still, and I saw it was an enormous Saka holding a long-handled war ax in both hands. The Saka was naked. His enormous body—he was at least seven feet tall—was covered in matted black hair and crisscrossed by old scars and fresh wounds. His upper arms were as broad as my waist. His legs were like tree trunks. His head was shaven bald, and he had a huge indent over his right eye, an ancient wound made by a war hammer or some other blunt weapon. At his belt flopped three gape-jawed severed heads, Greek heads.

This beast walked right up to me. When he was about ten feet away, he sniffed, licked his lips, and raised his war ax.

This monster is the instrument of my punishment.

Halfheartedly, I raised my shield. The war ax descended. It hewed my shield in two like paper, and the two shattered halves fell to the ground on either side of me. I raised my sword. It looked like a butter knife matched against this beast's war ax. I poked my sword at him.

He laughed—or you would have called it a laugh, were he human.

He raised his ax directly overhead for the killing blow. He would cleave me in half lengthwise skull to crotch. I wasn't afraid. I didn't care. I stared up at his ax head. It quivered, beginning its downward stroke.

Then out of nowhere, a slender brown arm and hand appeared and pinioned the giant's forehead. The giant frowned and grunted. Another brown arm and hand appeared. This hand held Kali's Tooth. Kali's Tooth plunged to the hilt into the giant's right ear.

The giant roared and whirled around with my Yasmine clinging to his back. Howling, he pirouetted three times, desperately trying to shake this demon from off his back. Then his eyes rolled back in his head. His knees buckled, and he fell on his face with an earthshaking crash. His tongue lolled out. It was long and black. Blood oozed from his eyes. His feet smashed up and down on the ground two times. His feet kicked, and he was dead.

Yasmine detached herself from the corpse, placed one dainty foot on the Giant's face, and yanked Kali's Tooth out of his ear. It made a sound like a plunger unclogging a toilet. She wiped the dagger carefully on her sleeve and replaced it in her belt.

"Thank you," I said.

She growled a deep, feral growl. Her eyes blazed with sex and death. Was she going to kill me or make love to me? I didn't know. In an instant, I had my answer. She reached behind her back and pulled some magical cord known only to her. Her clothes fell away and collapsed in a heap on the ground. She stood there naked, slick with sweat, her breasts heaving. She stepped over and stood astride me.

The clash of arms, the howls of rage, and the shrieks of mangled men behind the dust cloud were drawing closer again as I stood up. She charged, leapt, crashed into me, and wrapped her thighs about my waist in a rib-shattering grip. We crashed on my back into the dust.

From behind us, I heard shouts, cries, and a great thundering of running feet. Something—something enormous and not necessarily good—was almost upon us.

I wrapped my arms around Yasmine and pulled her down. "Play dead!" I whispered.

Out of the dust cloud stampeded the entire Persian army in a mad panic, yelling, screaming, throwing down their arms, and running for their lives.

They thundered by. One hapless archer tripped and fell over us. He stared right into my face and scrambled for his dagger. Yasmine slit his throat.

In a moment, they had passed.

"By Heracles's humping hammer, Keos, look here! Our boy roots like a mad beast in the very midst of battle! Have you ever seen such a thing?" It was Theos.

"We weren't …" I sputtered. "We didn't …"

"Never have I beheld such a hero!" Keos replied. "And look here: he slew this giant with one hand while squeezing her pretty little bottom with the other! What a prodigy!"

"We taught him everything he knows," boasted Theos to Aeschylus and Cynegeirus, who were standing beside him.

"I am truly impressed," Aeschylus remarked, goggling at Yasmine's backside.

"Is she for sale?" asked Cynegeirus hungrily.

Bernie arrived. "Boys, I told you the lad had talent. Have I ever lied to you?"

Yasmine leapt off of me, swept up her clothes, pulled her dagger, and swished it back and forth, hissing obscenities.

I lay flat on my back, a circle of filthy, blood-spattered hoplites staring down at me. "What happened? The battle?"

"The battle is won," said Bernie. "The barbarians flee to their ships."

"But we were beaten," I protested.

"The center—Antiochus and Leontis—was beaten and retreated," Bernie explained. "But the army was not. As you were driven back and the enemy advanced, your brothers on the flanks closed in around them and slaughtered them."

"It has been a memorable massacre," added Keos. "I slew thirty with my own hand."

"By Athena's immortal knockers!" exclaimed Keos, sneaking another look at Yasmine. "You are a liar and braggart. I counted your kills. There were twenty-six. I had thirty-four."

"Come, boy," said Bernie, giving me a hand up. "This is what we call the *pursuit*. It is the fun part when we chase down the fear-crazed enemy and slaughter him without mercy or risk to ourselves." He picked up the spear and shield of a fallen soldier and handed them to me.

I pulled my helmet back on and adjusted my lower clothing.

"You can play with your girlfriend later," he added.

"She's just a friend," I protested again.

"In that case, after you're done, would you consider sharing her with your stalwart comrades in arms?" asked Keos hopefully.

Yasmine glared and swished Kali's Stinger back and forth under his nose.

"Onward, Greeks!" Bernie cried. "There are barbarians to slay, camps to pillage, ships to burn, and women to violate!"

The Greek army roared like mad beasts.

I cast Yasmine a little air kiss, and we all trotted off into the dust cloud after the panicked Persians. In a minute or two, we emerged from the cloud and beheld a sight to gladden the black heart of any soldier. Before us was spread out a field littered with the products of the great god Pan's work. The Persians had abandoned their weapons to flee. Discarded bows, spears, shields, and wicker armor lay everywhere, mixed in with hundreds of corpses. Scattered among the dead, legless and armless Persians struggled to drag themselves along the ground into the safety of the camp.

A hundred yards beyond the field of battle was the great mob of retreating Persians. Half were trying to jam themselves through the single narrow camp gate, falling, trampling, and being trampled underfoot, clawing and hacking at each other to cram themselves through and reach the safety of their ships. The other half of the Persian army had given up on the gate and were trying to flee through the swamp. They were now sinking up to their chins in muck and quicksand as Greeks waded among them, methodically hacking off their heads or cracking their skulls.

To gate or swamp? Which barbarians to slaughter first? We elected to keep our feet dry. Theos, Keos, the two brothers, and I charged the gate.

The technique of slaughtering a panicked, fleeing, and disarmed enemy, for your information, differs markedly from the technique of fighting an organized foe. We abandoned the disciplined shoulder-to-shoulder work and went freestyle. When we had run to within ten yards of the mob, Theos and Keos hurled their spears. I followed suit. My spear skewered not one, not two, but four naked Indian archers through the back like a string of trout on a single line. They collapsed kicking and wiggling in the dust.

"Good arm, boy," Theos commented. "My record is three."

We drew our swords and waded into the crush. The barbarians didn't fight. They submitted. The preferred technique for quickly killing a submitted foe is to seize the victim from behind by his long hair, pull his head back and place your blade to his throat. He stops in his tracks and closes his eyes. Then you draw your blade across his throat. His hot blood gushes onto your hand and arm. His eyes roll back into his head. He goes limp. You drop his corpse aside into the dust and move on.

I slaughtered twenty men this way, and Theos and Keos slaughtered even more. It was murder, not war. My last kill, a slender Indian boy much like Ramesh—looked me in the eye just before I slashed his throat. He was no older than twelve or thirteen. His eyes, wide open, filled with tears. "Please," he whispered.

I killed him anyway.

That was enough. I felt sick and weak and utterly disgusted with myself. Perhaps I am a natural soldier. Bernie says I am—and so does my grandfather. A "genetic warrior," they call me. But I am not a natural murderer. I stopped in my tracks and dropped my sword. I would have turned around and walked back to Athens, but Theos cried out, "The fleet! I can see the fleet!"

That was where Apollonius and Hippias would be.

We had cut our way through the crush at the gate and into the open camp. The Persian tents had been trampled into the ground. The Persian survivors were in full flight before us. Half a mile away, we could see the beach and the Persian transports. Thousands of desperate Persians were crowding, splashing, and drowning to get aboard them.

"Let's capture a ship!" cried Keos.

"Yes, a ship!" shouted Cynegeirus. "I want a ship."

"Our yacht!" added Aeschylus.

The idea of capturing a ship inspired me not at all. What did inspire me was the realization that Hippias and Apollonius would unquestionably be on one of those ships trying to escape my wrath. I picked up my sword again, and we—the five of us and most of the rest of the Greek army—sprinted toward the beach.

The Persian boats that were drawn up on the sand at the Bay of Marathon were not sleek war galleys. They were scows: wide, high tubby things fifty or sixty feet long—no longer than many modern sailing yachts—driven by one big square sail or eight backup oars to be hauled out when the wind died. Fat, slow, and unarmed, they were manned by wharf rat merchant seamen from all over the Mediterranean. Normally they carried trade goods. The sleek war galleys crammed with soldiers were on their way to Athens.

"Booty!" a soldier shouted.

"Booze!" Theos cried out.

"Bimbos!" Keos yelled.

Our trot toward the beach became a race. Ugly and tubby though the Persians ships were, every soldier in the Greek army knew that their spacious holds must be filled with great barrels of prime Persian vino and compliant slave girls. The motivation for the army's charge was no longer patriotism or even military. It was a race to the hooch and the hookers.

But not for me. I sought a bigger, bloodier prize. Over the heads of the screaming, clamoring, and drowning Persians on the beach, I saw Datis and my old friends Hippias and Apollonius. They were scrambling up the ramp of one of the fancier transports, a broad-beamed vessel flying Datis's personal pennant. It was guarded by a ring of liveried guards warning off panicked barbarians with their spears. I burned with rage.

"There's Datis's yacht!" I shouted. "If we take it, we shall all be rich men!"

This idea had popular support. Only I wanted to revenge myself on Hippias and Apollonius, but everyone in the army wanted to be rich. We charged and waded into the guards, swinging and hacking. I felt strong, focused, and unbeatable again. I was back in my battle frenzy. One bodyguard lunged at me with his spear. He seemed to be moving in slow motion. I sidestepped as gracefully as a ballet dancer and sliced off both his arms at the elbows. Another lunged at my face. I dropped to my knees and lowered my head. His spearhead glanced harmlessly off my helmet, and I drove my sword into his crotch. He squealed like a little girl, clutched himself, and collapsed. On my right, Theos was beating a Persian's brains out with the man's own severed leg. On my left, Keos was chuckling at a Persian stumbling in his own intestines.

In seconds, Datis's bullies threw down their weapons and scrambled into the water, screaming like skinny-dipping high school girls. They had delayed us just long enough. Sailors strained to push Datis's yacht off the sand. Others were untangling ropes and pulling on lines to raise the single sail. I knew that as soon as they got the boat afloat and the breeze hit that canvas, Datis's yacht would scoot into the bay beyond our reach. I sprinted for the boat, but with all the armor on my back, my feet sank into the sand up to my calf. My breath was finally coming hard. My legs were screaming in agony. I saw Datis, Hippias, and Apollonius standing in the bow. They were laughing and pointing at us.

"Come on!" I yelled to Theos and Keos and gave a last desperate kick.

To my surprise, Cynegeirus, the fancy boy, reached the boat first. He charged into the water up to his knees, grabbed the anchor rope hanging from the bow, dug in his heels, and pulled. "Help me!" he cried.

Theos, Aeschylus, and I took hold behind him and pulled with all our might. A wave slapped me in the face, but I kept pulling. The boat slowed, and then it nearly stopped. Behind us, the whole Greek army was running up to give us a hand. If we could just hang on for a few seconds, I knew we had them.

Then, in the bow, I saw Apollonius's swarthy head appear over the gunwale. He peered down at us. He smirked and drew his sword. "Bon voyage!" With one blow, he severed both the anchor rope and Cynegeirus's right wrist. Cynegeirus cried out in agony. We all collapsed into the water. The yacht leapt from the shore. In seconds, it was under full sail and out of reach, with Cynegeirus's right hand still grasping the dangling anchor rope. Apollonius stared at the bloody hand in disgust and flipped it into the water with the tip of his sword. "Fish food," he cried out, laughing.

Cynegeirus sat in the shallows clutching his wrist, his face ghastly pale, blood pulsing out of his wound with every heartbeat.

Aeschylus knelt beside him and wept. "What do I do, brother? Oh, Apollo, what do I do?"

"A strap," Theos cried. He ran over to the brothers, unfastened one of Cynegeirus's greaves, removed a leather strap, and tied it around

Cynegeirus's upper arm. He seized a fragment of broken spear shaft off the sand, thrust it between the strap and the boy's arm, and twisted it tight. "Tighter. Tighter," he muttered. The flow of blood lessened to a dribble. "A tourniquet, we call it."

But Cynegeirus was gone.

"Oh, God! My brother!" Aeschylus exploded into tears.

"I'm sorry, boy." Theos gently put his hand on Aeschylus's shoulder. "I'm sorry."

To my other sins, I added the death of Cynegeirus caused by my pride and lust for revenge.

The remnants of the Persian fleet were disappearing over the horizon. The beach was littered with barbarian corpses and barbarian bits. Some Greek soldiers were dispatching the Persian wounded with a quick jab into the eye with their lizard stickers. Others were rummaging through the dead.

"No time for weeping," said Theos. "The boys are getting in ahead of us. Come on, junior. I shall now teach you the finer points of corpse harvesting."

"Of what?" I asked.

"Body robbing," Theos replied. "You don't think they pay us a salary, do you?"

"Well, no. I guess not."

"Here's a likely one." Theos guided me over to the nearest dead Persian, one of Datis's bodyguards, one I had killed. "Now, the first thing is to make sure your corpse is really a corpse. One doesn't want it to suddenly wake up and take offense at you stealing his wallet."

Theos drew his dagger, kneeled down, and slit the man's throat.

"So, go to it, boy," he said.

The man had rings on nearly all his fingers, and I set to work trying to slip an especially nice emerald off the ring finger of his right hand. It was sticky. I tugged.

"What are you doing?" he asked.

"Got any soap?" I replied.

"You want a bath? Boy, we're in a hurry here," he said. "The competition is out in force." Sure enough, the beach was crawling with Hoplite harvesters. He hacked off the ring, finger and all, with his dagger. "That's the way to do it." He flipped finger and ring to me. "Now get the others."

I ended up with a nice little pile of bloody rings and fingers lying beside me on the sand. There was a diamond stud in the man's nose. I carved off the nose but dropped it into the sand. A seagull swooped in, picked it up, and flew away.

"Damn thief!" Theos shouted and shook his fist. A trumpet blasted. "That's it. Gotta go. Mustn't offend the gods by being greedy." He scooped up the jewels, rings, fingers, and the nose stud and dropped them into a leather pouch he carried slung around his neck.

The whole business disgusted me. On the other hand, years later—about 2,500 years later—I sold that emerald to a jeweler in New York for $750,000.

We helped Aeschylus carry his brother's body to the Assembly and laid him down beside our other dead. We laid Cynegeirus beside old Callimachus, another casualty of the battle. I wondered where his gold had got to. Probably pilfered by some hoplite—or maybe Bernie had reclaimed it. You never know with old Bernie.

There were fewer than two hundred dead Greeks. Slaves stood by with shovels to quickly plant them. It was a very hot day, and they were growing ripe.

The Persian dead were left on the field to rot.

Beside the grave, Bernie stood on a stump and addressed the army. He said that we had achieved an immortal victory—but that it was not yet complete. Half the Persian army was still aboard ship. If they headed back to Asia Minor, we were victors. If they headed for Athens, we'd march to defend the city. He had posted, he said, a lookout on Mount Pendelikon. When the fleet's direction was clear, the lookout would send a signal with his shield. One flash meant the Persian fleet was sailing north for Athens—and we would march to relieve the city. Two flashes meant the Persians were sailing back to Asia.

Right on cue, a shield on the summit caught the sun and flashed. The army waited for the second flash. It did not come.

"We march!" called Bernie.

CHAPTER 31

The army trudged back to Athens. All of us were exhausted and suffering from that adrenal letdown that always comes upon soldiers who have fought a battle. Most of us were beaten up with wounds big and small. I had a serious gash on my right arm. Half the army was also blind drunk on Persian wine.

Bernie marched at the head of the column. Theos, Keos, Aeschylus, and I marched just behind him. Before we started, Bernie took Aeschylus aside and spoke to him privately. I asked Aeschylus what Bernie had said.

"The general said he was sorry Cynegeirus had been slain but that he was a hero and now dined with the immortal gods on Mount Olympus. And he said I now have the material for my first tragedy."

"Do you?" I asked.

"Yes."

"And what will you call it?"

"I will call it *The Persians*," he said. "It will be the tragedy of the great Persian king who brings ruin down upon himself by daring to attack the freemen of Athens. The general said it will be a bestseller and gave me the name of a good agent in Athens."

Keos had corralled four Persian prisoners to carry our booty. They were Babylonian slingers, stunted, emaciated creatures, naked except for piss-stained loincloths and covered with bumps and bruises. When anyone of them stumbled or lagged, Keos motivated him with the flat of his sword liberally applied to their backs. He said he'd sell them in the Athens slave market when we got home and split the proceeds with us. We didn't expect to make much for such sorry specimens. Theos said Keos should have chosen more robust types: a Saka or even a premium Persian guardsman, if available.

Yasmine and Ramesh were nowhere to be seen. I was sure nothing bad had happened to them. That girl knew how to take care of herself and her brother. I supposed that she was ashamed of her display of naked passion on the field of battle and was hiding at the back of the column. I knew she would find me when we reached Athens. *Love will find a way*, I told myself. I marched along, my steps quickened by fever daydreams of passion.

Bernie set a brisk pace. He never seemed to get tired. I was several hundred years younger than him, but I struggled to keep up. We had nearly reached the summit of Mount Pendelikon when he finally looked back.

"Why, Lex, you're alive and no limbs lost, I see," he remarked, looking me over in some surprise. He threw his arm over my shoulders. "So, how was your first real battle?"

"I screwed up," I said. "I really, really screwed up."

"Oh? And how did you screw up?" he asked.

"I ran before you gave the signal. And they followed me, the whole Antiochus and Leontis. Why did they follow me, Bernie? I'm a nobody."

"They followed you because you are a natural leader, Lex. The Greeks say it's a gift from the gods. They call it charisma. Men naturally want to follow you."

"No, Bernie. I nearly lost us the battle."

"Not at all. I tricked you."

"Tricked me?"

"Sure. I made a mousetrap."

"A mousetrap?"

"You were the cheese. I knew you would forget yourself and attack. You are impetuous as a puppy. You are as emotional as a hysterical teenage girl. You are disobedient, and you let your lust for revenge overcome your good sense. I knew you would disobey me and charge. I knew just as surely that you would be thrown back and the Persians would advance. When they advanced, I sent the army inward on their flanks like a mousetrap. The Persians panicked and ran."

"I was the bait? Bernie, I could have been killed!"

"Yup," he said without much interest. "And you would have deserved it. So, how was your first real battle?"

How could I answer that? I felt the rapture of my battle frenzy again:

cutting, stabbing, crushing, killing. Yes, killing felt wonderful. I had never felt as alive as when I was killing.

Then I recalled the slaughter at the gate and that boy whose throat I had slit. That was killing too, and I hated it. And I hated myself.

I couldn't answer Bernie's question. It was too hard.

"It's well that war is so terrible or we would grow too fond of it,'" he said. "That's what Bobby Lee said to me after Fredericksburg. He won that battle, but the slaughter of all those Union boys was almost too much for him to bear."

We marched on in silence for a time. Then he patted me on the back. "Still, it was a great victory, wasn't it, Lex?"

"Yes. It was a great victory, Bernie."

We reached the summit, and he stopped again and looked back. Just below us, our ten thousand soldiers—minus the 203 heroes lucky enough to have fallen on the field of honor, whether they wanted to or not—wound like a giant python up the narrow road. Two miles below them, the Marathon plain was carpeted with thousands of motionless specks, the nine thousand bodies of the enemy. Among them moved a few figures, local peasants, busy stripping the corpses of the few baubles our boys had left behind in their haste to depart. The beach too, was carpeted with corpses, some lying on the sand, some bobbing and rolling over and over in the gentle surf. Great billows of black smoke rose from the camp and from the smoldering hulks of the enemy's wrecked ships. Over this feast, black vultures circled and swooped. From time to time, one would land, peck, flap, and rise, carrying a dangling bit of man meat in his beak.

"Ah, war!" Bernie murmured. "Humanity's proudest achievement!" He took a deep cleansing breath of the stink of rotting Persian flesh on the plain. "God, how I love it!"

"My God, Bernie!" I exclaimed. "How can you love it? Look how terrible it is!"

"Oh, yes," Bernie agreed, sounding a bit too jolly. "Terrible, indeed. The most terrible thing of all."

We paused to watch the vultures at their work.

"So, tell me one thing, young Lex."

"What's that, Bernie?"

"If wars are so terrible—and all of you humans say it is—why do you keep having them?"

We were suddenly interrupted by a piteous braying from the side of the road.

I knew that bray! I looked and saw my Buster. The poor little fellow was standing stock still with his head downcast. A mountain of loot—from bags of treasure to gilt chairs and tables—was piled six feet high on his poor, bent back.

I rushed over to him. He planted a big, wet donkey kiss on my nose. I wiped my face and hugged him around the neck. "Buster! You're okay!"

"Get your hands off my donkey," someone shouted. "That's my donkey, and I'll thank you to take your hands off him, you filthy thief!"

It was that old farmer and his hideous crone of a wife.

"What do you mean, *your* donkey?" I protested. "This donkey's mine. I lost him."

"And we found him. Finders keepers!" shrieked the toothless hag. "He's ours. See? He carries our property honestly earned on the field of battle."

"Get going, you goddamned lazy ass!" The farmer whipped Buster hard across the rump with a stick. Buster yelped and jumped. I saw a tear in his eye.

Nobody hits my Buster. I gave the farmer a good shove and knocked him into his wife. They sprawled in the dust.

"That's assault!" the geezer croaked. "I'll sue! You'll see! I'll take you to court for assault."

"What do you mean by loading Buster up like this and whipping him? He's a very small donkey and very sensitive." I drew my dagger and cut the ropes that tied the booty. The sacks split open on the ground, spilling treasure into the dust.

"No!" screamed the farmer as passing soldiers threw themselves onto the treasure and began loading up their pockets. In a few seconds, it was all gone.

"Our retirement!" the farmer screamed. "Our pension! Our IRA! Thieves! Robbers! I'll sue!"

Theos stepped over. He lifted the geezer up by his collar and held him there, his feet dangling in the air. "Shut up—or I'll cut off your lips and nose and feed them to your wife."

"Yes, sir," the farmer said.

Theos dropped him on his butt in the dust and gave him a good kick in the ribs. He rolled over and over down the hill with his wife stumbling along behind.

Just as the farmer and his hag were disappearing, Bernie slapped himself hard on the forehead. "By Hermes, I must be getting dotty! I forgot to send Philippides ahead to warn Athens that the Persians are coming." He turned and bellowed back down the trail, "Send Philippides to the front!" The command echoed down the mountain.

Now, you probably have heard the story of how the marathon—the race, I mean—first came to be. The famous story told by Herodotus is that Philippides, the long-distance runner you will remember from Bernie's speech to the Assembly in Athens, trotted to Sparta to ask for their help at Marathon, jogged back to Athens again, jogged to Marathon, fought in the battle, then ran all the way to Athens to carry the news of the victory to the Assembly. As the story goes, he staggered to the podium, gasped, "We conquer," and then dropped stone-cold dead.

Herodotus was a liar. Here's the real story.

In a few minutes, Philippides limped up to us. A bloody bandage was wrapped around his right foot. He had blisters.

Bernie turned to me. "Lex, get on that beast of yours and ride like the wind to Athens. And don't spare the burro—or whatever that creature is."

"Yes, Lord Polemarchos. Buster is a donkey though, just so you know." I saluted, climbed up on Buster's back, and made myself comfortable. He turned his head and gave me a love nip on the hand. We started to walk. Three steps, and I leaned over, put my head on Buster's neck and breathed in the heady perfume of his gamey donkeyness.

"To Athens, Buster," I whispered. "And make it snappy."

Buster leapt ahead: a donkey leap, I mean. In two steps, he had broken into his donkey trot, which is considerably faster than I would walk to class for a math quiz for which I hadn't studied, but considerably slower than my energetic pace to the cafeteria when I knew pizza was being served for lunch.

We trotted along, dusty mile after dusty mile. I snoozed. My intrepid

Buster carried on. Finally, we reached Athens and made our way through the city streets to the Assembly. It was crowded with hundreds of anxious citizens, frantic to hear news of the battle. As usual, rumors were flying every which way. Some people were saying that the Persians had defeated us, stuck Bernie's head on a spike, slaughtered our entire army, and were on their way to burn the city. Others were saying that the battle still raged inconclusively with vast slaughter. Nobody was reporting that we had won.

I dismounted and led Buster up to the podium.

"What's the news from Marathon?" an elder croaked, wringing his hands.

"We conquer!" I cried.

I had just managed to blurt out the news of the Persian fleet headed for the city when both Buster and I were being borne on the shoulders of the mob through the streets, plied with overflowing jugs of wine, solicited by every lady of the night (yes, even Buster caught the eye of one or two harlots), and generally being celebrated as the heroes who had singlehandedly won the battle and saved Athens.

A few minutes later, Bernie and the army showed up, bedraggled and exhausted but still full of fight. They marched straight to the beach. We were drawing up in battle line just as the Persian fleet sailed around Cape Sounion.

"Put your game faces on, boys," shouted Bernie. "Look tough!"

The Persian flagship rowed back and forth just out of bow shot range for a time while the Persian admiral, a bald Egyptian with gold hoop earrings, examined us. We looked ferocious, bloodthirsty, and invincible. He conferred with Datis, Hippias, and Apollonius. For a half hour or so, it looked like the Persians might risk a landing. Then the admiral shook his head and yelled commands. Sailors scurried about and ran signal flags up the flagship's main mast. The whole Persian fleet sailed away.

Athens was saved.

CHAPTER 32

The city partied. For a week, nobody was sober. A fire broke out in one of the poorer districts. Everyone was too drunk to notice. Once again, blocks were leveled, and several hundred citizens were burned alive. A good time was had by all.

Bernie let me celebrate with Theos, Keos, and Aeschylus for two days and two nights, and then he corralled me. He said he found me passed out under a urinal in a public restroom near the Agora. I was stark naked. Thieves had stolen every stitch of my clothes, but they had otherwise done me no harm because I was the hero of Marathon.

Bernie had me carried back to his house and put to bed in his best guest room. I slept for twenty-four hours. Finally, four very young and more or less naked slave girls entered and escorted me to the baths. They washed me, anointed me with priceless unguents, brushed my green teeth, powdered me down, and dressed me like a prince in silk and satin raiment. Then they spoon-fed me a feast of sixteen courses, peeling the dessert grapes and popping them into my mouth while they giggled and their breasts bounced under my appreciative gaze.

Gorga supervised all of this. Once I ordered her to trot out to the stables and hand-feed Buster a particularly succulent piece of home-baked fresh bread with walnuts.

"Your wish is my command, O young lord," she said.

I was no longer her slave. She was mine.

Payback feels good.

I lolled around Bernie's place, resting up and thinking about Yasmine. On the third day of my vacation, I was sitting in Bernie's courtyard dangling my bare feet into his koi pond when Gorga waddled in. "These young people are here to see you, my master," she announced.

Standing beside her were Yasmine and Ramesh.

Both had cleaned up since I last saw them. They were spic and span. In fact, they looked like a pair of middle school kids on their way to a friend's birthday party. Ramesh wore a spotless white tunic. He carried his bow and a leather bag over his shoulder. Yasmine was dressed demurely in what, if it had been the twenty-first century in America, I would have called an adorable little sundress. It was a little on the short side for 490 BC, but it showed off her pretty legs. She was very well-scrubbed and wore a flower in her rich black hair. She was stunning. My heart leaped through the skylight.

Ramesh bowed, and Yasmine curtsied.

"Sahib Lex," said Ramesh. "We are overjoyed to find you well."

Yasmine said nothing. She kept her eyes modestly downcast. It wasn't like her at all.

"Ramesh, my old friend, how very good to see you," I said, playing my new role as the sophisticated Athenian aristocrat. "And you too, Yasmine, my dear. How lovely you look."

"Thank you, Lord Lex," she said.

"Where are you two staying?"

"That's just it, Sahib," Ramesh said. "We have been staying at an inn in another part of the city. It is it not what I would call a first-class establishment, Sahib. The innkeeper has been bothering Yasmine."

"No! The pig! He'd a dead man!" I reached for my dagger.

"Do not trouble yourself, Sahib. Last night, he crept into her room and tried to have his way with her. She took his head, of course, but we thought it best to seek lodgings elsewhere."

"Of course."

"But, Sahib, we are temporarily embarrassed for funds."

I pulled out my purse.

"No, no, Sahib." Ramesh waved the purse away. "We could never ask our friend, the Sahib, for money. I have come to claim the bounty that Lord Polemarchos so generously promised me for saving his life." Ramesh reached into his bag, withdrew the Persian champion's head, and held it up by the hair. The champion did not look his best. His eyes were gone, and Ramesh had to shoo off a few bloated green flies feeding in the empty sockets. "You remember, Sahib? Filled with gold, Lord Polemarchos said."

"Of course! Of course!" Bernie bellowed, ambling into the courtyard. "Welcome, my young friends! Welcome! Welcome! Come in! Come in! Come in!"

"Hail, Lord Polemarchos, victor of Marathon!" Ramesh bowed deeply as Yasmine curtsied. "May his fame live ten thousand years."

"Thank you, young man. Thank you. Thank you," replied Bernie. "Slaves! Bring my treasure chest!"

Seconds later, four muscular specimens struggled out onto the courtyard bearing a wooden chest bound with bands of iron. They set it on the floor at Bernie's feet with a clunk. Bernie pulled a ring of keys from under his cloak, selected a great brass model, and unlocked the six giant padlocks on the chest. He threw it open.

Ramesh and Yasmine's eyes goggled. It was overflowing with gold coins.

"Well, go ahead, kids. Help yourselves. Fill 'er up," Bernie cried.

Ramesh turned the champion's head upside down and gave it a shake. The Persian's brain had turned to none-too-sweet-smelling green goo, which oozed out onto the floor, leaving plenty of room for the gold. Yasmine stuffed coins into the brain cavity by the fistful.

When Bernie heard that Ramesh and Yasmine were homeless, he naturally invited them to stay with us. I could barely believe my good fortune. Yasmine and me under the same roof all night!

Bernie treated us to a feast. A platoon of slaves walked in and out of the dining room bearing delicacies—peacock under glass, roast sucking rock adder, hummingbird beaks with mushrooms, salamander au gratin—a feast fit for the king of Persia. I counted sixteen different wines. Everything was delicious, but I was careful not to overeat or overdrink. Yasmine sat across from me. She picked at her food and barely sipped her wine. Both of our thoughts were focused on the nighttime heaven to come.

The feast was done. Everyone retired to their bedrooms. I washed, brushed my teeth, squirted a little cologne in the right places, and climbed between the sheets. I lay there for a time listening to the clatter of dishes down in the dining room as the slaves cleaned up. Soon they finished. The house was silent. A few minutes passed. I heard a floorboard squeak outside my door. I heard the door swing open. I heard footsteps crossing to the bed. I heard the jingle of little bells. The sheets lifted, and I felt her satin body snuggle up beside me. She threw one leg over mine.

"I love you, Lex Sahib," she breathed, and her fingertips stroked the soft skin of my stomach.

I reached for her.

She said, "No, Lex Sahib, I'm not that kind of girl," and gently relocated my grasping paw.

She was saving herself for marriage, she said. She wanted me to respect her. My gropes and grabs were to no avail. She was just too quick for me. She fought me off all night.

I had no experience with girls, but in the morning, I guessed that what she wanted was for me to take her out on a date. Didn't girls always want to be wined and dined?

With my booty from Marathon, I took Yasmine down to the chic shopping street, the Rodeo Drive of ancient Athens, to pick up a few fashionable frocks and accessories. The saleswoman at the first boutique was snooty. She didn't want to serve us. Yasmine was dressed as demurely as a parochial schoolgirl, but somehow, she still had "assassin" written all over her. I flashed an egg-sized sapphire I had picked up on the field to the saleswoman. She instantly began curtsying and groveling.

"Only the very finest for the master's most beautiful lady." She cooed. "Our frocks are all the very latest fashions from Ionia now being worn by the very chicest ladies of the city. May I ask what size the lady is? A one? A two? Ah, a perfect figure to strike envy in Aphrodite herself."

The word that the hero of Marathon was on his way with a purse full of Persian jewels spread to the other shops on the avenue like a forest fire. When we stepped into the sandal shop next door, the entire sales staff was lined up at the door bowing and scraping. The manager assured us that her wares were also the very latest imports from Ionia at that very moment being worn by all the very chicest society ladies of the city. Yasmine couldn't make up her mind which style she liked best. She compromised by picking six pairs. That girl sure could punish a boyfriend's purse, but I didn't mind at all.

Next, we dropped in at Athens's most chic hair salon, and I bought Yasmine a complete makeover: hair, makeup, nails, and pedicure. I asked the staff to tone her down a bit from the Persian harem look. They cut her hair into bangs. Her makeup and nail colors were modest. I had a plan in mind.

We shopped all day and then stopped for a bite of supper at a five-star restaurant Bernie had recommended to test Yasmine's new look. The maître d' seated us immediately at a table just the right distance from the dance floor.

Aeschylus came over to say hello while we were having dessert. He said his script was going well. He was halfway through the first draft. He had an agent, the top woman in the city, who was speaking to a director. A couple of rich producers were very interested. He was expecting a sizable advance.

The streets of Athens at night were not always safe, so we hired a sedan chair to take us back to Bernie's. We got home at midnight and went to bed.

She was still too quick for me. She was still saving it for marriage.

But now I was fatally, desperately, head over heels in love.

Yasmine liked to sleep in. When I came down to breakfast the next morning, Bernie was reading *Pravda*. "We leave this evening, Lex," he said.

"What about Yasmine and Ramesh?" I asked. Despite my inner turmoil, I kept my voice even and controlled.

"Ramesh tells me he plans to purchase a farm outside of Athens for himself and Yasmine. With all that gold, they should be quite comfortable."

I said nothing more, but I made a plan.

A few minutes later, I proposed to Yasmine in the bedroom. I even went down on one knee and presented her with the first emerald ring I had sliced off that Persian's finger. Yasmine sat on the bed with her ankles crossed. "Yasmine, my darling, will you marry me?"

"Oh, yes, darling, I will." She threw herself into my arms.

It was the happiest moment of my life.

We hurried immediately down to the Temple of Hera for the "Ten-Drachma Economy Wedding." The ancient priestess and her even more wizened acolyte doddered out and sanctified our love over a slaughtered duck. The ceremony took five minutes. I tossed the priestess her ten drachma and tipped the acolyte one drachma, and we hurried back to Bernie's house to give him the good news.

Bernie was lingering over his decaf and a large red folder marked "Top Secret". Yasmine and I stood before him hand in hand.

"We're married." I said.

"Oh?" Bernie said, peering at us over his reading glasses. "Congratulations. What are your plans?"

"We'll stay here, buy a farm with Ramesh, and raise olives and six children."

"That's impossible," Bernie said.

"Why?"

"You know nothing about growing olives."

"We'll learn."

"You'll die of some vile pestilence to which Yasmine and Ramesh are immune. Just drinking the water will kill you."

"I'll drink nothing but Yasmine's love."

"In ten years, Emperor Xerxes will march an army of a million men to Athens and burn the city to the ground. On the way, they will burn your farm and kill all three of you. You cannot stay here."

I stuck out my chest. "Our love will be as a helmet and hoplon to us. Love will find a way." And to hammer my argument home, I added, "Love conquers all."

Bernie, stuck dumb by my eloquence, fell silent. A hush fell over the room.

Yasmine squeezed my hand, "My darling, if we can't stay here, couldn't I go back to your homeland with you? We could build a cottage. We could have many babies. Do they grow olives in your faraway land? We could live forever ever after."

Bernie gave in. Yasmine packed a pretty pink overnight bag. A few hours later, with Ramesh looking on, Bernie took my hand and hers.

"Bon voyage," said Ramesh, wiping a tear from the corner of his eye.

"Kiss Buster goodbye for me," I said, wiping a tear from the corner of my eye.

CHAPTER 33

Kitty whined.

"She's missed us," Bernie said. "She wants a little tickle."

I scratched the top of her head, then the top of her other head, and then the top of her other head.

Kitty growled at Yasmine.

Yasmine pouted. "I don't like those … whatever that is. They're dirty, and I'm allergic. Look at me. My eyes are streaming, and my makeup is running. I'm a mess."

I supposed it was a cultural thing. After all, in the ancient world, families did not normally keep three-headed monsters as family pets.

When we got to the house Bernie told us that the chauffeur would be there in an hour to take us to my grandfather's house. "Your grandfather would like to welcome you home," he said. "And meet your young lady."

In the limo, I expected Yasmine to ask me some sweetly innocent questions about the car: "Where are the horses hiding in this carriage, darling?" Instead, she didn't seem at all surprised by twenty-first-century technology. I supposed she was nervous about meeting my family.

When we pulled up at the house, the driveway was once again crowded with black limousines guarded by bodyguards holding Uzis and wearing earbuds.

"Your grandfather has many guards," Yasmine said. "Is he emperor of America?"

"No, but he has many famous and important friends. Our president—the emperor of our nation—is here today."

"Ah, I see," Yasmine said.

We got the once-over from the two bodyguards at my grandfather's study door and entered.

My grandfather sat at one end of the conference table with his black cat sleeping in his lap. My grandmother sat beside him pouring tea from a silver teapot.

"Will you take one lump or two, Mr. President," she cooed.

The president sat at the other end of the table, and the secretary of state sat in the middle. John stood behind my grandfather.

"Welcome back, Lex," everyone said.

"Everyone, this is my wife, Yasmine."

They greeted her warmly.

"Oh, she's lovely," my grandmother said.

Yasmine curtsied prettily. The president stood and kissed her hand. I stood beside her, beaming with love and pride.

The atmosphere in the room changed very quickly. Whipping Kali's Tooth out from a sheath strapped to her pretty thigh, Yasmine slashed at the president. I saw a thin red line appear across the top of his hand.

Bernie jumped to his feet, and Yasmine thrust her dagger at his midsection.

Bernie, despite his chubbiness, was too quick for her. He dodged away, and the tip of her dagger missed his tummy by a hair.

Everyone was on their feet—everyone, that is, but the black cat who had launched itself from my grandfather's lap like a furry guided missile.

Yasmine raised her dagger to thrust it down into Bernie's shoulder.

The cat shrieked like a thousand hell-spawned demons and sank its teeth into the tendons of Yasmine's wrist. Yasmine screamed. The cat raked her eyes with its claws.

Kali's Tooth clattered on the floor.

The room exploded.

Yasmine's pretty head went away.

My grandmother stood holding the smoking .357 Magnum Smith and Wesson she had drawn from beneath the needlepoint tea cozy on the table.

"Oh, my goodness," She said. "What a mess."

The president was examining his wound.

"Just a little scratch," he said.

"The poison!" I cried. "The cobra venom!" The president would be dead in seconds.

"Not to worry, young man," the president said. "All of us have been taking antivenom for weeks. A hundred times this little dose wouldn't give me a headache. I could use a Band-Aid though."

"You knew?"

"Of course," Bernie said. "We knew that Yasmine was working for Hippias the very day you and I arrived in Athens. We expected she'd seduce you. You are sixteen, after all. Your hormones are uncontrollable, and your desires are utterly beastly."

I hung my head.

"But we didn't expect it to go quite so far," said Deanna, who had changed back into Deanna and was licking blood from between her fingers. "I'm sorry, Lex."

"We're all terribly sorry." The secretary of state applied a Flintstones bandage to the president's scratch.

Three guards—two for her lovely body and one for her exquisite head—were carrying Yasmine from the room. A maid mopped up.

"Yasmine, darling. I love you." I wept bitter tears. "I can't live without you."

"I'm so sorry, Lex." Deanna was wearing a pretty flowered sundress, which I couldn't help noticing was fetchingly short. "But she really wasn't right for you." She threw her arms around me and pressed me close. "There are other fish in the sea, Lex. And time heals all wounds."

The president was busy tweeting. He looked up. "Are we done here?" he asked.

CHAPTER 34

I hung around my grandfather's house for a few days resting, eating Big Macs, and nursing my broken heart. Deanna kept me company. She was very kind.

One day, John told me that my grandfather wished to see me again in his study.

I found him sitting at his desk.

"Dr. Polemarchos tells me that you did an outstanding job," he said. "Never for a moment did I think you would do otherwise. Congratulations."

"Thanks," I said, not feeling particularly outstanding.

"I thought you'd like to know that the North Koreans backed off. There will be no nuclear war. We expect that their regime will collapse within the next month, and Korea will be reunified."

"Good, I guess." International relations really didn't interest me at the moment. All I could feel was heartbreak.

Ramesh and Buster got their farm. When Xerxes's army tore through Attica, Bernie arranged for the farm to become invisible. Ramesh fought bravely for Athens as a bowman in the sea battle off Salamis and later at the Battle of Plataea, which drove the Persians out of Greece once and for all. He became a famous general and died a rich and respected Athenian citizen.

Buster retired to stud. He fathered sixty-five little donkeys with ten wives. He grew quite fat.

Aeschylus's *The Persians* was a great popular and critical success. Aeschylus became one of the greatest playwrights in all history.

I poured out my heart to Deanna about Yasmine. Yasmine had joined the Others, the enemies of humanity. She had tried to slaughter all of us in my grandfather's study. I had loved her. She had betrayed my love. Most important of all—she had broken my heart. It was all about poor me.

Deanna listened patiently to my self-pity for a week of long walks on the beach and through the woods on my grandparents' estate, saying almost nothing in response to all my whining. Finally, she said, "Lex, have you ever given any thought to Yasmine and the life she had to lead?"

"Huh?"

"Well, her father sold her into slavery when she was only a little girl. You were a slave for a few days. How did you like it?"

"Not much, I guess."

"You swept the floors. What kind of work did her masters make Yasmine do?"

"I don't know."

"Yes, you do. Was Yasmine pretty?"

"Yasmine was smokin' hot."

"Yes. Men liked Yasmine, so her masters made her have sex with them. This is called *rape*. For years and years, they raped her."

I'd never thought of it that way.

"No wonder she became bitter and angry and looked for revenge. You know revenge, don't you, Lex?"

I did. And I came to look at Yasmine in a different way. I began to forgive her … little by little.

Hippias and Apollonius disappeared. I think about them often. Someday, we will meet again.

Bernie said we had saved history, yes, but it was rather more despite me, I knew, than because of me. I had nearly screwed things up completely. If Bernie's little mousetrap trick hadn't worked, Bernie said the Greeks would have lost the Battle of Marathon, you would never have heard of Athens as the cradle of Western civilization, or probably of Athens at all, America would have a great king not a president and a Congress, and the students at your high school would go to the temple and chant in Persian to Zarathustra on Fridays. Just about everything that counts would be different.

"Oh, come on, Berns," I said. "It wouldn't have turned out that bad."

"Let's see." Bernie sat me down on the plastic-covered sofa in his living room. The plastic squeaked and stuck to my thighs. He set a cracked bowl of Fritos Original on the coffee table in front of me, grabbed himself a generous handful, and stuffed it in his mouth. Munching away, he walked over to the fire-engine red RCA Victor Deluxe portable TV in the corner and switched it on.

The TV popped, winked, crackled, and came up all snow and static.

"These old-time TVs suck," Bernie said. "Outdated technology." He fiddled with the rabbit ears. The picture cleared to a test pattern: a great eye. It was the eye of Ra, the ancient Egyptian god of the sun.

Bernie walked back to the sofa, sat down next to me, and picked up the remote. He flicked rapidly through channels until he came to one labeled "2017."

"Thought you'd like to see how things would have turned out if we hadn't won," he said.

The great king looked like Datis, but he was twice his height and bulk. He sat upon an enormous golden throne set on a stone-step pyramid whose peak was wrapped in clouds. The steps of the pyramid were lined with soldiers in all outfits of the Persian army at Marathon. At the base of the pyramid was a giant pit boiling with fire and smoke. Into the pit, thousands of half-naked guards were whipping crowds of men, women, and children to their deaths. The television cameras zoomed in on the guards and their victims. The guards were Persians, wearing Persian dress. Their victims were all Americans, dressed in contemporary clothes. They were shrieking and tearing at each other to keep from falling into the fire pit.

The Persian conquerors of America were exterminating us.

So, history stayed on track … until the next time.

EPILOGUE

Following the disappearance of my father, Alexius (Lex) Whitney, I searched his office in hopes of finding a clue to his whereabouts. In doing so, I came upon a thumb drive hidden in a secret compartment in his desk. The drive contained a novel—or series of novels—some three thousand pages in length.

I never suspected that my father was a novelist. He had no apparent artistic interests or talent. I thought his creative writing was confined to regular contributions to the class notes in his boarding school alumni annual. To me he was a very conventional Boston State Street banker specializing in wills and trusts who left our house in Brookline promptly at seven o'clock and walked in our front door promptly twelve hours later, dropped his brief case on the foyer table, removed his hat and coat, and mixed himself a cocktail: one and only one Bombay Sapphire martini straight up, two olives.

Two or three times a year, my father went on business trips. He always returned with reproductions of museum pieces, usually of a military nature, with which he decorated his study. He brought back the splendid reproduction of a Corinthian hoplite helmet that now sits on my desk from a trip to Greece when he was a very young man.

My father never served in the military, but he was deeply interested in military affairs, an interest he apparently inherited from his own father and grandfather. He never read fiction. He read only newspapers and nonfiction. He filled the bookshelves of our house with hundreds of volumes on wars, some famous and many obscure. Other than his reading and the law, my father had few interests. He did not play tennis or golf like most of his legal associates. He did keep himself lean and fit throughout his life by jogging every morning at five o'clock in a tattered old weighted vest.

As you will see, my father's novels are written in the form of his faux memoirs. It was his delight to pretend that he was the hero of his fictional adventures. He was not shy about accurately describing intimate details of his own life in furthering his plots. It is a fact that he was raised in rural Vermont by eccentric parents who home-schooled him. He went to high school in Vermont. He did leave high school after his parents, his sister, and his brother were killed in the fire that consumed their farmhouse. He did go to live with his grandparents on Long Island and was privately tutored there until he entered Harvard College as a freshman.

I cannot say whether my father would have approved or disapproved of me publishing this first novel of his series. The fact that he hid his manuscript suggests that he was shy about exposing his art to the public eye. Nevertheless, this novel is my father's legacy, and I am publishing it privately, as part of his biography.

I hope you will enjoy his fanciful creations.